THE TEACHER OF NOTHING

USA TODAY BESTSELLING AUTHOR

K WEBSTER

The Teacher of Nothing

Editor: Emily A. Lawrence

Photographer: Michelle Lancaster @lanefotograf
www.michellelancaster.com

Cover Design: All By Design

Formatting: Champagne Book Design

DEDICATION

To Matt—my teacher of everything.

From USA Today Bestselling Author K Webster comes a new steamy age-gap, student-teacher forbidden romance!

He's a grumpy teacher with a chip on his shoulder. She's his much, much younger student who's completely off-limits.

Love broke me when I was a teen.
My dad not only slept with my girlfriend, but he knocked her up and made her my stepmom, too. Nearly two decades later and I'm still not over it.
How can I be when they're a daily reminder of what was stolen from me?

Being a teacher isn't necessarily my passion, but pissing my dad off is.
He thinks teaching is beneath our family and I love watching him squirm.

But the joke's on me.

I'm completely obsessed with the quiet, beautiful girl in my class.
Always staring at her perfect lips when no one's looking.
She's so young—*too young* for me.
Something about her, though, is just so sad and I can't seem to stop thinking about her.

I want to comfort her. To hold her.
To teach her filthy lessons while in the sanctity of my bedroom.

And yet, I can't.
Not only would I lose my job and bring humiliation down on the others in my family who don't deserve the heat, but I'd be just like him. My father. A sicko chasing some girl he has no business going after. I refuse to let that happen.

Until I'm forced to protect her when no one else will.
Everything changes and I cross a line I'm not sure I can come back from.

It turns out, I'm exactly like my father.
A selfish man hell-bent on ruining everyone's lives over a teenage girl.

This is a complete standalone novel with a happily ever after. Characters are of legal age.*

Trigger Warning

This book has some triggering scenes for some readers including bullying, sexual assault, domestic abuse, and other potentially upsetting subject matter.

These scenes do not happen between the two main characters.

CHAPTER ONE

Callum

LIPS SHOULDN'T BE SO CAPTIVATING. THEY'RE A PART of the body, not twins made of magic and beauty. But her lips are a work of art. I want to study them and discuss them. Marvel over their perfection—the exact light red shade of the inside of a sliced strawberry. Probably just as sweet too. Each time she licks them, I stifle a groan of need, wishing I could lick them too.

Look away, you fucking creep.

Somehow, I manage. I dart my gaze along every face in the room, lingering on the other fifteen or so females, wondering if it's me who's the problem here or *her*. When no one else captures my interest, I know the answer.

Her.

Always her.

The urge to drag my hungry stare back to her pretty mouth is almost uncontrollable. With each passing day, I find it more and more difficult to remain unaffected.

She makes it impossible.

Someone laughs and attempts to stifle the sound. This draws my attention to Levi Paulson. He's a little shit who gets on my last nerve. Normally, I'd be irritated, but I'm almost grateful for the distraction.

Almost.

"Is there a problem, Mr. Paulson?" I lean back in my desk chair and it creaks from the movement, echoing in the otherwise silent classroom. "I'm not sure what you think is so funny about your test."

Levi rolls his eyes but won't look at me. "No problem, Mr. Park."

"That's what I thought."

A few students snigger at my reply. Levi's features harden. I don't care if kids like Levi think I'm a dick. I *am* a dick. I have no problems with being a dick. It's kind of my thing.

Which makes this…*obsession*…so complicated.

Because I don't want to be a dick to her. Not even a little bit. I want to pull off all her petals, expose whatever hides beneath her outer layers, and know every sweet piece of her.

But I can't.

I won't.

She's a student. *My* student. This makes her untouchable. I refuse to be like my father.

Don't look at her. Don't look at her. Don't fucking look at her.

Against their own accord, my eyes abandon the shit starter, Levi, to travel their way back to her.

Willa Reyes.

My dick stiffens as soon as my gaze is back on her lips. She has her plump bottom lip captured between her teeth, her brows furled in concentration. Willa is the best student I have in any of my classes. Not because I crave her mouth like my next breath. It's because she's quiet, studious, and always outperforms everyone else.

It's not her performance that has me so captivated, though.

There's just something about her that taunts me. It

provokes carnal desires inside me that have no business being poked at. Her innocence is like blood dragging its way through dark ocean waters. I'm the shark desperate for a taste—the predator who will tear through her sweetness and devour her whole.

Fuck.

My dark gray slacks tighten around my cock, the material unable to keep the hard flesh from straining for freedom. Beneath my desk, I push against it with the heel of my palm, needing relief but unable to find it.

I'm going insane.

All semester, this girl has lured me closer and closer. She doesn't mean to do it. She can't help it. She doesn't know I'm a monster with an unquenchable thirst for her. Her only fault is being present, day after day, and chewing on her supple lip that distracts me beyond reason.

Levi coughs and I'm forced to look at him. He's smirking at one of his friends in class. He's seventeen and on his way to prison. At least, that's my deduction. I'm not usually wrong. I have the foresight of knowing where kids like him will land well before they do. A teacher's sixth sense.

"If you'd rather take your test to the office, I'm sure Mr. Erickson would love the company," I grind out, my patience withering like a flower without sun. "That's two, Mr. Paulson."

His nostrils flare, but he gives me a clipped nod. I'm still glaring at him when warmth washes over me. I cut my eyes over to Willa just in time to see her wide dark green eyes fixated on me.

She immediately glances down at her paper and her skin colors to a soft pink. My unruly dick twitches. Is she embarrassed? Was she checking me out?

I try to ignore that line of thinking, but it won't go away. A million thoughts tangle together in my mind.

How old is she?

Does she find me attractive?

Was she thinking about me inside her?

I'm out of control. A selfish fuckwit like my dad. It wasn't supposed to be this way. I was supposed to be everything he's not. The exact opposite. Yet, here I am lusting over a girl half my age and who's still in high school.

There's a special place in hell for men like us.

My phone buzzes, vibrating my desk.

"No phones allowed," Levi mocks under his breath.

I've had enough of that dipshit today.

"Out," I bark. "Take your things and go see Erickson. Now."

Levi's face burns crimson with a mixture of embarrassment and fury. I don't care. He's pissing me off, interrupting my class during a test—interrupting my favorite part of the day.

"Whatever," he grumbles as he stands. "Peace out, losers."

This earns him some nervous laughter from his buddies but is silenced when I stare each of them down. Levi storms down the aisle, bulldozing over backpacks and knocking into desks, making sure to display how pissed off he is about his marching orders. When he shoves Willa's test off her desk, sending the stapled papers fluttering to the ground, I have to grip onto the arms of my chair to keep from charging after him.

Willa wilts and frowns at her papers on the floor. She presses her sexy lips together, stifling a groan of irritation.

I sear my gaze into her, watching her body move as it slides out of her chair.

She's not short, but she's not tall either.

Average height, average build, average looks.

There's nothing about her that should have me obsessing like I do. But I'm here, aching to bury my face in her dark brown hair so I can inhale her scent. I crave to cradle her soft jawline and taste her sweet lips.

I want her.

I just fucking want her.

With every cell in my body.

Today, like any other day, she's wearing something plain. A fitted pair of jeans, a scuffed-up pair of black Converse, and a gray knitted sweater. On any other person, it would make them blend in. On her, she somehow makes it sexy.

Someone fucking shoot me now.

Take me out of my misery.

As much as I want to strip this girl, bend her over her desk, and fuck her into tomorrow, I can't. I refuse to. I absolutely won't.

She quickly grabs the papers up and gathers them into her small hands. I expect her to sit back down, but her eyes have found me.

What is it that she sees?

Her perverted, evil teacher salivating over her every move?

I focus on her eyes, careful not to look anywhere else that might give away my ravenous need for her.

"Miss Reyes," I rumble, hating how hoarse the sound is to my own ears. "Did you need help?"

Her cheeks blaze red-hot and she gives a quick shake of

her head. "N-No. I just...I'm through with my test." She extends her arm out over my desk, offering me the pile of papers in her hand, her sugary scent enveloping me and making my mouth water.

It would be so easy to take hold of her dainty wrist and drag her over the surface into my lap. Would she let me hold her? Would she rub her ass against my needy cock until I came in my pants?

"So soon?" I arch a brow at her, not making any moves to reach for the papers because I might grab her instead. "Did you rush through it?"

I don't mean to sound like an asshole, but it comes naturally to me.

Her nostrils flare and a flicker of irritation dances over her features. "I didn't rush through it. It was just easy."

All the blood in my body seems to drain to my cock, filling it and making it thicken impossibly more. That tiny bite of sass in her voice only manages to send me spiraling further into the madness that is her. It's an unexpected layer. Another piece of her being revealed to me.

I need to see it all.

"Easy?" I purr, my voice low enough that only she can hear. "Awfully confident, Miss Reyes."

She fidgets, shifting her weight from foot to foot. The crimson on her cheeks only seems to grow more saturated as the seconds tick by with her on display in front of my desk. "Easy A," she says in a breathless, unsure voice, though it's still a taunt.

"Hmm." I carefully take the papers and pluck them from her hold. "Perhaps I'm not challenging you enough."

Her lashes bat against the apples of her cheeks quickly, as though she can't seem to make sense of my words.

Yes, sweet thing, I am absolutely flirting with you.

"I'm not insulting your instruction," she says quickly, dipping her gaze to my desk. "I just don't find statistics very hard."

If she were mine, I'd tell her to get on her hands and knees so she could crawl around the back side of my desk and find something else instead that's very hard.

She's not mine.

She will never be mine.

Because I am nothing like my father. I won't pluck an innocent girl out of her world and turn her into the queen of mine. My family is still dealing with the ripple effects from when Dad did the very same thing.

And not with just any girl.

My high school girlfriend.

Sourness settles in my gut and I don't want Willa to see the hatred that lives inside me. Hatred for Nathan Park, my father.

"Sit down, Miss Reyes. You're distracting the class."

Her entire body flinches, which is a kick to the nuts. I don't like being the one to make her wither. It's on the tip of my tongue to apologize and attempt more of this innocent flirting, but she's already walking away.

So I don't stare at her cute ass and land my own ass in trouble, I pick up my phone to see what message I missed earlier. It's from my brother Hugo.

Hugo: Spencer has a D in chem. Can you go sprinkle some Park magic on your girlfriend so she'll up his grade?

Me: I don't have Park magic, remember? I'm the family prick. And Lisa's not my girlfriend.

I dated Lisa Collins for like a fucking second. She was needy and kind of bossy. As nice as she was to look at, we had zero chemistry. No pun intended.

Hugo: Fine. I'll ask the golden child. Dempsey owes me a couple of favors…

I nearly groan at his suggestion.

Me: You're the golden child, dumbass. He's the black sheep. Our baby brother is in enough trouble as is. Don't encourage him into bribery or prostitution too.

Hugo: Like I'd let him go to prison. He's too pretty for that shit.

I smother a laugh.

Me: How about I find Spence and put the fear of God in him to bring up his grade? He listens to me better than he does you.

Hugo: That works. I owe you a beer. Friday?

Me: We could always get shitfaced before Sunday dinner with Dad…

Hugo: Dinner and a show? Count me in.

Since I'm done ribbing Hugo, I set my phone down and pick up Willa's test. Even her handwriting is sexy. All cutesy swirls and curves. I trace her name, written in black ink, with my finger, memorizing the feel of it.

As much as I want her to draw her name with the tip of

her tongue all over my body, I know I have to quit that line of thinking. I've worked too fucking hard my entire life to be everything Dad is not. I'll be damned if I let a sweet girl like Willa Reyes transform me into that motherfucker.

Not happening.

Not now. Not ever.

The seconds crawl toward the end of the hour. It's agony forcing myself to look at anything but her. Like an alcoholic desperate for a drink, my hands tremble and the urge overwhelms me.

Just one look won't hurt.

A little taste to get me through.

As soon as I give myself permission, my eyes are on her pouty pink lips, learning, memorizing, studying.

I need a distraction.

And soon.

Or else I'll do a lot more than just look at Willa.

A helluva lot more.

CHAPTER TWO

Willa

WHY DOES TIME FLY WHEN YOU DON'T WANT IT TO?

It's been nearly twenty-four hours since my… encounter with Mr. Park and it's about to happen again. Except, this time, I have to live with the humiliation of knowing there's nothing between us.

Just my wild imagination.

Wishful thinking is more like it. Men like Mr. Park don't want girls like me. They want voluptuous and funny and clever.

Not shy and fearful and sad.

We might as well add awkward to that list too of what he won't like.

Somehow, yesterday, I convinced myself that he saw through to me. The person buried so deep, alone and afraid. I'd allowed myself to paint him as my chivalrous hero, saving me from the life I hate, showering me with love and protection.

I'm a dreamer.

And it sucks when I wake up to this wicked reality.

Someone barks out a laugh in the hallway, drawing my attention. Dempsey Park is messing with his twin sister, Gemma, near a bank of lockers. They're the younger siblings of my stupid-hot teacher. Everyone in the Park family, as far as I know, is gorgeous.

Especially Mr. Park.

Speak of the devil.

He steps into the threshold of his classroom door, filling the walkway with his massive, muscular frame. A tiny whine crawls out of my throat. Not because he terrifies me. No, because I find him so sexy it hurts.

It's a thing.

I physically ache when I look at him. It starts in the center of my chest and pulsates this fiery, painful throb all the way down my appendages. It's frustrating, to say the least.

"Hey," Mr. Park calls out as he leans a shoulder on the doorframe to make room for someone entering the classroom. "Have either of you seen Spencer?"

Dempsey, a younger, but still handsome version of his brother, gives Mr. Park a chin lift. "Yeah, I think he was getting high in the bathroom earlier."

Mr. Park doesn't take the bait. "Tell him I'm looking for him."

"Is he in trouble?" Gemma asks, brows scrunching together. "What did he do?"

I find myself drawn to the three of them, slowly approaching as though by being near them, I'll somehow become one of them.

The Park princes and princess.

Royalty among the average townspeople.

More money than God.

If the rumors are true anyway...

"He's trying to fail Miss Collins's class." Mr. Park frowns at Gemma. "What's your grade in there?"

She scoffs, huffing in an indignant way. "Seriously, Callum? You're my brother not my dad. It's none of your business."

Callum.

The name suits him.

Just thinking of it has my heart fluttering and my stomach twisting.

"Watch where you're walking," a girl hisses, bumping into me. "Freak."

I recoil at her words. I'm not a freak. Just quiet. I don't have friends, though. My stepbrother made sure of that. There's no telling what he whispered in everyone's ears to make them treat me as an outcast. I don't exactly help the situation. Rather than trying to prove to them I'm someone else—someone better than he says—I turned into a silent ghost who quietly haunts the hallways and classrooms, mostly keeping to myself.

Except for yesterday.

Except with Mr. Park.

Callum.

I actually worked up the nerve to speak to him. To attempt to be playful and flirting. All because I caught him staring at me with an intensity I couldn't ignore even if I'd wanted to. It emboldened me. For once in my powerless life, I felt like I held the hand with all the cards.

But I was wrong.

He snuffed out the flickering fire all too easily and I've been obsessing over it since.

Mr. Park's deep voice cuts through my self-deprecating thoughts. "Grades are important, Gemma."

Dempsey cackles, playfully tugging on his sister's long, silky mahogany-colored hair. "Did you hear that, Gemmy-Lou?" He lowers his voice, mocking their brother. "Grades are important."

Mr. Park stalks over to them, jaw clenching. Dempsey, despite being half his size, doesn't back down. Gemma's face is red from humiliation. Whatever Mr. Park says to them is in a low tone and through gritted teeth. I can't make out what he's saying, so I take a second to admire him before I have to actually face him in class.

The man is a mountain.

Not some burly guy with a thick neck and thunder thighs. No, Mr. Park—*Callum*—is like a castle wall. Firm. Solid. Impenetrable. Power and authority are cut into every sculpted muscle on his body so that his presence is not only felt but also seen in the way he carries himself. Expensive suits are always molded to his fit body, the fabric stretching slightly over his biceps and back. On the rare few times he's removed his suit jacket, the entire class is rewarded with the way his slacks hug his tight ass.

He's just so...manly.

Arrogance and confidence war for the lead. I think, deep down, he's more than some rich prick whose name this city was built upon. I can see it in the gruff, yet concerned way he deals with his younger siblings. There's more to Mr. Park than a sexy body and heart-stopping face.

I thought...

I thought maybe I was going to learn what all lurks beneath him.

I thought maybe I was special.

The bell rings, jarring me from my daydreaming and forcing me into the present. Dempsey and Gemma are gone. Mr. Park remains near the lockers, intense blue eyes searing into me. His nearly black hair with a few rogue strands of gray is styled in a casual way despite his professional, bespoke three-piece charcoal suit. Dark scruff lines his sharp jawline and his dark brows dip. Like he's angry to see me.

My heart stutters to a stop and bile creeps up my throat. I do everything in my power to be a good girl and stay off everyone's radar. The thought of being on Mr. Park's radar sends terrifying chills down my spine. Shuddering, I hug my arms to my chest and hurry into the classroom.

With my head down, I make my way to my seat. I drop my bag onto the floor and sit down, hoping to disappear completely.

"Psst. Willa."

So much for disappearing.

I gnaw on my bottom lip, pretending I don't hear Levi call for me. A wadded piece of paper bounces off my head and scuttles across the floor. Unable to ignore him, I look over my shoulder to find Levi grinning evilly at me.

As if having to live with the monster wasn't enough, I've been forced to share my statistics class with him.

He's the absolute worst.

"What?" I ask, frowning.

One of his friends barks out a laugh. "Dude, your sister doesn't like you."

I'm not his sister.

I'm his *step*sister.

Other than sharing a house with him, we may as well be strangers.

"She likes me," Levi argues. "She just got her period, though, which is making her kind of bitchy. Didn't you, Willa? Bloody panties all over the bathroom floor—"

Even though it's stupid and he's made it up, it doesn't stop him and several friends to roar in laughter. At my expense. I cringe, quickly turning to avoid his mean teasing. This time, I'm desperate to see Mr. Park. Not because I want to relive the embarrassment of yesterday, but because he is one of the few people who can shut my stepbrother up.

"Mr. Paulson," Mr. Park snaps, slamming the classroom door shut behind him. "I suggest you spend less time clowning around and more time studying. Fs on exams mean you won't pass my class. Do you really want to spend the summer retaking this statistics class?"

Levi mutters something, but it can't be heard past the raucous laughter of our classmates. Mr. Park walks over to his desk, opens a drawer, and tosses the tests on his desk.

"Nearly half of you will be going into winter break with failing grades in my class." He points at one of Levi's friends, Nick, and then thumps the pile of tests. "Pass these out, Mr. Henson. Your F is on top."

Nick groans as he stands and then saunters over to Mr. Park's desk. He winces when he sees his grade. As he begins passing out the tests, I attempt to keep my eyes averted anywhere than on my teacher.

It's useless.

He looks like a vengeful god perched on the edge of his desk, pulsing with authority and dominance. One of the things I find so attractive about him is how he makes people like Levi seem weak and worthless.

Our eyes clash, seemingly against their will, and all sound fades around me.

I'm not imagining this.

Mr. Park's gaze is cutting into me, hot and unapologetic. The fiery heat of it leaves a trail over my skin. The urge to look away prickles through me, but a stubborn streak, hidden deep within keeps me motionless.

I'm not imagining this.

His brows deepen in their frown and his lips press together. A sudden wave of panic skitters through me as I wonder if I said those words aloud.

Smack!

I jolt in surprise when Nick slams my test down on my desk. Precise red ink mars the top of the paper. ***100% - Nice work, Miss Reyes.***

Nice work.

My stomach flutters at the note. He's never written anything on my work before. It feels like a secret message between the two of us. Glancing up, I find him watching me intently. A rare smile tugs at my lips. His own lips twitch and then he winks at me.

Winks!

Heat floods through me. I'm not going insane. My teacher, *Callum*, is flirting with me. This isn't some fantasy or dream. It's real.

"Willa got the only A," Nick grumbles, tossing the last test on someone's desk. "I wonder how she got that."

The room erupts in a cacophony of sexual grunts and moans. Humiliation burns hot in my gut. My test—that I'd been elated over just moments before—crumples in my tight grip. Tears threaten, but I blink hard, fiercely keeping them at bay.

"Out," Mr. Park growls. "Get out of my classroom right now."

"Mr. Park," Nick whines. "I was just kidding—"

"OUT!"

I flinch at the booming order. My palms are clammy and my heart is beating a hundred miles per second.

Nick mutters under his breath about what a dick Mr. Park is but doesn't speak it loud enough for him to hear. The classroom grows deathly quiet as Nick leaves.

Is everyone staring at me?

I just want this day to be over with.

"Now that you've all had your childish fun, open your Chromebooks. You'll find today's assignment waiting. After the lecture, I expect you all to complete the assignment and pass it with flying colors."

With shaking hands, I shove my test into my backpack and then pull out my computer. It feels like everyone is watching me.

Except for Mr. Park.

It's almost as though he's avoiding looking at me. Is he embarrassed too? To be called out for our flirtatious exchange?

Dread coils in the pit of my stomach.

Maybe I should request a schedule change. I'll have him next semester too. Can I really put up with another several months of feeling like this?

Each of my breaths grows more shallow than the previous ones. I'm lightheaded and dizzy. Panic attacks aren't unusual for me, but they don't often happen at school. Home is where these feelings tend to render me immobile.

Breathe, Willa. Breathe.

It's hard to breathe, though, when you feel your world closing in around you. My vision darkens around the edges and I fear I might pass out. Because that won't be embarrassing or anything.

Mr. Park's deep voice draws me out of my inner turmoil.

As he begins his lecture, discussing statistical inference and confidence intervals, the tension in my neck and shoulders slowly releases. I fall victim to the hypnotic, calming cadence of his words.

All my worries, for a moment, have ceased to exist.

The only thing remaining is him.

His rumbling, authoritative tone. The expensive, manly scent of his cologne that fills my nostrils each time I enter this classroom. A comforting presence, warming me to my core.

When I glance up, a flash of heat rushes through me. He's no longer wearing his suit jacket and stands with his back to us, writing out a few terms we'll need to know. The writing on the smartboard is the same neat scrawl that he'd written "Nice work" on my test.

As much as I want to stare at his ass that seems to be the real object of study right now, I buckle down and focus on his notes instead. My life might be a mess, but above all, I'm a good student. Especially for him.

I'd give just about anything for another wink.

Anything for more of his praise.

CHAPTER THREE

Callum

RAGE BUBBLES UP INSIDE ME. IT'S TAKING EVERYTHING in me not to lose my shit on the entire class. I need to focus on my lecture, but I'm physically vibrating with fury. My voice is tight and clipped as I recite my notes. I wish I'd had a pop quiz prepared that I could give them so I could cool off a bit.

As much as I want that innocent, sweet thing on her knees with my aching cock in her pretty mouth, it's not the reason she's passing my class with nearly a perfect grade. She earned it. Studied while all the other idiots in here were goofing off.

Times like these, I'm reminded why it probably wasn't a good idea for me to become a teacher. Where most people go into education because of honorable intentions, I'd done it to piss off my father.

We're Parks.

That means we make money, not shape the futures of others.

But, since he knocked up my goddamn girlfriend my senior year of high school, I made it my sole mission to do the opposite of his wishes.

Rather than become an attorney like Hugo or a finance

mogul like Jude, I decided to teach. It pleases me to no end that I'm an embarrassment to my father.

The feeling is mutual.

Riotous laughter explodes from behind me, chasing off thoughts of my father and bringing me to the present. I swivel around to face the class. It takes considerable effort not to look at Willa, but I somehow manage. Barely. Instead, I focus on the source of the disruption.

Levi.

He's not-so-discreetly showing his phone to one of his friends. While he's distracted, I storm over to him. A shocked grunt escapes him when I snap his phone out of his hands.

"Dude, hey, give it back," he grinds out. "Seriously."

"I'm curious, Mr. Paulson, what could be so important on this phone." I look down at the screen and frown. "What is this?"

Levi shrugs. "Nothing."

Nothing?

There's a picture of a woman sleeping face down on a bed, her white shirt riding up to reveal a pair of pink panties.

"Porn?" I demand.

"She wishes," Levi mutters.

Something in his tone unnerves me. "She?"

"I said it was nothing," Levi grunts. "I'll put my phone away. Scout's honor."

Ignoring him, I swipe to the left. A different picture, but the same person based on the fact the bedding is the same. This picture is of a naked breast, a man's hand in the picture as he lifts a black shirt to reveal it. I swipe again and my blood runs cold.

Pretty pink lips parted in oblivious slumber.

My brain can't compute what I'm seeing. It's her. It's Willa fucking Reyes. Why in the hell does Levi have these pictures of her?

I'm going to kill this kid.

Murder him with my bare fucking hands.

"I'm keeping this. We're discussing it after class." My voice is cold, cutting through the air like an ice blade. "You too, Miss Reyes."

Her sharp gasp of surprise is such a sexy sound, but I'm too pissed to get aroused. I need answers. I don't understand what her relationship is with this fuckface. Whatever it is, I'm going to get to the bottom of it.

The rest of class goes by in a blur. Levi's phone, now resting in my pocket, burns against my thigh. I'm dying for this period to be over so I can deal with this shit.

Finally, I'm given the reprieve I need. The bell rings and everyone bolts like their asses are on fire. My statistics class is notorious for being the most difficult at this school, so no one sticks around any more than they have to. When it's just Willa and Levi, I walk over to the door and close it.

My hand clutches the door handle tight enough that the metal creaks. I release it before I do something psychotic like rip it off in a fit of rage. Somehow, I manage to keep my fury in check.

"Miss Reyes," I say, allowing myself to look at her.

Her dark green eyes glisten with unshed tears. She's confused as to why she's being held after class. My guess is she's always been a good girl and probably thinks she's in trouble.

"Are you in a relationship with Mr. Paulson?" I grit my teeth. "I want the truth."

Her eyebrows knit together in confusion and her nose scrunches. "I don't understand the question."

My patience, already wire-thin, snaps. "It's a very simple question, Miss Reyes. Yes or no?"

She recoils at my harsh words. I want to recall them back, but I can't. We're not a "thing" because she's my student and I won't fucking go there. However, I still feel the sting of betrayal. Like I've been cheated in some way.

"Don't be sick, Mr. Park," Levi mutters. "She's my sister."

The room spins for a long second. His what?

"Step," Willa corrects icily. "His dad married my mom."

"So you live together?" I demand.

She studies me as though she wishes she knew what was going on inside my head. If this situation weren't so fucked up and we were alone, I might offer her my thoughts.

"We've lived in the same house for a few years," Willa murmurs. "Why?"

I sit down on the edge of my desk, contemplating what to do next. Smashing my fist through Levi's face isn't an option that'll allow me to keep my job. And, in order to keep my eyes on my lovely obsession, I need this job.

"Come here," I instruct, my eyes narrowing on her. "Please."

Her body relaxes slightly and she nods. As she gets out of her seat, I cut my glare over to Levi and pull out his phone.

"Passcode."

He shakes his head but mutters out the code. Once I have it unlocked, it opens back to the pictures. The one of her pretty mouth. She approaches, frowning as she notices Levi's phone in my hand.

"What is it?" she asks, voice breathy and soft.

My dick thumps in my slacks. I try hard to ignore it. "There are photographs of you on Mr. Paulson's phone. Were you aware?"

Her face pales and her pink lips part. "What kind of pictures?"

Sliding off the desk, I stand and show her the one on the screen. While she looks at the picture, I look at her. This close, I can smell her shampoo. Honey and cream. If Levi weren't watching our every move, I might dip my head and nuzzle her hair with my nose so I can inhale her.

"There are...more." My voice catches, raspy with barely contained anger. "Have a look."

A horrified mewl crawls out of her throat and her entire body shakes. On the screen is a picture of her tit. It's such a disgusting violation of her privacy.

"I take it you weren't aware of these pictures?" I ask in a gentle whisper. "Hmm?"

A tear races down her cheek and she shakes her head. Hastily, she swipes at her cheek. "N-No. I didn't know. W-Why?"

Levi deserves her hatred and rage.

Not her whispered questions and humiliation.

"Meet us in Mr. Erickson's office," I bark out to him. "You're in serious trouble, Mr. Paulson."

He gets up and stomps out of the room, muttering curse words along the way under his breath. As soon as he's gone, I pluck the phone from her hands and pocket it once more.

"Are you okay?"

Willa remains frozen, her body trembling. She manages a slight nod. Her chin quivers and she hugs her arms around her body.

I wish my arms were the ones doing the comforting instead.

"He'll be suspended for this," I assure her. "The police will want to get involved because of your age."

"I'm eighteen," she breathes.

Those two words send fire spearing to my groin and settling in my nuts.

Eighteen.

Legal. Legal. Legal.

Clearing my throat, I attempt to be professional. It's a sad attempt because I can't fucking think straight when she's so close I could touch her. When her scent is camping out in my nostrils, intoxicating me.

"Then it'll be up to you if you want to press charges. I understand with family—"

"He's not my family." Her tone is sharp and her green eyes flicker with a fierceness I haven't seen before. "I'll need to talk to my mom."

"Of course," I agree. "When we get to Mr. Erickson's, we'll give her a call."

I'm itching to grab hold of her hand and guide her to the principal's office, but I can't. That won't sit well at all. The last thing I'm going to do is put her in a position that might have this entire situation turned on her. She needs me to protect her right now. At least until her mother arrives.

Unable to be a complete gentleman, I press my fingertips to her lower back, urging her forward. "Grab your bag and let's go."

Her shock seems to wear off and she jerkily makes her way over to her bag. Once it's on her back, she follows me out of the classroom, waiting for me to lock up. Since this class was my last hour of the day and my planning period is next, I don't have to worry about anyone but her right now.

The bell rings for final hour and a few straggling students rush into their classrooms. It quickly grows silent as I walk Willa to the office. When we arrive, Levi is sprawled out in a chair like the lazy slouch he is, not at all bothered by what he's done.

"Have a seat," I instruct. "Mr. Erickson and I will be talking to both of you shortly." I stab a finger in the air at Levi. "Do not speak to her."

He snorts in derision but wisely doesn't argue. I give Willa a soft, encouraging smile before letting myself into Wayne's office. Wayne's laughter booms as he chats to someone on the phone. I clear my throat, making my presence known, and wait for him to end his call. As soon as Wayne sees my murderous expression, he groans and hangs up.

"Callum," he says with a nod. "What can I do you for?"

I'm not fooled by Wayne's friendliness. He's a two-faced schmoozer. Nice to your face and talks shit behind your back. The Ericksons and Parks aren't exactly friends.

"Levi Paulson," I say and wave off Wayne's annoyed groan. "It's more than disrupting my class."

Wayne frowns. "I'm listening."

"He has pictures of Willa Reyes on his phone."

"And?"

"They're of her in her bed."

"Isn't that her stepbrother?"

"It is."

"Hmph."

I glower at him, not liking his response. "They're partially *nude* pictures of her. She didn't know they'd been taken of her."

"Boys are little perverts. You know that. At least they're not blood related because that'd be pretty sick."

"I want him suspended," I snap, the fiery authority of my words vibrating the entire room. "He's lucky she's not underage."

"Do you have proof?"

"I do, but I'm not about to violate that girl anymore by showing you."

His lips purse together. "I understand. Call them in."

"Miss Reyes," I bark out. "Mr. Paulson."

She enters the office first, head down and cheeks blazing crimson. Her dark hair curtains around her face as though she can hide from the embarrassing situation. If we were alone, I'd tuck her soft hair behind her ears so I could see all of her features.

"Mr. Paulson," Wayne says with an exasperated sigh. "Your dad isn't going to be happy to have to come up here again."

Levi shrugs like he doesn't care, but I don't miss the clench of his jaw. Sounds like the apple doesn't fall far from the tree with this dipshit.

While Wayne calls both of their parents, I lean against the wall, shamelessly staring at Willa. What is her home life like? Living with this idiot can't be good, especially after this stunt. If he's ballsy enough to take naked pictures of her, what else is he ballsy enough to do?

Images filter through my mind, providing me with suggestions, and it takes an act of God to keep me rooted in place when everything in me screams to knock that fucker's head off his shoulders.

"Your father is on his way," Wayne says and then shoots

an apologetic look at Willa. "Your mother said your stepfather can deal with both of you."

Willa deflates, losing all the air in her sails, and shoots me a resigned expression. It's clear she's used to this stepfamily getting away with crap like this.

Her mom doesn't want to come up here and fight for her?

Then *I'll* do the fucking fighting for her.

CHAPTER FOUR

Willa

DREAD POOLS IN THE PIT OF MY BELLY.

Mom's not coming. Of course she's not. Since when does she ever come out of her Xanax haze long enough to show me any sort of attention or affection?

I'd hoped...just this once, I was important enough.

Levi pops his knuckles slowly in the chair beside me. The action never ceases to unnerve me. There's just something so threatening about the way he does it. Like it's a promise of pain. I attempt to ignore it, instead choosing to place my attention on Mr. Park.

He's leaning against the wall, muscular arms crossed over his chest. Since he left his jacket in the classroom, the white material of his dress shirt visibly strains to encase his biceps. It's much easier to fixate on his physique than allow Levi to get under my skin or to worry about my mom's neglect.

Mr. Erickson lectures Levi on the harm to not only my reputation but his too. *Gag.* This statement in particular has Mr. Park tensing. I peruse my stare up his chest to his jaw muscle that ticks furiously as he glowers at Mr. Erickson.

Mr. Park is pissed.

On my behalf.

That is what gets me through the next half hour. Knowing I'm not all alone through this. He's too engrossed in ensuring

Levi's harshest punishment possible that he doesn't notice my openly gazing at him.

I try to imagine what having Mr. Park as a boyfriend would be like. Would he be growly and impatient like he is with the other students in class or would he be sweet just for me? Until today, I might not think it was possible for him to be sweet to anyone, but then he winked at me. We shared a moment and it was charged.

I wonder if we'll ever get an opportunity like it again.

"Dad!"

The room that had felt deliciously warm a second ago drops to a chilly temperature. I force my stare down to my lap and pick at my nails. It feels like I'm in trouble, but I didn't do anything. And now Darren is here, dragged from whatever scummy thing he was doing before he was called to deal with us.

Mr. Erickson lays it all out, explaining to Darren the entire story. Blood rushes in my ears and I miss most of what's being said. My only hope is that Mr. Park speaks up on my behalf if need be.

"Miss Reyes."

Mr. Park's deep voice hooks into me, tugging me from the darkness I'd settled into. I skate my eyes over to him and take in the way he motions for the door.

He wants me to leave.

No problem.

I shakily stand and grab my bag. Levi's legs are stretched out, blocking the path. I make the mistake of looking at him. His blue eyes burn with hatred for me—a hatred I've yet to understand.

"Excuse me," I murmur, tearing my eyes from his to look at his feet.

He doesn't move them.

Smack!

"Ow, fuuu—dge. Dad, what the hell?" Levi's feet jerk back and he rubs at his arm.

"Are you okay, cupcake?" Darren asks, voice dripping with faux concern.

I jerk my head up, looking at him in confusion. Is he talking to me? Cupcake? Since when?

"She's fine," Mr. Park assures him, an unidentifiable edge in his tone. "Miss Reyes, I need assistance making copies for an assignment tomorrow. Can you help and I'll return you to your stepfather once they're done here?"

Darren's eyes are burning holes into me. I sense that he doesn't want me to go, but it's not exactly like I have options right now. Besides, I'd rather escape with Mr. Park than spend another second in this office, suffocating in his stifling presence.

"Yes, sir," I say, avoiding Darren's attention. "Happy to help."

I rush past Mr. Park, unsure where to go, just knowing I need to escape. Mr. Park catches up to me and gently grips my arm, guiding me out of the front office and into the hallway. He doesn't let go but instead tightens his hold. The action doesn't hurt. It feels possessive. As though he's laying claim to me. This sends a wild thrill down my spine.

"In here," Mr. Park murmurs, pushing through a door marked *Staff Only*. "Copy room."

The *room* is nothing more than a closet. A giant copy machine sits along the wall and the other two walls are floor-to-ceiling shelves covered with reams of paper and other supplies. There's space for both of us, but adding a third person would be a tight squeeze.

He pushes the door closed behind me, leaving his palm on the door, caging me in. My heart rate kicks up at his proximity.

"Do you really need help?" I ask, my voice breathless and faraway.

Amusement briefly dances across his features, lighting up his eyes and making the corners of his mouth twitch like he might smile. "I'm quite capable of making copies myself. You, on the other hand, needed a breather."

I note that he doesn't drop his hand. If anything, it feels as though he's leaning closer into me. He's so near I can smell his cologne—a hint of spice and maybe apples. Whatever it is, it reminds me a little of Christmas. That makes my heart swell.

"You're smiling," he murmurs. "I was just sure I was going to be met with tears."

I grin, chancing a look up at him through my lashes. "I'm stronger than I look."

Too bad I don't believe those words. I want him to, though. I want this man to see me as someone who could be his equal. Someone he would want to take to bed with him. I want to be seen as a woman, not some helpless girl.

"You shouldn't have to be." He lifts a hand like he might touch my face. I hold my breath, praying he does, and then exhale a disappointed sigh when he fists his hand and drops it back down. "Your family is supposed to look out for you."

"We're not exactly close." I hate that the conversation has moved from our almost playful banter to his concern for my familial relationships. "Darren didn't like that my mom came with *baggage*."

Mr. Park's eyes narrow. "You are *not* baggage."

His fierce tone sends currents of buzzing electricity through every nerve ending. I shift on my feet and chew on my bottom lip. The copy room is completely silent aside from our breathing that seems to be heavier than before. It feels as though all the air has been sucked from the room, leaving me hot and desperate for a cool breath.

The door bumps into my ass and I yelp in surprise. Mr. Park's features harden and he barks out, "May I help you?"

"Callum?"

Mr. Park's nostrils flare and he curses under his breath. Not like he's ashamed of being in here with me, but as if he's annoyed we've been interrupted. I give him a knowing smile. This moment feels like our little secret and I want him to know I won't give him away.

"I'm teaching Miss Reyes to use this dinosaur of a machine, Miss Collins. You'd think Mr. Erickson could find a way to budget for a better copier machine," Mr. Park says. "Do you need in here?"

Mr. Park grabs a handful of papers off the shelf and pushes them into my hand. He motions with his head for me to go over to the copy machine. I wriggle past him, my body brushing against his in the process. He stiffens and I can feel the heat of his stare burning into me. As soon as I'm at the machine, he opens the door.

With my back to them, I try not to look guilty. But I am guilty. I've been flirting with my teacher all alone. Given the time, who knows what would have happened. My skin flushes as they talk in friendly voices behind me.

"Let's get you back to Mr. Erickson, Miss Reyes."

I jolt at being addressed and set the papers down on a shelf. If I don't make eye contact, maybe Miss Collins won't see how badly my mind is still racing with steamy fantasies about Mr. Park.

Once we're in the hallway and traded places with Miss Collins, I shoot him a questioning look. I'm not sure why I need reassurance, but I need it. I need to know what I felt in that room wasn't my imagination. That he felt it too.

His penetrating stare bores into me, his expression giving nothing away. My heart sinks until he tugs at the knot on his tie.

"They should also see about fixing the air conditioner in there too," he grumbles, though it sounds teasing. "We could have suffocated in there."

My skin flushes and I fight a smile. "I did find it hard to breathe."

Oh my God.

We're absolutely flirting.

Shamelessly and in the hallway. At school.

"It's probably good we escaped when we did then." He winks at me again before growing serious. "Are you going to be okay? At home?"

I deflate like a balloon, dropping my attention to the scuffed linoleum. "I will."

He steps closer, enveloping me with his faint cinnamon and apple aroma, until his shiny dress shoes come into view. "You'll tell me if you feel...unsafe?"

I tilt my head up, searching for his eyes, to discover him towering in front of me. So close it feels intimate. So close the heat of his body washes over mine.

"Yes," I whisper. "I promise."

His nostrils flare and he leans closer. My eyes flutter closed as I imagine him dipping for a kiss. Instead, his murmured words tickle over my face rather than his lips. "Good girl."

Male voices from down the hall have Mr. Park stepping away from me. I pop open my eyes just in time to see Darren and Mr. Erickson round the corner.

"Willa," Darren calls out. "I've checked you both out for the rest of the day."

I wince at the thought of riding home with both Levi and Darren after everything that's transpired today. But it's not like I have a choice. Nodding, I quickly make my way over to him. Darren places a heavy hand on my shoulder and squeezes. It makes my skin crawl. He's not exactly the fatherly or affectionate type.

Feeling helpless, I glance at Mr. Park. He watches with a blank expression that leaves me hollow inside.

Darren ushers me out of the school and away from Mr. Park. The cold, wintery air blasts into me, making me wish I'd worn a coat today. His suped-up black Camaro is parked in the fire lane out front. Levi is leaning against the car, arms crossed as he waits.

"In the car. Both of you," Darren growls, releasing his hold on me. "I've had enough bullshit today without having to deal with this."

He hits the fob, unlocking the vehicle. Levi opens the door and lifts the seat, motioning for me to sit in the back. "Ladies first."

I ignore him and slide into the back. Once they're both

seated and buckled in, Darren peels out, his lame rock music blasting through the speakers.

I wait for him to yell, like he's known to do, but he doesn't. It's not until we're home and making our way inside that he finds his voice again.

"Are you a fucking idiot?" Darren snarls at Levi. "I could go to prison for that stunt!"

Darren backhands Levi, sending him crashing against the wall. Levi grunts, rubbing at his cheek, a fearful glint in his normally mean blue eyes.

"I'm sorry, Dad," Levi mutters. "I was just having some fun."

"Fun?" Darren's eyes narrow and the vein in his neck throbs. "When were these pictures taken? Before or after Willa's eighteenth birthday?"

"After," Levi says quickly. Too quickly. "I swear it."

"And you," Darren snaps, turning his venom on me. "Stop traipsing around our house half-naked like a little whore and maybe this shit won't happen. For Christ's sake. Go to your rooms before I beat the fuck out of both of you."

I shudder at the threat. Darren hasn't hit me, but he's hit Levi and my mom both enough for me to know he would do the same to me.

"I'm sorry," I croak out. "It won't happen again."

It won't.

I don't care if I have to blockade the door every night while I sleep. I'm never letting that prick catch me at a disadvantage ever again.

CHAPTER FIVE

Callum

I ALMOST CROSSED A LINE I WOULDN'T BE ABLE TO COME back from.

It's like I can still smell her—honey and sweet cream, so real I can nearly taste it. This is going beyond an inappropriate crush. This is a maddening obsession. When I had her alone with me in the copy room, it was wrong, but it felt so goddamn right.

I need a drink.

Or an ass kicking.

Maybe both.

I could visit my father. It'd be a good reminder of why I can't allow myself to fall down this rabbit hole with Willa. I'll be just like him. And I *cannot* be just like him.

Park Mountain Lane is quiet this late afternoon. In the spring, it's bustling with lawn care workers as they fuss over my father's immaculate lawn, but since it's winter, it's devoid of workers. Even with the flowers and grass dead from the cold, the house is otherwise perfect, custom built to Dad and Jamie's specifications. You'd never know nearly two decades ago a different house stood—the house I grew up in.

"Miss you, Mom," I mumble under my breath.

The fire that destroyed our home and took my mother from us also nearly took my brother, Jude.

Don't think about bad shit.

But that only leaves Willa and I'm trying not to think about her at all. Not her supple bottom strawberry lip as she bites down on it. Not her slightly pink cheeks that flood crimson when my gaze falls on her. Not her long, dark lashes that flutter when I'm near.

I pass Dad's house and then Hugo's next. Even after what my father did to me, I still couldn't escape him. Our family populates Park Mountain Lane from the turn off the main road that runs through Park Mountain, Washington, all the way to Grandpa's old house at the base of Park Mountain itself. My house is situated between Hugo's and Grandpa's, where Jude lives with him. Parked out front is Dad's golf cart, reminding me no matter how hard I try to avoid him, he's always there.

Maybe I should take a page from my uncle Theo's book and move to the other side of the mountain, far away from Dad. Then I wouldn't have to see him on a daily basis, constantly reminded of how wrong he did me when I was Willa's age.

Willa.

Fuck.

The last thing I need is to have a stupid conversation with Dad while thinking of Willa's tight, young body I remember with precise detail from those photos.

So much for that.

At least having to speak to Dad will kill my stupid boner.

I pull into my garage, attempting to keep my anger at bay. If living on the same street wasn't bad enough, he infects my life as though he has the right to.

Hell, I suppose he does.

This is his town after all.

Sucking in a few deep breaths, I attempt to calm myself. Talking to Dad while I'm on edge is never a good idea. I'll say rude shit and he'll remind me of his authority over me. Jamie or Hugo will get involved, both of them peacemakers, and I'll end up backing off like I always do. The chip on my shoulder will grow and the cycle will continue.

I step into the house from the garage to the scent of coffee. Taking my time, I pull off my coat and hang it, along with my laptop bag, on a hook before making my way into the kitchen. Dad—also dressed in an immaculate suit—is seated at the bar.

"Afternoon, Cal."

"Dad."

I toss my keys on the counter and then set to making myself a cup. Dad's stare bores into me. For him to show up at my house like this, it means either he wants something or he's here to demand something.

"It's been a long day," I say once my cup is brewed and I've dumped enough sugar in it to make my teeth fall out. "What do you need?"

Dad chuffs and sets his cup down on the black-and-white granite with a clink. He stretches his arms out in front of him, loosely threading his fingers together. His titanium wedding ring glints in the overhead lights, always mocking me.

"Have you spoken to Hugo?"

"About Spencer?"

Dad smirks. He doesn't look a day over forty, often getting confused as our brother rather than our father. As if he needs anything else to make his head swell.

"Spencer. Ahh, that boy. So much like you at that age."

Spencer is a shit starter. We both know this. Dad's dig doesn't hit where he intends it to. I'm able to ignore it, quirking an impatient brow at him to move the conversation along.

"No, Cal," Dad continues. "About Washington State Attorney General."

I frown, racking my brain for the information about who Washington's AG is. Melinda something, I think. "He didn't mention her."

"Not her," he says with a chuckle. "About the upcoming campaign."

"I'm afraid he didn't." I scowl at my father, hoping he lays it on me rather than delivering his demand in tiny spoon-fed doses. That shit is annoying.

"Hugo's running for AG. He'll be making the announcement soon at a press conference."

"Attorney General? You sure he's ready for that?"

Dad waves me off with his hand and then picks his mug back up, slowly sipping. "Hugo's been ready for politics his entire life. He's always kept his nose clean and his past is flawless. The people of Park Mountain admire and love your brother. He's ready."

"But..."

Dad's lips press into a firm line and his brow furrows. If he knew this expression aged him ten years, I doubt he'd do it. I'm not going to tell the bastard.

"But Spencer is not ready."

"And you want me to keep Spencer in line? You know that kid doesn't listen to anyone. He's as bad as Dempsey."

"I'll handle Dempsey," Dad bites out. "Your baby brother will step in line. You all will."

"Does Hugo even want this position?"

"Hugo knows what's best for this family. It's why he went into law, like me and your grandfather."

It's always about control with our family, my dad being the one tugging on all our strings.

"I'll speak to him about his grades," I grunt out. "Is that all?"

"Our family, more than ever, will have a magnifying glass upon us. We don't need anything popping up out of the blue. Hugo can achieve this, but it's going to take everyone doing their parts to get him to the top."

"Noted. Is that all?"

Dad slides off the bar stool and stands. He's not nearly as tall as me, but he's just as solid. I sip my sweetened coffee, attempting to relax my muscles. Whenever he's near, I get tense as fuck.

"Your mother—er—*step*mother." He chuckles. "Jamie wants everyone to meet at the house on Sunday for a celebratory dinner honoring Hugo's new endeavor. You'll be there of course."

My hand tightens around the handle of my mug, my knuckles turning white. "Of course, Dad."

He studies me for a beat, clearly disappointed that his little jabs haven't resulted in an outburst he can belittle me for. With a quick nod, he excuses himself and leaves the kitchen, exiting through the garage door. Every time I change the code, the fucker cons one of my brothers into giving it to him. My bet is on Hugo.

I whip out my phone and fire out a text to him.

Me: Thanks for the warning, dick.

Hugo: Yeah, about that. I was going to tell you the news over a drink. Guess Dad beat me to it.

Me: Waiting eager as fuck in my house like a kid on Christmas Eve.

Hugo: I'm sorry, man. I should have known better.

Me: AG? Really?

Hugo: Not all of us have big dreams of being a high school statistics teacher.

I send him several middle finger emojis.

Hugo: Seriously. This could be good for me. For our family. I didn't tell you because you always get pissy when Dad is involved.

He'd get pissy too if Dad stole the love of his life, put a couple babies in her, and then married her, making her his stepmom.

Me: What do you need from me?

Hugo: Get along with Dad. Be happy for me.

Me: I'm happy for you.

Hugo: Liar.

Me: I'll get there. As for Dad...I'll work on it.

Also a lie.

Hugo: Just help me keep an eye on Spencer. The last thing we need is some scandal popping up when I'm knee-deep in this campaign and have dumped a shit ton of money into it.

Me: Spence isn't going to cause trouble. I'll keep an

eye on all three of those brats at school. You have my promise.

Hugo: Let's have that drink soon. Tonight?

Me: Long day today. Friday?

Hugo: I'll pencil you in.

Asshole.

Me: What did Jude say when you told him?

Hugo: Jude is Jude. He rarely replies to my texts and never responds to my phone calls. I'll feel him out on Sunday.

We text back and forth for a bit while I make dinner. It's not until he's done chatting and I'm alone with my thoughts that they drift back to Willa.

Is that monster of a stepbrother of hers going to take more pictures?

My blood boils at the thought of him lurking over her sleeping form, moving the covers away to reveal naked parts of her. If he wasn't seventeen, I'd whip his ass for the hell of it.

I should check on her.

Grabbing my laptop from my bag after dinner, I make my way into my home office and sit down. I have assignments to load, but first, I need to make sure Willa is okay. I open up my inbox, skip over some student questions for the time being, and draft an email to Willa.

Just making sure you're okay. If you ever need to talk, my number is on the syllabus.

I should delete the email, not send it. But I'm not being perverted. I just want to know that she's okay. It's platonic. Any teacher would check in on their student after going through something like Willa did today. It's completely normal.

She doesn't respond, so I busy myself with my work. If I let my mind drift, I'll get pissed at Dad or annoyed with Hugo hiding shit from me, or obsess over Willa. Once I'm finished for the evening, I grab a quick shower. I'm just coming out of the bathroom in a towel wrapped loosely around my waist when I hear buzzing from my phone. I pick it up, expecting more yammering from Hugo, but instead discover a number I don't recognize.

Unknown Number: A little freaked out if I'm being honest.

A flash of heat ignites in my gut, burning its way through every nerve. It's Willa. She responded. It's such a simple text, answering my question. Benign. It assures me she's fine. No need to delve further.

Except, I do.

Me: That's natural. It was an invasion of your privacy, and quite frankly, criminal.

I quickly save her name on my phone. I'm waiting on pins and needles for her reply like a desperate teenage virgin talking to a girl for the first time.

Willa: Thank you for what you did today. It means a lot. I don't have anyone who cares enough to fight for me.

Her words are a punch to my chest. How can someone so sweet and beautiful be treated that way?

Me: You're welcome. It was my pleasure.

Willa: Good night, Mr. Park.

Me: Call me Callum when we're not at school.

Fuck.

The dots move and stop a couple times, making me regret my last text. It's too late to take it back now.

Willa: Does this make us friends, Callum?

My dick thickens at her text. I can almost imagine her lips curling into a flirty smirk. This is wrong. We've crossed a line here and I need to gingerly step back over it, creating distance between us.

But she just fucking admitted she has no one.

No. One.

Me: Yeah, I suppose it does. Get some rest.

Willa: Yes, sir.

Me: Good girl.

Jesus Christ. Do I have to keep flirting with her?

Willa: See you tomorrow. Thanks again.

I toss my phone away from me onto the bed. The last thing I need to do is reply and call her sweetheart or beautiful or anything else to get my ass in trouble. With a grumble of annoyance, I yank off the towel around my waist, grab a bottle of lube, and fuck my fist in an effort to relieve some of this built-up tension.

All it does is make me crave her more.

Fantasize about my dick inside her and her lips on mine.

I'm going to have to figure out something to get this girl out of my head. This is getting out of control.

CHAPTER SIX

Willa

FRIENDS.

Such a loaded word, especially for someone who doesn't ever make friends. Maybe to someone like Mr. Park—er, Callum—it's a word that's tossed around easily. But for me, it actually means something.

A friend is someone you can depend on.

Yesterday, not only did he defend me and do his best to protect me from what Levi had done, but he also checked on me later.

I'm sure texting with your student is a big no-no.

I certainly won't be telling anyone. It can be our secret.

My skin flushes. I'm going to see him soon. With thoughts of Callum next period comes the dread of having to see Levi. I'd managed to escape this morning without a run-in with anyone in my family, including Mom, but I can't avoid my stepbrother forever.

As the clock ticks by too slowly, I agonize over texting Callum again. Was our conversation last night just a one-time thing? Would he reply if I texted him today? I'm itchy with nerves, once again confused about this thing between us.

"Psst."

I jerk my head to the left to find Dempsey Park smirking at me. He's like a younger version of Callum—same floppy dark hair, though minus a few grays at the temples, same icy blue eyes, same intensity that clearly runs through the family blood. But where Callum is all fitted suits and impeccable perfection, Dempsey is the opposite.

He wears a lot of black. Black concert tees. Black, holey jeans. Black boots. Even the leather bracelets he wears around his wrists are black. Every bit the bad boy his reputation warns of.

"What?" I mouth, frowning at being the object of his attention in the middle of class.

"Got a pencil I can borrow?" His eyes flash with mischief. "Pretty please."

I study him for a moment, wondering if he's messing with me. Hot guys like him don't normally talk to me. But, then again, hot teachers don't talk to me either. Seems like it's just one of those weeks.

"Uh, sure," I mutter. "In my, uh, bag."

For some lame reason, my skin flames red-hot. I lean down and dig in my bag, hunting down a pencil. A cool draft skates across my chest. It's then I remember the V-neck shirt I wore today in my effort to be "sexy" for Callum.

And I just gave Dempsey an eyeful.

Jerking my head up, I discover him peeking right down my shirt. He bites down on his bottom lip, clearly satisfied at the show. I gasp, pressing my hand to my chest, ending his view. Mortified, I grab a pencil and offer it to him.

"Here."

He takes the pencil, a grin tugging at his lips. "Red bra. Nice. Who are you trying to impress today, Reyes?"

Oh my God.

I want to crawl into a hole and die. Kill me now.

If I were like his sister, feisty and confident, I might tell him, "Your brother." But I'm not. Instead, I discretely flip him the bird. He barks out a laugh of surprise, earning him a warning from the teacher.

Thankfully, the bell rings and I'm rescued from this whole stupid incident. It's a reminder of why I wear baggy clothes a lot of the time. I don't like bringing attention to my appearance. I like blending in and going unseen.

Except with Callum…

"Wait up!"

My hasty exit out of the classroom was a waste of effort. Dempsey easily catches up to me, slinging an arm over my shoulders. He smells like a hint of tobacco mixed with blueberry muffins, which is an odd, yet nice combination.

"Sorry," Dempsey says with a chuckle that begs to differ. "I swear I didn't do that on purpose."

"Right," I mumble. "Everyone knows you're a manwhore."

He laughs again. "Do they now? My reputation precedes me. I bet my dad's super proud."

I'm not sure why Dempsey is showing a sudden interest in me, but it unnerves me. People don't notice me. I've managed to fade into the background for years. Why the sudden interest in Willa Reyes, school nerd?

"Can't you go bother someone else?" I say, making the mistake of peering into his blue eyes that match Callum's almost identically.

"Technically, I am." He winks at me before turning his attention down the hallway. He does a chin lift and says, "'Sup?"

I follow his stare to Levi. My stepbrother. His narrowed stare is on me, furious and accusing.

"Willa," Levi growls, coming to a stop in front of us. "Stay away from Park."

My skin burns hot. How dare this prick. He photographs indecent poses of me while I sleep, gets caught having them by our teacher, and then has the audacity to act like the moral hero in my story. Excuse me, but no.

"I can see whoever I want, Levi." I adopt the bitchiest face I can muster. "Walk me to class, babe?"

I don't know what's possessed me to poke at Levi, but it actually feels good. Dempsey could blow my cover and I will die of humiliation.

Dempsey kisses the top of my head. "Yeah, *babe*. Of course."

Being called babe, even by the wrong Park brother, does wonders for my ego. I stand taller and face off with the monster I live with. Levi blinks at me, a mix of confusion and rage.

"When you get knocked up or crawling with STIs, don't come home looking for support," Levi snarls at me.

"Don't be a prick," Dempsey snaps, his easygoing persona disappearing in an instant. "And stay away from my sister."

Levi's nostrils flare. "Is that what this is about? I fuck your sister, so you fuck mine?"

Dempsey vibrates with anger and drops his hold on me. He steps forward until he comes nose-to-nose with Levi. If I don't do something, there's going to be a fight.

"Stay. Away. From. Gemma."

"Or what?" Levi taunts.

"It'll be the last thing you do."

A crowd has formed around us, a combination of curious students and those who are laughing, entertained by the impending fight.

"Come on," I say, grabbing Dempsey's bicep. "He's not worth it."

Dempsey considers my words and then steps back. He takes my hand, threading our fingers together. It's all a ruse, but Levi doesn't know that.

I tug at Dempsey's hand, dragging him past my fuming stepbrother. The eyes of every student in the hallway are on me and Dempsey, quickly forming their own shocked conclusions. That we're a couple.

"Care to fill me in?" I ask when we're no longer in Levi's earshot.

"Your brother is a dick."

"Tell me something I don't know. And he's my stepbrother."

Dempsey squeezes my hand. "Right. Step. Sorry about all that. I just..." He huffs. "He pisses me off."

"That's something we both have in common." I glance up at him. "Is he really messing around with your sister?"

"Doubtful, but he wants to. My dad won't let Gemma date, but that doesn't mean Levi won't take every opportunity to get with her. The last thing my family needs right now is Gemma causing a scandal by getting mixed up with Levi. No offense."

I don't know what half of that means, but I nod in understanding, because any way you shake it, Levi is a bad apple. The Park family is not only wealthy, but they're the backbone of this community. Levi would be the bad seed that poisons them all. Just like he and his father are at my house.

"I don't think he's watching anymore. We can stop pretending." I go to tug my hand away, but his grip tightens.

"This might work." He comes to a stop, shooting me a

teasing grin. "I mean, we've already practically been to second base."

I roll my eyes, unable to smother a laugh. "You're a brat."

"*Your* brat."

"Ha."

"Seriously."

"No. I will not be your pretend girlfriend."

"I'm wounded, Reyes. What about my for real girlfriend?"

As enticing as that might sound, my heart isn't in it. It's his brother I can't stop thinking about.

"How about friend?" I offer, arching a brow at him. "I don't have too many of those."

"Friend. I guess I can handle that label until I woo you out of your clothes and make you beg for girlfriend status."

I playfully shove at him. "Asshole."

My heart is light. A friend. And not just any friend, but one of the most popular kids at this school, too. Not to mention, imagine all I could learn about Callum through Dempsey.

"You chose the right side, Reyes."

"Yeah?"

"The Parks take care of their own."

He messes with my hair before sauntering away. I stare after him, a little unnerved by our whole encounter, but not hating it.

Dempsey Park is my friend now, just like Callum said he was my friend last night.

Interesting.

This is by far the weirdest week of my life.

"Bell's about to ring, Miss Reyes."

I jolt at the deep timbre of Callum's voice, jerking my attention to where he stands just outside his classroom. Today, he's handsome as ever in a three-piece navy suit that accentuates his electric blue eyes. His dark hair is tousled like he's been running his fingers through the thick strands. My own fingers twitch to do the same.

"I see you know Dempsey," Callum says, his stern features unreadable.

Flames lick up my neck and heat my cheeks. "I, uh, he..." I bite down on my bottom lip, trying hard not to continue to ramble out words that make no sense. "He's my friend."

Callum doesn't react to my words. I guess I expected to see relief in his features. Or maybe jealousy. He wears the same almost-scowl he always has on. No secret smiles or winks. I'm thrown for a loop, questioning everything that happened yesterday.

I didn't imagine it.

I have proof of his texts on my phone.

"Call—er—Mr. Park, it's not what you think," I whisper, unsure why I feel like I need to make him understand the situation.

Callum's jaw ticks, like he's clenching his teeth, but then he motions for me to go into the classroom. I've been dismissed. His blatant rejection or refusal to hear me out is a punch to my chest.

"Don't be tardy," he says in response.

My gaze falls to my feet. I'm unable to look at him. Why do I have to fall for someone so completely unattainable? Why not give in to Dempsey's advances? Weeks ago, I'd have jumped at the chance of being the girlfriend of Dempsey Park.

But that was before I realized my teacher likes me.

He does like me.

I'm not insane.

Ignoring Callum's cold words, I leave him, entering the classroom. The other students are babbling, creating a dull roar that makes my temples throb. I'd been looking forward to this class all day, but now I want nothing more than to run away and hide.

Levi saunters in just seconds before the bell rings with one of his douchebag friends. The room falls nearly silent when Callum enters, closing the door behind him. Every nerve ending in my body comes alive at his nearness. It's as though even the hair on my arms is attracted to him, standing on end, pulling toward him.

"Who here read the case study last night?" Callum asks by way of greeting, his voice clipped and serious.

Of course I did, but I've had enough attention on me today. The last thing I'm going to do is add more by being the teacher's pet.

"Mr. Morris?" Callum asks. "Do you even know what class this is?"

The emo kid up front, Casey Morris, shifts in his seat. "Eh, statistics?"

"I'm the one asking questions, Mr. Morris. Either it is or it isn't."

"Statistics, bruh. Yeah."

Callum walks over to his desk, peering down at the blue-haired kid, power and authority radiating from him. "I'm not your *bruh*."

The class sniggers.

"I didn't read the case study," Casey mutters in defeat. "Sorry, Mr. Park."

"The only thing sorry is your grade." Callum steps aside,

no longer interested in humiliating Casey. His attention falls on me. "How about you, Miss Reyes?"

With his intense gaze blatantly boring into me, a flash of heat prickles over my skin. I, too, shift uncomfortably like Casey, but probably for entirely different reasons.

I like being the object of Callum's burning stare.

"I read it," I admit with a whisper.

"Of course she did," Levi utters loud enough for me to hear. "Probably fingered herself all night to it, too." He barks out a laugh before mocking me in a voice that's supposed to sound like mine. "'*Statistics is so hot, Mr. Park. Make me come.*'"

CHAPTER SEVEN

Callum

I WANT TO PUT MY HANDS AROUND THIS KID'S NECK AND choke the life out of him. Watch his face turn purple and his eyes bug out as he gasps for air. He must sense the rage bubbling up inside me, despite my apathetic expression, because he drops his gaze to his desk.

Good.

He can shut his damn mouth and leave my girl alone.

My girl.

Stupid fucking man. She's nothing to you. Nothing.

But that's a lie. Last night, when I made the decision to text her, I made her mine. My friend. Or so I'd agreed to.

It's not…enough, though.

Friends seems like the wrong word to label what we have.

"May I be excused?"

The object of my obsession's voice draws me from my inner turmoil. I find Willa's eyes shiny with unshed tears and her chin slightly wobbling. Everything in me begs me to go to her, pull her into my arms, and not let go.

"You may."

She grabs her stuff and is out the door in a flash. Without Willa in my presence, I can think and focus. I manage to get through the entire lesson uninterrupted, keeping the class busy taking a ton of notes. It's not until the bell rings do I realize she never came back.

I need to talk to her. It wasn't until that dickhead started saying shit to upset her earlier that I really understood how difficult this is for her. He betrayed her trust, in a place she's supposed to feel the safest, and continues to mock her. I don't know what all Levi's father said to Wayne to keep him from being suspended, but it's not fair to Willa. She's a victim who's being forced to face her perpetrator.

When every last person has left my classroom, I lock up and make a beeline to the closest women's restroom. I wait until the bell rings, sending a few straggling girls rushing out the door, before pushing inside.

"Miss Reyes?"

Something clatters in the farthest stall. "Mr. Park?"

"You going to hide in there all day?"

"The day's practically over."

I walk over to the stall door and peek in through the crack. It probably makes me a creeper, but she's *my friend* and I'm worried about her.

"Come out of there, Willa."

The door unlocks, but she doesn't open it. I take it as an invitation to join her. Some invitations should be declined, but I'm a selfish man. We're alone and she needs me.

She. Needs. Me.

I push into the stall and close it behind me. The lock engaging echoes in the empty bathroom. Willa stands with her back leaned against the wall, her backpack at her feet. Her eyes are red, obviously from crying, and her brows furl as she meets my gaze.

"I swear, I'm not always this pathetic," she whispers, her voice caught between a laugh and a sob.

I take a step toward her, bringing my body nearly flush with hers in the small space. "You're not pathetic."

She tilts her head up, green eyes searching mine. "I can barely talk to him."

"You shouldn't have to," I rumble, swallowing down my anger that threatens to resurface. "He should be suspended."

"I still have to face him at home."

"Which is fucked up."

This earns me a shy smile. "You cursed. You shouldn't do that at school."

"Oh, Willa, I do a lot of things I shouldn't do at school." Like hide out in the girls' bathroom with one of my barely legal students. "And yet, I do them anyway."

Her cheeks turn crimson at my words. "Will you get in trouble for being in here with me?"

Yes.

Absolutely fucking yes.

Worse, my father will find out. Then, I'll be just like him. He'll take great satisfaction in making my life hell for the next lifetime.

"It's our secret," I murmur.

We're not doing anything wrong. We're just talking. She admitted to not having any friends. I'm being this for her. The girl can't go at this shit alone.

"I won't tell anyone." She smiles, mischief gleaming in her usually innocent stare. "About any of it."

The inappropriate stares. The alone time in copy rooms and bathrooms. The late-night texting.

"What did your mother say?" I ask, fisting my hand so

I don't do something stupid like cradle her face in my palm. "About yesterday."

She flinches at my words, dropping her stare to my azure silk tie. "Nothing."

"Nothing?"

"I didn't see her." She sighs. "I hid out in my room all night. She was still in bed when I got up this morning for school."

Anger swells up inside me like a red tide, threatening to drown me. Her mother should have gone to her the second she heard what Levi did.

Unless...

"Your stepfather didn't tell her?" I ask, hoping like hell that's the reason.

"I don't know." She shrugs. "If he did, though, she won't care."

The anger is back, like a surprise smack to the face. "Why the fuck wouldn't she care?"

Her jade eyes are back on mine, filled with heartache and pain no girl her age should feel. It ages her. Makes her more relatable to someone like me. A kindred spirit.

"Willa..." This time, I don't restrain myself. I reach up and delicately run a finger over her smooth jawline. "Why wouldn't she care?"

She swallows and starts to look down, but my finger curls under her chin, keeping her face looking up at mine. I lean impossibly closer, the warmth of her body so close I can feel it radiating through my suit, but not enough to feel the softness of her breasts.

"Tell me," I implore. "I need to understand."

"Ever since..." She pauses when her voice quavers.

"When she started seeing Darren, she started popping pills. For anxiety and depression or whatever. I don't know exactly. But when she takes them, she just sleeps and…"

Her eyes fill with tears and she closes them, wetting her lashes. I know it's wrong, but I can't help myself. I draw her into my arms, hugging her to me. At first, she's stiff, maybe surprised, but then she melts into me, her hands gripping the back of my suit jacket as she holds me tight. With her cheek pressed to my pectoral muscle, I'm able to bring my mouth to the top of her head, pressing my lips there.

"She doesn't care about me anymore, Callum."

Her muffled words against my chest coupled with the natural way she says my first name has my heart twisting painfully. It makes me want to keep her locked in my arms, safe from all the people who've hurt her or plan to hurt her.

"I'm sorry." I kiss her head again. "I really am so sorry."

I refuse to lie to her—to tell her it will get better or that her mom is going through a hard time. She just needs to know that someone is here for her. Even if that someone is old enough to be her father and who's in charge of teaching her statistics.

"I'm late for class," she murmurs after a long beat. "I missed yesterday and now today."

"I'll write you a note." Reluctantly, I pull away from her, ignoring the way my cock twitches, unhappy with no longer being pressed against her. "Are you going to be okay?"

She nods and offers me a brief smile. "I will be. This helped." Her cheeks blaze bright red again. It makes me want to see where else I can make her turn colors. "Can I, uh, call you later?"

No. Absolutely not. Texting was crossing the line.

"Of course," I say instead, offering her a comforting smile. "I need to catch you up on what you missed during my lecture."

Fuck, her smile is beautiful.

I want to kiss her so bad it hurts.

She licks her lips, as though she's thinking the same thing, but neither of us moves. Thank God. I do not need to start down that path. If I kiss her, it won't be enough. I'll cross many more lines before we ever step foot out of this stall.

"Were you mad at me?" she asks, her voice hoarse. "Earlier, I mean."

"What could possibly make you think I'd be mad at you?"

She narrows her eyes, like she can see right into my mind. "Dempsey."

Ahhh, that.

Yes, I do remember now.

Levi pissed me off so badly when I'd overheard him shit talking to Willa that I'd nearly forgotten what I'd seen in the hallway. I admit, when I saw my fucking brother with his arm around Willa, I was confused. Momentarily outraged. Not at her, but at the unfairness of it all. The fact that I've got my dick in a knot over a girl who's around the same age as Dempsey. That I couldn't do what he was doing with her because of my position of power over her.

"I didn't realize you two were friends," I admit. "You told me you don't have any."

"I don't. Well, didn't." She shifts on her feet. "We just started talking in class today and then I think he wanted to piss off Levi, so he put his arm around me, pretending to be my boyfriend. It's stupid."

Not completely.

"You know my brother has a reputation for being a player, right?"

She nods. "I don't want Dempsey…" Her teeth bite into her bottom lip. "You know that."

I do know that. I can see how she feels about me. This thing brewing between us is chaotic and confusing, but it's also incredibly powerful. It's not a crush or an infatuation.

I'm drawn to this beautiful, quiet, broken girl.

"It's okay if you did," I lie. "He may be popular with the girls, but he's a Park. He'd never hurt you. Dempsey isn't like Levi."

"I like someone else," she whispers. "Someone I shouldn't."

This fucking girl.

"You need to leave," I croak out. "Now."

My words strike her and she flinches. "Okay, Mr. Park."

I grab her shoulders, stopping her from moving past me. "Not because I want you to. It's because I don't want you to. Do you understand?"

Her eyes are wide and innocent. "I understand."

Dipping my head down, I bring my mouth to her ear. "You have to leave because if you don't, I might put my lips on yours, sweetheart. And that would be only the beginning."

She turns her head, lips brushing over my stubbly cheek and stopping near my mouth. "Would that be so bad?"

The heat of her taunting words sends fire traveling straight to my dick. My fingers bite into her arms as I force myself to keep them there rather than letting them travel down and around her body.

"It would be very, very bad."

"How come?"

"Because I wouldn't know how to stop." I close my eyes, inhaling her sweet, honeyed scent. "I'd become addicted."

Her lips press against the corner of mine. It's brave and maddening all the same. I want to chide her for doing it and reward her for her boldness. A savage groan of need rips its way up my chest. Without thinking of the repercussions, I open my mouth and nip at hers, capturing her plump lip between my teeth.

I'm jerked from my lust-filled haze at the sound of the bathroom door opening and a teenage girl making furious sounds as she stomps inside.

"Ughhh! I hate him!"

Willa freezes, gasping sharply. I reluctantly release her lip and pull back. Slowly, I hold a finger to my lips, signifying she be quiet. I peek out the door and am annoyed to find that I know the person standing at the mirror.

"Stay here," I mouth to Willa. "Lock the door behind me."

She nods and crosses her arms over her chest. Worry flashes in her eyes. Not for herself, but for me. It warms me to know she doesn't want me to get into trouble.

Before I can second-guess myself, I slip out of the stall and storm over to Gemma. Her eyes widen in the mirror, taking in my appearance.

"What the hell, Callum?"

"You should be in class," I grind out, grabbing hold of her backpack and physically guiding her to the door.

"Let go, asshole!" She squirms to no avail. I manage to push her out of the bathroom and toward my classroom. "What were you doing in there?"

"Nothing," I lie.

She scowls at me. "Liar."

"Nothing that concerns you," I say instead. "Now get to class before I tell Dad you're cutting."

Her nostrils flare, but I know I've hit my mark. She's Daddy's little girl. Does nothing wrong in his eyes. He already shelters her. If he knows she's skipping class, he'll want to know why and double down his efforts to keep her safe and protected.

"You're a real dick, you know that?"

"It's not exactly news, Gemma."

She shoots me the bird before stalking away but stops just shy of the corner of the hallway. "I'll find out what you're up to. Or who you're doing it with."

Her threats, though they make my skin crawl, don't work.

"Go before I assign you detention."

"Fuck off, Callum."

Holy shit. I barely dodged a bullet.

What the hell was I thinking?

I wasn't. That was the problem. My dick was calling the shots and it's fucking brainless. The moment I shared with Willa will have to be enough because it can't happen again.

It. Just. Fucking. Can't.

But, oh God, do I hope it does.

CHAPTER EIGHT

Willa

HE BIT ME.

My teacher bit me.

I'm still in a daze, even as I walk home from school.

That really happened. Callum came to check on me, comforted me, and then…lost control. It was hot and thrilling. I've been aching ever since.

More. I want more.

It's easy to focus on Callum rather than my crappy life because he's such a big presence. Not just his height or muscular frame. It's him. Something about him commands attention. I can still smell his masculine scent clinging to my clothes. It's intoxicating.

My phone buzzes in my pocket. Eagerly, I pull my phone out, hoping it's him. I deflate at seeing my mom's name instead.

Mom: Have you seen my black clutch?

All pleasure at my encounter with Callum disappears in an instant. I glare at her words, angry at her for not being the mother I need her to be.

Me: I don't exactly go to black tie affairs, so I don't have it.

The dots move as she responds. I'm not normally bitchy to her, but being with Callum has left me energized.

Mom: You don't have to be a brat about it.

It's always like this. When she comes out of her pill fog and decides to be a parent again, I'm just supposed to bounce into line right along with her.

Me: I'll be home soon to help you look for it.

An ache forms in my chest. Everything in my life seems to be in turmoil lately. Almost daily, I wish we could go back to the days when Darren and Levi weren't in our lives.

Another buzz from my phone has me scowling. But, instead of Mom, it's him.

Callum: Sorry about earlier.

I frown in confusion before tapping out a reply.

Me: When you bit me?

The dots move and stop a couple of times before he responds.

Callum: Not sorry about the bite. I meant I'm sorry about making you hide while I dealt with my sister.

Me: You were protecting me.

Callum: I like protecting you.

Energy buzzes through my veins.

Me: It was nice forgetting everything around me for a little while. You're distracting.

Callum: You're distracting too. Trust me.

A car honks as they drive by and I recognize Dempsey.

He waves his hand through the window before he guns it. I can't help but wave back.

Me: Maybe I should meet you somewhere. You could give me the lecture notes.

Callum: Bad idea. Seriously. The worst idea ever.

Me: Because you'd try and bite me again?

Callum: Absolutely.

This is flirting. We're actually flirting. Callum Park is actually into me.

Me: I don't see the problem.

He makes me feel comfortable enough to put myself out there, especially since he's doing the same.

Callum: The problem is…I can't be with you.

His words sting. I frown as I stare down at them.

Me: I'm eighteen.

Callum: Very well aware, sweetheart.

Sweetheart.

Me: So?

Callum: Aside from me being your teacher, there are other reasons why I can't allow myself to go down this path with you.

Me: You have more reasons than that?

Callum: My brother is announcing that he'll be running for attorney general. They're going to pick apart everyone in his life. Politics are fucked up like that.

I'm not an idiot.

If the press discovered a salacious scandal like this, they'd turn it against Callum's brother and use it on him during the campaign. Not only would that be humiliating to Callum, but it'd be humiliating for me as well. And there's no telling what Darren would do if I embarrassed him by being involved in an affair with my teacher.

Callum: Say something…

Me: It's fine.

Callum: It's not fine, though. It's not fair.

Me: I knew you were too good to be true.

Callum: I'm sorry. I still want to be your friend, but even that will have to be kept on the down low.

I'm not exactly in a place to deal with his second thoughts and rejection of what happened earlier, so I pocket my phone, unable to reply. The walk home is a blur. I want nothing more than to run to my room, barricade the door, and hide.

Of course, that's when Mom would choose to parent.

"Willa," Mom calls out from her bedroom. "In here. We need to talk."

Grumbling under my breath, I make my way to her room. She's dressed to the nines in a fitted black dress, impossibly high heels, and her makeup perfectly applied. Her dark hair that matches mine has been twisted into an updo that makes her seem much more elegant than the wife of a weasel of a man who lets his son get away with being a pervert.

"Hey," I say in greeting. "I see you found your clutch."

Her eyes narrow on me. When she's not zoned out on Xanax or whatever is helping her cope for the day, she can be kind of scary. It's what made her a fantastic attorney before she met Darren.

"What's going on with you?"

I gape at her in disbelief. "What?"

"First that nonsense with your brother and then—"

"My brother? Mom, he is not my brother." My voice is shrill and shaking. "He's my stepbrother."

"Don't be a child, Willa. This is exactly what I'm talking about. Your dramatics are always over-the-top."

I'm stunned, which is dumb because it's not surprising. When it comes to Darren and Levi, she's always sided with them. It's like, when she married Darren, she turned into someone else. Someone pliable. Whatever Darren wanted, Darren got. She wasn't like this when Dad was alive, nor after when it was just the two of us. Something changed.

"Mom," I croak out. "I'm not being dramatic."

Her lips press together as she disregards my comment. I notice, despite her flawless look, her hands tremble slightly. "I'm going to a gala with Darren tonight. Get along with Levi, please. We have enough going on in our lives without you two adding to it."

"He took pictures of me, Mom. While I slept." Hot tears burn at my eyes, but I'm too angry to let them fall. Why is she taking their side? "He violated me."

"Enough," Mom snaps, her voice rising a few octaves. "Don't you think you're blowing this a little out of proportion?"

"He had half-naked pictures of me on his phone and was showing his friends!" I cry out, choking on a sob. "My teacher saw them!"

She flinches at my words. Barely. Almost imperceptible.

Then, she straightens her spine and points a manicured finger toward my bedroom. "You live in the house with a teenage boy. Learn to lock your door at night."

"Mom…"

"I can't afford for you to ruin my marriage. Not now."

I shake my head in confusion, tears racing down my cheeks. Unable to face her any longer, I turn on my heel and run to my bedroom. Slamming the door shut, I make sure to throw the lock, that Levi no doubt can pick, and then push my nightstand in front of it. I toss my backpack to the floor and fall face first onto the bed.

I'm eighteen now.

I should just pack my stuff and leave.

It's silent and dark when I wake, but when I check my phone, I realize it's only seven. Mom and Darren must be at their gala and Levi, if home, is being quiet. I take a quick shower, ignore my grumbling stomach, and crawl back into bed.

I have many missed texts from Callum.

Callum: Willa, we can talk about this.

Two missed calls follow that text.

Callum: I get that you're upset with me, but don't ignore me. We were having a discussion.

Another missed call.

Callum: Let me know that you're okay. Please.

His concern makes me physically ache. My mom doesn't care, but Callum does. Even if he doesn't want to let our feelings take us somewhere together, he still cares about my well-being. I finally text him back.

Me: I'm okay.

Callum: Thank fuck.

Me: Sorry I left you hanging. I had a fight with my mom.

The phone starts ringing, but it's Callum calling me on FaceTime. I panic for a second, knowing he'll see me look like a pathetic mess. With a sigh, I answer it anyway. I need to hear his voice. He'll have to get over my messy, wet hair and bloodshot eyes.

I mash the accept button and then his handsome face fills the screen. "Hi."

His brows crash together. "You've been crying."

"Yeah." I swallow hard, looking away from his penetrating stare. "It's been a rough day."

"Is that why you're in bed so early?"

"I had to get away from her—from them." A humorless laugh escapes me. "She actually said I need to remember to lock my door."

The line goes silent.

"I lock it, Callum. I do. He obviously gets in anyway." Hysteria crawls up my throat. "The best I can do now is block the door with my nightstand."

He growls. My sexy teacher growls like he's a mountain lion or a bear or a rabid wolf.

"Your home is supposed to be safe," he bites out, fury crackling through the line. "You shouldn't have to barricade your door."

"I have no choice."

"Have you been locked away in your room since you got home from school?"

"Yep," I say with a nod.

He scowls, his blue eyes flashing with rage. "I have to go."

And then the call drops.

Umm, what?

I sit in silence for several moments, wondering what would make Callum hang up on me. Did I make him mad? No, he was most definitely angry on my behalf. I try and text him.

Me: That was abrupt…

Nothing.

This really has been the worst day. First the fight with my mom and now all these mixed messages with Callum. On top of that, I'm getting a serious headache from skipping dinner. All I want to do is roll over, bury my face in my pillow, and forget this day even happened. I'm not sure how long I lie there, obsessing over the day's events, but I'm startled when I hear a tap on glass.

Someone's at my window.

I climb out of bed, taking my blanket with me and wrapping it around me since I'm not wearing much aside from a T-shirt and shorts, and head for the window. Pushing the curtains aside, I pray like hell it's not Levi come to terrorize me.

It's not Levi.

The man wearing jeans and a black hoodie is too big to be Levi.

"Open the window, sweetheart. I brought you food."

I leave the window to turn on a lamp. When I return, Callum's face is illuminated. With his hood pulled up over his head, he seems more mysterious than usual. I want to pull it down and run my fingers through his hair.

He brought me food.

Sure enough, in one hand is a fast food bag and a Styrofoam cup is in the other. I open the window, ignoring the chilly air that rushes in, and smile at Callum.

"How did you know where I live?"

"I have my ways." He winks at me. "Are you okay?"

"I am now. You brought me food. That better be a cheeseburger and fries."

He grins, wide and flirty. My heart flops around inside my chest. "And a chocolate milkshake."

"My hero." I climb through the window and sit on the edge, my legs dangling. He hands me the milkshake.

"I didn't know what you liked on your burger, so I had them put everything on the side. Just in case."

I'm in awe at his thoughtfulness. Not only did he take care while ordering my food, he brought it to me. Even though so much is at risk for him, he's still here because I need him.

"Thank you," I say, setting the shake on the ledge beside me. "You're the kindest person I know."

"Only to you. To everyone else, I'm an asshole."

"I feel special."

"You *are* special."

CHAPTER NINE

Callum

SO MUCH FOR STAYING AWAY.

This girl makes it nearly fucking impossible. Aside from the fact I have to see her every day in class, now I'm so far gone obsessing over her, I'll never escape this madness.

How could anyone be cruel to her?

Willa is a vision, perched on her window ledge, wrapped in a blanket, and wolfing down a burger like it might be her last. So fucking perfect.

"What?" she asks around a mouthful of food.

"I just like looking at you."

She bats her lashes and drops her gaze. I know my forward nature with her catches her off guard sometimes, but I can't help it with her.

"You're risking a lot coming to my house," she says after she swallows. "Someone could see."

I parked down the street and wore a hoodie. I'm not terribly worried about being caught.

"You needed me." I shrug my shoulders and step closer. "I had to see you."

She peers up at me and cocks her head to the side. "You confuse me."

"Likewise, sweetheart."

"Why fight this then?" She sighs, frowning at me. "We like each other."

It's far more than like with this girl.

It's need and desire and obsession all wrapped up in a pretty little bow.

"You know what's at stake," I remind her, hating how bitter and childish my tone is.

She finishes her meal in contemplative silence. After she bags everything up and tosses it inside her room, she turns to look at me.

"I would never do anything to risk anyone finding out." She hugs the blanket tighter around her. "You can trust me."

The thing is, I know I can trust her. She wears her intent so obvious for all to see. Willa Reyes likes her old-ass teacher and is willing to sneak around for him.

It's fucked up.

She deserves to be with someone like Dempsey. Even I can admit she looked good—natural—tucked under his arm. They're the same age, for fuck's sake.

With me, there's too much drama involved.

The school would have a shit fit if they knew I was romantically involved with a student. And the press? They would love to smear my family's name through the mud. Just in time for Hugo's campaign. Worst of all, Dad would find out. He'd find out that I'm a sick fuck like him, lusting after a girl still in high school.

"I know I can trust you," I assure her, my voice gruff. "It's everyone else I'm worried about."

She reaches her arm out of her blanket cocoon and grabs the front of my hoodie. I allow her to tug me closer. Her thighs spread, inviting me between them. Because I can't think straight with this girl, I go, nestling my body against hers. Neither of us says anything about the fact my dick is hard as fuck sandwiched between us.

"I can keep a secret," she whispers. "I won't tell anyone, Callum. I just…" Her chin wobbles once. "I'm so alone and you make everything feel…better. So much better."

I'm losing this battle between us. My palms find her face, delicately cradling her. I could stare at her round eyes, so full of innocence, and parted pink lips for hours.

"You're so fucking beautiful."

A sweet smile curls her lips up. "So are you."

I've been called a lot of things, but never beautiful. This amuses me. My heart thunders in my chest, aching and yearning to get swallowed up in this girl.

"Can I kiss you, sweetheart? I promise not to bite. At least not this time."

She nods, eyes twinkling with wonder. I tilt her head up, angling her so I can dip down and capture her mouth with mine. Earlier, I'd been given the slightest tease of her lips before we were interrupted. Now, I get to finally partake in this forbidden fruit.

A soft moan escapes her when my tongue plunders into her mouth, seeking hers. She tastes like chocolate milkshake and it's the most delicious thing I've ever had. I devour her mouth, hungrily sucking and teasing her tongue. I consume every whimper and moan. It's safer if I keep my palms on her face, but it soon feels like torture not being able to touch her.

Pulling back, I meet her lust-filled stare and admire her swollen lips still wet from our frantic kiss. I want to see her like this but naked and spread out before me in bed. I need to see the way her eyes roll back as I take her sweet cunt in my mouth, driving her to new heights with my tongue.

"What?" she rasps, eyes hooded. "Did I do something wrong?"

"No," I growl with more force than necessary. "You're so fucking perfect it does my head in."

"I'm not perfect."

"To me, you are." I rest my forehead to hers. "May I touch you?"

"Y-Yes."

I slide a hand inside her blanket and groan when my palm finds silky bare flesh on her thigh. Her leg is smooth, freshly shaved, and I want to run my tongue along every inch.

"We shouldn't be doing this," I remind her, but neither of us is listening.

"No one knows. It's our secret."

Fuck.

For such a good girl, she really feeds my bad side.

I slide my palm higher until I find the hem of her shorts. I run my thumb beneath the material. My dick twitches when she whimpers. I've barely touched her and she's melting.

"I'm not some sick fuck who preys on young women," I tell her. I'm not my father. "I don't do this. Ever. There's just something about you, Willa. I can't get you out of my head. I don't want to."

"You're a good guy," she assures me. "I know this is something special."

I trail my thumb over the outside of her shorts, seeking out her pussy. She jolts when I rub my thumb over it.

"Have you done this before? Let someone touch you, sweetheart?"

"N-No."

She's innocent as fuck. And I'm salivating at the thought of wrecking her completely. I want to make her scream and stretch her untouched pussy to the point of pain. I need inside her, claiming and owning this sweet girl.

"You're a virgin?"

"Yes."

"Good." I lean in and kiss her pouty lips. "I love the idea of this pussy being mine and only mine."

She makes a strained sound, somewhere between embarrassed and turned on. I'll show her how to talk dirty with time.

"I'm going to fuck you," I murmur, trailing kisses along her cheek to her jaw. "And when you're exhausted from coming so hard, I'm going to sleep with my dick buried deep inside you. You want that, pretty girl?"

"Yes."

I reward her compliance by massaging firm circles on her clit over her shorts. She squirms and whimpers. I'm desperate to have my face on her needy pussy, but I'll be damned if I do that here in the window where anyone could walk up and see what's mine.

"Can you come like this?" I ask, not stopping my frantic pace. "Quiet like a good girl."

"I t-think so."

Our mouths crash together as I massage her to ecstasy. Her moans are silenced by my kiss. I revel in the way her entire body shudders from her orgasm. If we were alone in my bed, I'd remove her shorts and run my tongue along the seam to taste her pleasure.

"You came so beautifully. A+."

She laughs. "Thanks. I have a great teacher."

I pull my hand away from her pussy and tuck the blanket back around her. She's still dazed from her orgasm, so she doesn't seem disappointed at my retreat.

And I have to retreat.

Because if I keep going, I'll end up fucking her against the side of her house. She deserves more than that for her first time. Willa is a treasure and needs to be treated like one. Her first time will be romantic and gentle. It's the least I can offer her.

"I need to go," I say with a sigh. "I'm meeting my brother for a drink."

Her shoulders slouch, but she nods. "Oh. Okay. I'll see you tomorrow then."

"Keep the door locked and check your email. I sent you the lecture notes so you don't fall behind."

I lean forward and kiss her pretty lips again. I'd spend hours worshiping her mouth if I could.

"When can I see you again?" she asks between kisses. "Besides class."

"We'll figure it out," I promise. "We just have to be careful."

"We will be."

I kiss her once more, savoring her essence before pulling away. My dick is stone in my jeans, but I do my best to ignore it. "Go back inside and close the window. I want to make sure you're safe before I go."

She melts at my words, offering me a cute grin. "Yes, Mr. Park."

"You're not making it easy for me to leave. Go before I do something insane like kidnap you."

An adorable laugh rumbles from her. She obeys, though,

and slips back into the house. After she moves her milkshake off the ledge, she leans back out the window.

"One more kiss for the road?"

God, this girl is going to kill me.

"Yeah, sweetheart. One more kiss for the road."

One turns into three more before I finally drag myself away from her addicting presence. It's not until her window is down and the curtains are drawn do I finally breathe normally again.

The best bar in town is a little shithole called Knock It Off near PMU. Park Mountain University is one of the town's historical landmarks. Every time the university tries to revamp the area surrounding the college and buy out Knock It Off to no doubt replace it with a bougie-ass coffee shop, the patrons of Knock It Off show up in droves, making it impossible for the owner, Kitty Robbins, to sell. She has a cash cow and knows it. No one can afford to make her move. You'd think with all the money rolling in, she'd update the eyesore.

Kitty calls it vintage.

Me and Hugo call it a dump.

But it's our favorite dump, so we deal with it.

I push through the glass door and am met with a wall of heavy smoke. Neither me nor Hugo smokes, which is another reason why we should hate this place, but we don't. I find him seated at a booth in the back, fiercely texting on his phone with two bottles of locally brewed beer on the table in front of him.

Rat or some other equally heinous '80s metal band rages through the speakers. A woman with huge tits and bleached white hair wriggles her fingers at me as I pass. I give her a tight smile but don't stop. I'm not in the mood to socialize with the locals.

"Hey, man," I bark out, earning Hugo's attention.

My brother, though older by two years, wears his age better than I do. Where I'm all scowls and frowns, giving me wrinkles on my brow, he's always smiling, which gives him the appearance of being younger.

"What's up, Cal? Why do you look sketchy as fuck?"

I snort out a laugh and shove my hood off my head and sit across from him. "Just prowling the neighborhoods, checking in to see if my students are doing their homework."

"I feel like you're not joking and that makes me worry for you." He smirks. "How've you been, little bro? I haven't seen you in ages."

Hugo is always dramatic. I see him every Sunday without fail.

"Been busy. From the looks of it, so have you, AG."

He straightens and flashes me a politician smile that'll take him places one day. Probably all the way to the goddamn White House. "Tomorrow we're making the announcement. I'd like everyone to be there. Naturally, Jude won't come, but I'd like my other two brothers there."

Jude never leaves his house unless it's for Sunday dinner. Other than that, he stays holed up in his dark, outdated house, feeling sorry as fuck for himself.

"I'll be there," I assure him. "I'll even be nice to Dad."

He winces. "You know I'm sorry, right? I wanted to be the one to tell you."

"It's fine. Dad gets off on catching me off guard.

Remember that time he surprised me by fucking my girlfriend and knocking her up?"

Hugo's humor fades and he looks down at his beer bottle. "That was fucked up, man, but it was nearly twenty years ago. Don't you ever just want to move on?"

His words are a punch to the gut.

"Kind of hard when you have to see the betrayal every week," I remind him. "Dad hasn't taken anything from you, so you don't get it."

He picks up his bottle and takes a long pull, avoiding my stare. "Do you still love her? Is that why you're still so mad?"

"Jamie?" I bark out a laugh. "Fuck no. Jamie slept with my father and got pregnant with his babies. I stopped loving her the day I found out."

"Then why do you let it pull you down every day, Cal?"

I'm not exactly in the mood to mull over the past. Of course Hugo doesn't get it. I'd thought I was going to marry Jamie. We had plans to go to college together and live in an apartment near campus. She was my high school sweetheart. Four years we were together. Dad and Jamie mindfucked me. They broke my fucking heart.

No one understands.

And quite frankly, I don't have the energy to try and explain this tonight.

Besides, I'm still high from seeing Willa. From kissing her and touching her. My mood improves considerably. I force a smile for Hugo.

"Yeah, yeah. So tell me what's up with Neena. What does she think of you running for AG?"

Hugo's face darkens and he grinds his teeth. "Neena's gone off the grid again."

"Again?"

"Spencer is pissed, hence his issues at school and with me. If I could keep Neena chained to the house, I would, but that woman has always been a free spirit."

"I'm sorry, man. Are you calling it quits this time? Will you finally serve her with divorce papers?"

Hugo's features tighten. "No. Not now. The last thing I need is to go through a complicated divorce while I run for office. I'll wait until I've won before I make that move."

"Neena is a skeleton in your closet," I warn. "You sure you don't want to clean it out first?"

"Nope." He shrugs his shoulders before downing his beer. "I want to lock that door for now. I'll deal with it later."

I don't push the subject because I have my fair share of skeletons too.

Sometimes shit just needs to stay hidden.

CHAPTER TEN

Willa

All morning, I've been floating on a cloud as I get ready for school. Callum Park came to my house, brought me food, kissed me senseless, and gave me an orgasm.

It's surreal.

I'd almost think it was a dream if it weren't for the way my chin still tingles from the way his scruff rubbed against me last night.

I'm so caught up in my daydream, I nearly run right smack into Levi, who's standing just outside my door. I squeak out in surprise before shooting him a scathing glare.

"What?" I demand, lifting my chin.

He studies me for a beat and then his lip curls up in a sneer. "Dempsey Park? Really?"

My mind spins for a moment. Yesterday, when Dempsey and Levi had their argument, feels like a lifetime ago.

"Out of my way, Levi."

Ignoring my command, he steps closer until he's towering over me. My skin grows cold and my knees wobble beneath me.

"I told Dad." He flashes me a triumphant grin. "He wants to talk to you before you go to school."

"Why does Darren care who I date?"

"Because it reflects badly on him. Especially when his client is in a lawsuit with the Parks."

He laughs in that cruel way he has down so perfectly and then saunters down the hall toward the living room. With my heart in my throat, I trail after him. Darren is in the kitchen, fussing with the coffeemaker. Mom is at the table, makeup smeared from last night, and eyes glossed over.

Great.

"Willa," Darren says with his back to me. "We need to talk."

I freeze, stopping near the table, staring at my mother. She's so up and down. It's maddening. Does she not see that I need her? That I hate these people we live with and this life she's carved out for us?

"Okay," I murmur. "About what?"

Levi sits beside Mom and pretends to scroll through his phone, though we both know he's listening to every word. Darren sets down his coffee mug and approaches. His suits are expensive, but he doesn't wear them like a god the way Callum does. Darren reminds me of a snake. A fancily dressed snake.

"You. Fraternizing with the enemy."

"The enemy? I don't even know what you're talking about." My tone is shrill and I sound defensive. Well, I am defensive. I don't want to get into trouble for something I don't even understand.

"Don't take that tone with me, young lady."

"What tone?" I shriek.

Darren moves so fast, I don't have time to think. His hand swipes the air, connecting with my cheek. It's not hard enough to bruise, but certainly hard enough to not only sting but bring instant tears to my eyes.

"You hit me," I say with a whimper.

Levi smothers a grin. Mom doesn't even look at me.

"You're out of control, Willa," Darren snaps. "And I won't have you messing things up for me."

I touch my cheek, still in shock that I've been hit. "Mom?"

"Your mother agrees," Darren bites out. "Don't you, honey?"

She mutters out her agreement. It's a knife to the chest. In this house with three other people, I've never felt so alone as I do right now.

I want Callum.

I need Callum.

"I'm sorry," I say because I don't know what else he wants from me. "I won't see Dempsey anymore."

"No, you won't," Darren replies. "You will also not bring attention to our family anymore. I expect you and Levi to be on your best behavior while at school."

"Yes, sir." I focus on the hardwood floors, unable to look into Darren's hard eyes.

"Good. You can start today by riding with Levi to school. It's about time this family becomes a united front."

I stare through the windshield, thankful that Levi is blasting his music. At least I don't have to make conversation with him. I've never had a problem with walking to and from school, so it's frustrating that I'm being made to take a ride from my douchebag stepbrother.

I've never liked Darren or Levi, but it hasn't reached this degree of hatred before. I feel like Darren's prisoner and Levi's plaything.

I'm nothing to Mom.

Not anymore.

I have one semester left of school and then I can leave. My grades are good enough to get into any college, really, though I never saw myself ever leaving Park Mountain. Freedom, to me, was getting my own place near PMU and studying finance. It just feels like a lifetime away now.

I'm itching to text Callum. To tell him what transpired this morning. I refuse to do it in front of Levi, though. I can't risk him seeing. If Darren has a problem with me fake dating Dempsey, he'd lose his mind if he knew who I was really spending my time with.

The music cuts off as Levi pulls into the school parking lot. We're bathed in uncomfortable silence. As soon as he parks, I go for the door handle, but his hand on my thigh stops me.

"Don't touch me," I bite out, smacking at his hand.

His fingers dig into my thigh, making me yelp. "Remember what Dad said. Dempsey is off-limits."

"Fuck you."

Levi scoffs. "You wish, bitch."

I claw at his hand until he releases me. Then, I snatch my bag and fly from the vehicle. Levi's footsteps behind me have me hightailing it to the school, hoping to blend into the crowd. I'm so focused on him following me that I nearly knock over some guy.

"Slow down, speedy," the guy says, humor in his tone.

"Sorry," I mumble. "Can you pretend to be my friend for like two minutes? Please?"

The guy's eyes lock with mine and I recognize him.

Spencer Park.

I go my entire life in Park Mountain without encountering the Park family, and this week, I've spoken to three of them.

Spencer looks past me and his eyes narrow. Where Dempsey is a bad boy, very visibly on the outside, Spencer is not. He's preppy and popular but has a vicious glint in his eyes that should terrify me. Luckily, it's not aimed at me.

I expect Levi to attempt to pull me away from Spencer, but he keeps walking. Like he doesn't even see Spencer. It's not until Levi is inside the building that I am able to relax.

"You okay?" Spencer asks.

"Yeah, uh, thanks for that. Sorry."

"Nothing to be sorry for. I'm Spencer Park." He offers me his hand. "Pleased to meet you."

I don't tell him that we've been in several classes together over the years, instead offering him my hand. "Willa Reyes."

"You're new here?"

I nearly groan in exasperation. "Nope. Been here all my life."

He smirks. "Then where've you been all mine?"

Someone playfully jumps onto Spencer's back from behind. The two wrestle around until Spencer cries "uncle" and the other guy lets him go. Dempsey. Oh, lovely.

"Stop mackin' on my girlfriend."

Spencer laughs. "Dude. You couldn't get a classy hot girl if you tried."

"Fuck off. You're my girl, right?" Dempsey asks, grinning at me.

"We're friends," I remind him.

"She friendzoned you, man," Spencer says gleefully. "That

whole punk vibe doesn't do it for the entire female population. Some girls like a good guy."

"Good?" Dempsey snorts. "You're a Park. No one in our family is good."

"Can I walk you to class?" Spencer asks, layering on his charm. "I'd be happy to."

"Get lost, cuz. I saw her first."

"I'm not some toy to fight over," I say, scowling at Dempsey. "But you both could walk me if you want."

The guys seem perfectly satisfied with that, falling into step on either side of me as we head inside. Spencer, the apparent gentleman of the two, steps ahead to open the door for me. I flash him a thankful smile. Walking into school with two of the most popular guys earns me a lot of confused looks and whispers. If only they knew who came to my house last night. Who kissed me until I was dizzy and then rubbed me until I came.

"I'm having a party Friday night at Park Mountain Lodge," Spencer says. "You should come."

Did I seriously just get invited to a party?

This never happens.

Ever.

"I'm not sure I can. My stepdad probably won't let me."

Spencer waggles his brows at me. "We'll sneak you out. Here, put your number in my phone. Demps and I will pick you up."

I stop to take his phone. I'm not exactly sure if this is a good idea, but the prospect of having friends is exciting. Plus, if they're Callum's family, they've got to be cool to hang with. After I plug in my number, he flashes me a satisfied grin.

"Spencer," a deep voice booms in the hallway. "My classroom now."

Spencer grimaces. "My uncle is such a dick."

"Technically, I'm your uncle too," Dempsey offers.

"Whatever, cuz," Spencer grumbles. "See you around, speedy."

I give him a little wave before sneaking a glance at Callum. He's pretending to look unaffected by my presence, but I don't miss the way his gaze sweeps over my entire body or the way he runs his tongue over his bottom lip.

"Spencer isn't your cousin?" I ask once we start walking again.

Dempsey laughs. "I'm younger than Spence, but still his uncle. My dad had me and Gemma late in life."

I have a million questions, most of them revolving around Callum, but I manage to keep them bottled up.

"I'm not supposed to be hanging out with you." I frown at him. "I've been banned."

Dempsey raises a brow. "Because of Levi?"

"Technically, yes. We can thank him for tattling. My stepdad says I'm not allowed to."

"Your stepdad sounds like a dick."

"He is," I agree. "Our fake dating made its way back to him and he's pissed."

"Because he thinks I'll defile his little girl?"

I grimace at being called Darren's little girl. "No. This has nothing to do with me and everything to do with him."

"It's not a crime to be friends with someone."

Callum's stare hasn't left me. I can feel it cutting into me like a hot knife. I want to look back at him, but I also don't want to be obvious. My cheeks heat knowing I'm the object of his attention. Dempsey is rambling, but I can't focus on him.

It's not until Callum steps into his classroom that I finally manage to suck air back into my lungs. I quickly catch up to what Dempsey is saying, something about how wasted they're going to get on Friday, and nod as though I never missed a word. He walks me to my first hour, gives me a mock salute, and then saunters away.

By the time I've settled into my seat and checked my phone, I notice a missed text.

Callum: Should I be worried my family is going to steal you away from me?

He adds in an eye roll emoji that has me smiling. Despite his joking, I think he's jealous or at the very least feeling insecure. My chest tightens, knowing he's just as vulnerable as I am. This thing between us has the potential to go sideways or blow up in our faces.

Yet, we're both here for it.

Me: They invited me to a party Friday night. Even offered to sneak me out of the house.

Callum: And?

Me: It's kind of nice to have friends. That's what friends do, right?

I'm eagerly awaiting his reply, but he doesn't respond. As my teacher starts the lecture, I remain focused on my phone. Finally, it buzzes.

Callum: I just gave everyone a pop quiz so I could get back to this conversation.

Me: You're so evil.

Callum: You have no idea. And, yeah, that's what friends do.

Me: So you don't care if I go?

Callum: Are you asking my permission?

A thrill shoots through me.

Me: Yes.

Callum: Good girl. Let me think on it. Now pay attention in class. I wouldn't want to have to give you detention for texting in class.

Since I want to please him, I dutifully put my phone away and get busy taking notes. Sure, detention would be fun, especially with him, but obeying him is better.

I don't want to be the teacher's pet.

I want to be the teacher's good girl.

His sweetheart.

CHAPTER ELEVEN

Callum

I'VE NEVER DONE THIS BEFORE.

Certainly not with a student.

But this whole flirting gig is new to me. Maybe, when I was in high school, I flirted like every other guy. After Jamie and my dad did me dirty, it skewed the way I see dating and relationships. Since then, I've gone out with women, but usually only as a means to an end.

Sex.

It's not like I'm a total asshole who fucks and runs, but I certainly don't stay. If I need to get laid, I go out or meet up with some friends, and then find someone to share a night with. By morning, I'm not keen on the hopeful look in their eyes.

I just want them gone.

Because if you stupidly give your heart to just anyone, they might break it. Jamie destroyed mine. It hurt worse because the man she was fucking behind my back was my own goddamn father. Maybe if they'd had this affair and then broken up, I'd have gotten over it. Since they married and had children together, it's been a constant reminder for the past eighteen years.

Willa is different.

I don't know why, but she is.

I can feel it. It's like I know she won't fuck with my feelings. She's too sweet for that.

Jamie was sweet too once…

Shoving that thought from my mind, I reply to Willa's newest text.

Me: Stay after class. I need to see you alone for a minute. It's driving me crazy not being able to touch you.

The bell finally rings. She'll be in my classroom soon. I'll have to put up with her annoying shit of a stepbrother too, but it'll all be worth it seeing her again. I don't have to wait long. She's one of the first students to arrive.

"Hi, Mr. Park," Willa greets, a wide, silly grin on her face.

I can't help but match it. "Hello, Miss Reyes. I take it you had time to look over your notes from yesterday."

Her face turns bright red and she darts her stare to her feet. "Uh, yeah. Looked at them late last night."

"Why so late?" I can't help but taunt her, even as more students file into the room.

She jerks her chin up, eyes round like saucers. "I was busy."

"I see." I smirk at her. "I hope it was worth it.'"

"Absolutely."

I discreetly check out her ass as she makes her way over to her desk. Once she's seated, she sits up straight, eagerly awaiting the lesson. Her obedient nature makes my dick super fucking hard. Which, naturally, is a problem considering I'm sitting at my desk with a near-full classroom of teenagers.

My phone buzzes on the desk with an incoming text.

Willa: I wish this class were over already.

Me: Me too, sweetheart. You're fucking hot today and it's doing my head in.

She squirms in her seat, shooting me a small smile.

Willa: You think I'm hot?

Me: Is that a rhetorical question? Of course I do.

Willa: I think you're hot too.

Me: Hotter than Spencer and Dempsey?

She smothers a laugh, which douses my spike of jealousy.

Willa: Umm, yeah. Have you seen yourself? I keep thinking I'm going to wake up and this will be a dream.

I could keep texting with her, but the bell rings and I'm forced to teach. I'm going to have to dig down deep and focus if I have any chance of making it through this class. It's difficult, but I manage to turn off my emotions and my brain, instead tearing through a shit ton of notes for my lecture. No one is goofing around, which means they're too busy trying to write down everything I'm barking out.

Finally, *finally* the bell rings.

These annoying bastards can't leave fast enough for me.

Willa stalls, pretending to be reading back over her notes. I busy myself with my laptop, barely nodding at a few students who tell me bye. When Willa is the only student remaining, I walk over to my classroom door and close it.

"Come here," I command, my voice a deep growl. "I don't want you to be late for class."

She tosses everything in her bag, pulls it on over her shoulders, and then walks over to me. Her pink lips are parted and her moss green eyes are hooded. I'm damn near salivating for a taste of her. It's reckless to kiss her at school, but I'm unable to refrain. I will go insane if I don't have her in my arms in the next three seconds.

When she's near enough to me, I grab hold of her delicate face and tilt her head up as I step close to her. A small, satisfied sigh escapes her.

I dip down, crashing my lips to hers. Our kiss goes from tender to frantic in half a second. Her fingers grab hold of the lapels of my suit, drawing me as close as she can to her. My dick is stone between us and the urge to grind it against her is overwhelming. I pull a hand from her face to bring it to her ass and squeeze it hard enough she yelps.

"Sorry," I growl, though I'm not exactly feeling remorseful. I nip at her swollen bottom lip and rock my hips against her. "Feel what you do to me, sweetheart? You make me so fucking hard."

One of her hands leaves my chest, snaking its way up to my neck. Her fingernails find the nape of my neck, tugging at the short strands of hair there.

"There isn't enough time," she whines. "I want to stay in here with you all day."

I reward her words with a deep kiss that makes her knees buckle.

"If you stay any longer, I'm going to do something regrettable. Something that could get me fired on the spot." I devour the moan that escapes her. "I want inside you so damn bad I can't stand it."

"I want that too," she breathes. "Just lock the door."

"My good girl is so bad." I tug at her bottom lip with my teeth. "You're a bad influence on me."

"Please…"

Pulling back, I stare into her pretty green eyes. "We can't and you know it. This is crossing the line."

She pouts and fuck if that doesn't make me horny as hell. I grab her wrist, dragging it down to where my dick strains in my slacks.

"Feel this?"

Her tongue darts out, sweeping over her bottom lip and leaving a trail of wetness there. "Y-Yes."

"You're a virgin, Willa, and my dick, as you can see, is thick. I can't just fuck you against my classroom door. I'll hurt you. We'll need more preparation."

"Oh," she murmurs, brows furling. "When?"

God, this girl kills me.

"Soon. I'll figure something out."

"I can leave my window open." Her eyes search mine, almost pleading. "You could come as soon as it gets dark."

The temptation to have her tonight is almost too difficult to ignore.

"I'd like that," I admit, smiling at her, "but I don't want this to be just about sex."

She blushes. "It's not. We don't have to do that. I just…I want to see you. This isn't enough."

"Get to class before I get us both in a lot of trouble." I rest my forehead to hers. "Okay?"

"Okay."

We kiss once more before I physically wrench myself away from her. Her lips are puffy and her chin is red from my scruff. I want to turn her entire body red as I devour each inch of her.

"Be careful with Spencer," I say before I can stop myself.

Her lust-filled haze fades and she frowns at me. "Why? Isn't he your nephew?"

"He is. I just…" *Can see him stealing you away from me.* "Just be careful. Tell me you'll do that."

"Of course," she replies with a sharp nod. "Does this mean I can go to the party on Friday night?"

My gut sours at the thought of them alone with her. "I'm still thinking about it."

Disappointment washes over her features, making me feel like an instant prick. I distract her by stealing another kiss. It's chaste and ends too soon, but it makes her smile again.

"Have a good rest of your day, beautiful. I'll see you again soon."

The press conference announcing Hugo's run for attorney general is being held in the lobby of the Park Mountain Lodge, owned by my uncle, Theo. There are cameramen and journalists everywhere. When a Park makes an announcement, everyone wants to know about it. Even though Theo and Dad don't get along as well as me and my brothers do, Theo always shows up when it's time to support the family. Like now, offering his rustic, yet stunning lodge as the backdrop for this announcement.

Everything the Parks do is ostentatious and over-the-top.

The lobby is packed with people and I'm dying to get out of here. All I want is for the night to fall so I can go to my girl.

She *is* my girl.

I was a dumbass to think I could even stay away. Or, hell, even be friends. Our chemistry is an unstoppable fire. I've already gone this far, so I don't plan on stopping now.

"Quite the turnout," Hugo says, sidling up beside me. "Our brother cleans up well."

Dempsey sits next to Dad, dressed in a charcoal suit, glaring at the floor like it could open up and swallow him, saving him from this nonsense. Spencer, beside him, is dressed nearly the same but wears his suit like he was born with it on. Gemma, beside Jamie, could pass for her mother's twin, both of them wearing similar black dresses.

All that's missing is Jude.

"I take it Phantom isn't coming," I rumble low enough for only Hugo to hear.

He nudges me. "Don't call him that."

"How come he gets a free pass to all this shit anyway?" I cross my arms over my chest, feeling indignant that Jude doesn't have to come, but I do. "Maybe if I get a mask to hide my ugly mug and become a hermit, I could stay holed up too."

"Don't be a dick."

"I was born a dick, man."

Hugo turns on the charm as an elderly woman approaches. She looks familiar, but I can't place her.

"Mrs. Jackson," Hugo greets. "What an honor for you to show up this evening."

"You know I've always had a special place in my heart for you Parks." Her green eyes glitter. "How's your grandfather? Jude still living with him?"

Ahh, Gretchen Jackson. The woman my grandfather, Wyatt, broke up with for our grandmother, Catherine. Gretchen since went on to marry the second wealthiest man, Richard Jackson, though I feel like she still holds out for a reunion with our grandfather.

"You know those two," Hugo says cheerfully. "Can't separate them."

He fails to mention that Jude only tolerates Grandpa because he lets him live in his house. They're both mean as snakes, which is kind of hilarious that they choose to cohabitate.

"Tell Wyatt I said hello. Can you do that, son?"

Hugo promises that he will and then bids her goodbye. When she's out of earshot, he groans. "He's a dinosaur and I still can't go anywhere without the old ladies in this town asking about him. Was he a damn stallion in his day or what?"

We both grimace at the thought of Grandpa fucking... well, anyone.

"Mr. Park," a woman in a pencil skirt calls out to Hugo. "We're about to begin. You can head for the podium."

I clap a hand on Hugo's shoulder and grin at him. "Make it quick. I don't have all night."

"You know," Hugo grumbles, "most guys would tell their brother, 'Good luck.'"

"You're a Park." I shrug. "You were born with good luck. This position is yours. You just have to take it. Now hurry the fuck up or I'll go Jude on you and vanish."

"You're such a dick, Cal. I better see your ass after for a celebratory drink."

One drink.

And then I'm going to see my girl.

CHAPTER TWELVE

Willa

It's like I'm under a microscope now. Darren, since he got home from the office, has been watching me like a hawk. Peeked in on me while I was doing homework and then stared at me all through dinner as if he could see right inside my mind.

He didn't kill me, which means he can't.

If he could, he'd see me replaying this afternoon over and over and over again.

I touched Callum's cock.

He was huge, just like he warned. Rather than terrifying me, I craved it even more. I can't stop thinking about the feel of him in my hand. How the heat of his erection was hot to the touch, burning through his slacks and warming my hand.

I'd wanted to unzip him and pull his cock out. To kneel before him, licking and sucking until he came. Of course, we didn't get that opportunity, but I wanted it nonetheless.

"Levi, help your sister," Darren barks out, making me jump and nearly drop the sponge.

I cringe as Levi enters the kitchen and starts collecting dishes. When Mom isn't drugged off her ass, she's a good cook. On the days she's beyond cooking, like today, one of us does the task. Tonight, Darren made tacos.

"Spencer is one of them," Levi mutters under his breath. "You do realize that, right?"

His body is too close to mine. I can feel his warmth at my back. I don't like not having him in my line of sight. Tossing the sponge, I whirl around to face him.

"No way," I deadpan. "I had no idea."

Levi's nostrils flare. "They're turning you into a smartass."

"Maybe I'm finally just tired of putting up with your crap."

He snorts. "Too late to find your backbone now."

"I can do the dishes alone." I wriggle my fingers at him. "Bye."

"I *should* let Spencer have his way with you." Levi sneers at me. "Dempsey's too dumb to fuck with you, but Spencer…" He whistles and shakes his head. "He would ruin you."

I'm having difficulty combining the charming Spencer I met with this one Levi is warning me about.

"I can handle Spencer." I lift my chin in defiance. "Are you going to tell your daddy?"

"Watch your mouth."

"Or what? You'll slap me too?"

His eyes narrow. "You know what? Have at it. Learn for yourself what kind of guy Spencer Park really is."

"Don't let Darren hear you encouraging me to go against his word."

We both glance toward where Darren is shuffling through the mail in the dining room. Despite our heated argument, neither of us seems keen on bringing Darren into it. I certainly don't want to get slapped again. And Darren hits Levi a lot harder than he hit me, so I know he doesn't want his attention either.

"I've seen what Spencer does to girls he likes. He makes them fall in love and then he breaks them."

Good thing I don't have to worry about that.

"Maybe," I allow, shrugging, "but that still makes him ten times nicer than you."

"He's only nice because he wants to fuck you. I don't, so you get this." He motions to himself and smirks. "Don't come crying to me when he pops your cherry and then leaves you heartbroken."

As if I would ever come to Levi for anything.

Ignoring him, I go back to doing the dishes. My mind returns to Callum. With him infiltrating my every thought, I don't feel like such a prisoner in my own home.

Callum Park is my escape.

Me: Is your event over with yet?

I delete the text before I send it. It'll make me sound stupid and needy. And while I'm definitely needy, I'm not stupid. I won't push Callum away by being a whiny girl, waiting for him to acknowledge her.

He's a grown man.

Thirty-five.

Only two years younger than Mom.

The last thing he needs is someone half his age pouting when she doesn't get his undivided attention. Even if I am pouting, I certainly don't want him to know about it.

I've done everything since dinner to distract myself. I'm ahead on my homework, deep cleaned my room, and even took a long bath to relax. I'm still on edge, though.

I miss Callum.

The stolen moment in his classroom today was nothing but a tease. A tiny bite of what could be.

Time crawls by and when midnight finally hits, I give up.

Did he forget?

Text him, idiot.

I want to tell him I'm hurt that he hasn't even checked in on me but decide against that as well. Emotion clogs my throat. I'm unable to swallow it down, instead my eyes filling with disappointed tears.

Tap. Tap. Tap.

A strangled cry of surprise claws its way out of my throat. My heart goes from painfully throbbing to thundering inside my chest. I rub my eyes with the heels of my hands and then walk over to the window. When I draw the curtain, I find Callum, once again dressed in a black hoodie and jeans. I lift the window and manage a croaked "hello."

"What's wrong?" he demands, his voice a soft whisper that I feel in every nerve ending.

I chew on my bottom lip, feeling ridiculous. I'm definitely an idiot. Still, the tears are close and it's taking everything in me to keep them at bay. Callum clearly grows tired of my silence because he takes it upon himself to climb into my bedroom.

Callum Park is in my bedroom.

Holy crap.

He shuts the window behind him and closes the curtain. Then, he steps toward me, crowding my space. "You're upset. What happened?"

Guilt surges through me.

Here he is thinking I'm upset over my home life, and really, I'm just pining over him.

"I'm fine. I promise." I still can't look at him. "Callum, I swear."

His fingers bite into my jaw, not as gently as usual. I can smell the faint aroma of liquor on his breath. It makes my mouth water. I wonder if he tastes as heady as he smells.

"Look at me," he commands. "I said, look at me."

My eyes snap to his, becoming trapped in his intense stare. "I said I'm fine."

"You're lying. Don't lie to me, pretty girl. I can always tell."

I attempt to kiss him, hoping to distract him, but he slides a hand into my hair and grips a handful. The sharp sting on my scalp makes my eyes water for a different reason.

"Tell me," he croons. "You're supposed to be my good girl. Good girls don't evade the truth."

I do want to be good for him.

I want to fix this rawness I'm feeling. This hurt. Even if it is all in my head. I trust he'll do it for me.

"I thought you forgot about me," I whisper, tears flooding my lids and blurring him. "Or..."

He presses his lips to my cheek, stopping a tear from its fall. His tongue lashes out, licking the salty wetness away. "Or what?"

"Or that maybe you'd changed your mind."

"I keep my promises," he growls. "Understand?"

"Y-Yes."

"I'm upset you gave up on me so quickly."

More tears roll out. "I'm sorry."

"It pisses me off, Willa."

Not sweetheart.

Willa.

"I want to punish you so you'll remember it the next time you think I'm giving up on you." His breath is hot against my cheek. "You think I'd risk my career or my brother's campaign to just fuck around with my student?"

"No."

"No, sweetheart. I can't get you out of my goddamn mind."

"I'm sorry."

"Those are just words." One of his hands finds my ass and he squeezes me over my sleep shorts. "I'd rather you show me how sorry you are."

I pull back and frown at him. "How?"

His grin is wolfish. Decadent. Evil. "Your innocence is a temptation I'm obsessed with. I want to strip it away piece by piece."

I'm not sure what that means, but I'm there for it.

"How do you feel about a spanking?"

I want to laugh in indignation, especially considering my stepfather smacked me today, but my pussy clenches. Warmth floods through me as images of Callum bringing his palm to my ass flash through my mind.

"Will it hurt?"

"Not terribly. Just a stinging reminder that I'm not going anywhere."

"Okay."

He tilts my chin up and kisses my lips softly. "You can't cry out. I don't want anyone to hear."

Levi's music is vibrating through the walls like usual, so I know no one is going to hear.

"I'll be quiet."

"I believe you," he murmurs. "Lie across the end of your bed and put your pretty ass in the air."

I obey, shivering at his commanding tone.

"Do you wear these shorts around the house?" His words are icy. It's on the tip of my tongue to lie, but he says he can tell.

"Sometimes if I'm running to grab a water from the fridge or something."

He palms my ass. "Thank you for telling me the truth, sweetheart. But..."

I tense up. "But what?"

"But you're not allowed to anymore. Your legs are too pretty for your stepdad and stepbrother to see. Understand?"

"Y-Yes."

"Good, good girl."

I'm not sure why I like his possessive edge, but I do. It makes me feel wanted and cared for. I'll wear pants when I leave my room if he wants me to.

"Push your shorts and panties down," he instructs. "Let me see your ass."

My skin burns with embarrassment, but my desire to please him overrides it. With my face buried against my comforter, hiding my shame, I hook my thumbs into my shorts and panties before shoving them down my thighs. When I go to push it down more, he stops me with a gentle squeeze to one of my wrists.

"That's good. Right there." His fingers delicately dance over my naked flesh. "So creamy and white. Untouched."

I squirm at his words.

He smacks one of my ass cheeks. I bite down on my

comforter to stifle my yelp of surprise. It stings but doesn't actually hurt.

"How many swats do you deserve, sweetheart?"

"Ten?"

He chuckles, dark and devious. "It's your first offense. I was thinking three."

Disappointment rushes through my veins, which makes no sense whatsoever.

"If you question the way I feel about you again, though, it'll be double that." He smacks me again, this time harder. "Understand?"

I nod, breathing heavily against the covers. "What happens if I do something else to upset you?"

"Depends on what you did." He pauses as though to think. "If it were bad enough, I might even take my belt to this pretty, flawless skin."

A soft moan escapes me, giving away how I feel about that intimidating statement. I should be worried or argue. Wanting to get spanked with a belt is really messed up, right? Then how come I'm practically squirming at the idea?

He strikes me once more, the hardest of the three swats. My ass clenches, but it's nothing I can't handle. In fact, I feel like he went easy on me.

"Now. I want you to flip onto your back so you can see exactly how much I want you. There shouldn't be any confusion by the time I'm done with you."

Are we going to have sex?

My heart is throbbing out of control. I feel lightheaded and dizzy. I'm going to lose my virginity to this man. This ridiculously hot older man.

I roll onto my back, blushing hard as I meet his gaze. His

intense blue eyes are cutting into me like razor blades. He pulls my shorts and panties off, tossing them to the floor. His large hand wraps around my ankle and brings my foot to his cock.

"I'm always so goddamn hard around you."

I attempt to rub at him with my foot, but he gently pushes it away. He parts my knees for me. Cool air kisses my pussy as it waits for a whole other kind of kiss.

"Holy fucking shit," he growls.

"What?"

"I've never seen anything so perfect."

"I feel awkward like this."

"With your pussy open and waiting?"

"Yes."

"Nothing to feel awkward about." He cocks his head, studying me. "How often do you pleasure yourself?"

"Sometimes," I admit in a whisper.

"Does it feel good?"

I've been able to make myself come two, maybe three times tops. My fingers don't seem to move fast enough and when I'm coming, I stop moving them, which ends my orgasm. It's on the tip of my tongue to tell him all this, but it sounds lame.

"Sweetheart," he says in his authoritative tone that makes me hot. "Your expressive face tells me you have a lot to say, but you're choosing not to say it. There will be no secrets between us."

My heart aches at the idea of him being disappointed in me again. I give my head a sharp shake. "N-No secrets. It's just weird."

"Tell me."

"I'm not good at making myself come. Right when I get close, I…lose it."

He stares at me for a long, silent beat. I want to crawl into a hole after admitting that. What is he even thinking right now? That he'd rather be with someone more experienced?

"One day, I'll bring you some presents to help with that."

He wants to buy me a vibrator? The thought of masturbating with something he gave me has me blushing furiously.

"Okay."

"Tonight," he says with a wicked grin, "I'll do it for you again since you have no problem coming for me."

"I want that," I murmur quickly. "Please."

"You deserve it for being my good girl. You'll learn, sweetheart, I can give rewards just as well as I can give punishments."

Words never sounded so wonderful.

CHAPTER THIRTEEN

Callum

I'M STILL BUZZED FROM THE AFTER-PARTY HUGO CONNED me into staying for at the lodge. He made it damn near impossible to leave, dragging me around from person to person for a meet and greet. If I didn't love my brother so much, I'd have abandoned him much sooner to get to my girl.

And knowing what I do now, I should have.

Since she hadn't heard from me, she thought the worst. That I wasn't coming or no longer cared. I'm irritated with her that she'd jump to those conclusions so quickly. I have to remember, though, she's just eighteen and has no social life. These things are learned with time.

I hadn't expected to spank her, but now that I have, my mind spins with other reasons to put my hand on her ass. She was so…into it. I probably could have kept on smacking her and she'd have taken it.

She wants, so badly, to be my good girl.

"Do you trim this hair yourself?" I ask, running my thumb over the strip of dark hair on her pussy.

"I do." She frowns. "Should I shave it all off or wax it?"

"What do you want?"

"Whatever you want."

"I like it like this. It's sexy." I tug at one of the hairs. "I think it'd be sexy bare too. One day maybe I can shave your pussy for you. Would you like that?"

She nods.

I kneel down in front of the bed, leaning forward to inhale her clean, soapy scent. She gasps when I tongue the inside of her thigh. I trail open-mouthed kisses up her thigh to the apex. Her whimpers make my cock weep with pre-cum.

"Fuck, I can't wait to taste you."

"Taste?"

"Yes, pretty girl. I'm going to eat your pussy until you cry for a reprieve."

Her eyes grow wide and her mouth parts. "Oh."

I kiss along her pussy lip, bypassing her clit and seeking her slick hole. She groans as my tongue teases her tight opening. Testing what I'm working with here, I gently push my tongue into her. Her hands slam down onto my head, grasping my hair so tightly I'm sure she's ripping half of it out. I pull my tongue out and look at her.

"Thread your fingers together and rest them under your head. When I make you come, I don't need you stopping it right when I get to the good part. Are we clear?"

She quickly obeys, locking her hands behind her head. Gripping her thighs, I push them farther apart so that her pink hole peeks open. It just begs to be licked and worshipped. Dropping my mouth back down to her pussy, I begin sucking the sweet, untouched flesh, learning every inch. Her whimpers and moans are hot as fuck. So quiet and restrained. One day, I'll have her in my bed and she can make all the noise she wants to.

I work my thumbs along her pussy lips and then pull them aside. Her hooded clit is on full display, dark pink and ready for attention. I flatten my tongue, tasting her slick arousal, and then drag it all the way along her slit until I reach her clit. She jolts at the touch, her hands flying out from under her head.

"Hands," I growl.

She quickly stuffs them back under her head. "S-Sorry."

"Do it again and I'll restrain you."

I blow on her pussy gently and then lick her again. Harder. Faster. And then I suck on her. I nibble and bite and tease until she's writhing so hard the bed is squeaking. Her arousal and my saliva are making quite the mess on her pussy.

"I like the way you taste," I murmur before sucking on her clit again. "So fucking delicious."

She moans and spreads her thighs farther as though she wants more but doesn't know how to ask for it. I obey her silent request, teasing her opening with the tip of my finger.

"Do you wear tampons?"

"N-No," she murmurs. "I tried once and it hurt."

I push inside her body to my first knuckle. "My finger is bigger than a tampon, I'm afraid."

"I want it."

"You say you do, but your body needs training." I lap at her pussy, teasing her closer and closer to the edge of ecstasy. "Let's try one finger for now."

She gasps as I push it deep inside of her. Her body grips my finger tightly. This girl is small and not quite ready for a man of my size. In and out, I work her pussy, lazily rubbing against her G-spot on each near retreat and simultaneously sucking on her clit.

I attempt to work another finger into her but fail. I'm not going to hurt her. We need lube and more time. Focusing on her orgasm, I lick and bite until she comes so hard the entire bed vibrates beneath her. While she's still shaking, I kiss my way up her body, easing my finger out of her pussy as well.

"Are we—"

I silence her with a kiss, letting her taste her sweet honey. She groans against my mouth. I fumble with my belt and jeans, needing to feel more of her.

"Callum?"

"We're not having sex," I assure her. "I'm just so fucking hard for you. I want to rub against you. Can I do that, sweetheart?"

"Yes."

"Good girl."

She whimpers the second I get my jeans down and grind against her. Her pussy is soaked, drenching me through my boxers. Our breaths come out in ragged pants as we have the wettest dry-fuck known to man. I work her into another orgasm, just from friction alone, and the way she claws at my biceps has me losing the final thread of control.

Cum jets out of me, soaking the inside of my boxers. It's messy as fuck and yet I don't care. I just want to rub my scent and seed all over her. I want to fucking claim her in the most primal way.

Thunk.

Something hard bangs on the door as though someone is trying to get in. I jolt up, glaring toward the door. Her nightstand has been pulled in front of it, and someone is pushing against it.

"Oh God," she whispers.

I snatch up her shorts, unable to find her panties, and

toss them at her. Holding a finger to my lips, I prowl over to her closet. She jerkily yanks on her shorts.

"Who is it?" she croaks out. "I'm trying to sleep."

"Open this door, dammit," Darren snarls.

I feel like a fucking twat hiding in the closet, but it'll be worse on her if I'm discovered. I stand in the shadows with the door cracked so I can see into the room. Willa smooths her hair and then moves the nightstand out of the way.

Darren pushes into the room, nearly knocking her over. "What are you doing in here?"

"I was sleeping."

He sweeps his stare over her. "You look like…" His hands land on his hips. "Like you've been up to something bad."

If only he knew her teacher was in her closet with jizz-soaked boxers and his jeans hanging off him, there's no telling what he'd do.

"Nope, just tired." There's an edge to her voice. "Did you want something?"

"What happened this morning…" He clenches his jaw. "You know better than to speak of it, right?"

Her face turns bright red. What the fuck happened this morning? My hands curl into fists. If this motherfucker put his hands on my goddamn girl, I will kill him.

The thought is filled with such evil hatred, I don't even recognize myself.

This is what this girl does to me.

Makes me crazed.

"I don't tell anyone our family's business," she mumbles. "Your reputation is safe."

He approaches her, towering over her smaller frame. "The sass coming from you this week is beginning to piss me off. Who do we have to thank for this? One of the Park monsters?"

My blood runs cold.

Does he know?

"I stayed away from Dempsey. We're not dating." She huffs and retreats a step. "That's what you wanted. I'm trying to be good for you."

The only man she needs to be good for is me.

"Keep it that way. This lawsuit is too big for you to fuck with, kiddo. It's the kind of money that makes or breaks people. If it breaks me, there's no telling what *I'll* break as a result."

She flinches at his words. He pats her on the head and then storms from the room. It takes every fiber of self-control for me to stay rooted in the closet. Once the door closes and she's moved the nightstand into place, I emerge from the closet.

Her chin wobbles and she won't look at me. I track her movement as she picks up a damp towel from the floor. She hands it to me to deal with my mess. I take the towel from her, shove it into my boxers to mop up the sticky cum, and then drop it to the floor. Once I've righted my clothes, I grab her hips and pull her close to me.

"What did he do to you?" I demand, my voice a whisper.

She closes her eyes. "He smacked me."

I start for the door, but she flings her arms around my neck and brings her lips close to mine.

"Callum, don't."

"Give me one reason why I don't go whip his ass right now."

"Because he'll hurt my mom." She presses kisses to my

mouth, pleading with her eyes. "If you hurt him, he'll destroy your family and mine. He's that vindictive."

"We'll talk about this later," I vow. "You tell me the second he even looks at you wrong. Understood?"

"Yes," she agrees. "I promise."

I kiss her deeply and then shake my head. "If he touches you, you call me. Any time, any night."

"I will."

"Good girl."

By the time I make it back to my car, I'm vibrating with rage. Darren Paulson just went from my girl's awful stepfather to my number one enemy. And for him to jump over Dad, that's quite a feat. It's time I start learning a thing or two about this prick.

I pull out my phone and text Jude. Since he hides out in Grandpa's house all the time, he has a way of making things happen from afar. Right now, I need him to find someone to dig into Darren.

Me: I need you to get everything you can on someone so I can ruin their fucking life.

Jude: Just take both Dad and Jamie out at Sunday dinner with a steak knife.

I fight a smile because it's surprising that Jude would reply right away. Usually, if he does respond, it's hours, or sometimes days later.

Me: I'm saving double homicide for a rainy day when I get bored and need entertaining.

Jude: Can I watch?

Me: You're my brother. Hell, I'd even let you help.

Jude: Who's pissed you off now?

Me: Darren Paulson.

Jude: The attorney? Why not just ask Hugo about him? He knows everyone in that circle.

Me: See, you've already helped me. I didn't know he was an attorney.

Jude: My work here is done.

Me: Not quite. I need you to track one of my students.

Jude: That sounds illegal.

Me: Discussing a double homicide isn't?

Jude: What's the name?

Me: Willa Reyes. I think Darren might be hurting her and her stepbrother is shady as shit. I'd feel better if I knew where she was at all times.

Jude: Do I want to know?

Me: Nope. Just track her phone. I have her number if that helps.

Jude: Yeah, man, send it. I'll be cashing in a favor soon. You owe me. This shit is big.

Me: I've got your back.

I know this is all kinds of wrong, but so is everything I've done this week with Willa. If I'm going to be wrong, I might as well be really good at it, too.

Now that I have Willa, I'll be damned if I let anyone hurt a hair on her pretty head.

CHAPTER FOURTEEN

Willa

I'VE BEEN DRIFTING TODAY, HEAD HIGH IN THE CLOUDS as I keep letting my mind wander to last night. Not the part where Darren burst into my room, nearly scaring the crap out of me.

The other part.

Callum.

I'd gone through a rollercoaster of emotions, up and down and upside down. It wasn't until he had his mouth on me and assurances rumbling from him that I fully realized something.

He's completely and utterly lost with me.

It's far from one-sided.

We're in this together.

This morning, when I woke up, I was greeted with a sweet text.

I want and need you, sweetheart. Don't ever forget that.

Even though his words and subsequent spanking helped drive home the fact that we're good, it really wasn't until that text that it sank in.

Callum Park likes me. Really, really likes me. And I like him. This thing between us is a powerful storm that keeps spinning 'round and 'round, gaining traction and speed. There's no stopping it. It just is.

We. Just. Are.

The students I walk past in the hallway all seem so immature. Laughing and joking about dumb stuff. I'll bet none of them are secretly seeing a man—a teacher—like Callum. None of them lost their minds with pleasure the way I did. I just know it. It's a vibe I'm getting.

No one gets it but him.

We get each other.

"Not so speedy today, speedy," Spencer says, coming into step beside me. "You're walking like a turtle. You okay?"

I'm rudely kicked out of my daydream. I can't be mad, though, because Spencer is a friend. I have friends now.

"I'm fine," I say, smiling at him. "Just tired."

"Same." He groans and shakes his head. "I had to schmooze last night."

"Schmooze?"

"My dad announced his running for attorney general."

I stop to grin at him. "Congrats. Are you excited?"

"I've been told to be on my best behavior." His blue eyes gleam with wickedness. "It's like they don't even know me."

"Spencer," I admonish. "Don't do anything dumb."

His grin turns into something equal parts boyish and terrifying. "Never."

"Ew, Spence, go away. You can't dick down every girl at school. It's gross."

We turn to the sound of a female voice. Gemma prances our way, lip curled up in disgust at her cousin—er, nephew. Spencer laughs at her and shrugs. I'm assuming the insult is for him, not me, so I smirk at him.

"For fuck's sake, Gemm. You can't turn this one. I like her." Spencer pulls me over to him, making an over-the-top move of hugging me and sniffing my hair. "She smells like honey."

Giggling, I try to shove him away, but he's really strong. Someone starts playfully punching him from behind, which has him releasing me. Dempsey shoves Spencer away and flashes me a bright grin.

"You're welcome." Dempsey winks at me and then he turns to Gemma. "You can't sink your claws into her. It will get you nowhere."

Gemma huffs, crossing her arms over her chest. "You guys get to be friends with the new girl, but I don't?"

"Lovers," Dempsey corrects as Spencer says, "Yup."

"I'm not new," I mumble. "You guys just didn't see me until now."

Gemma gasps, clearly affronted by my words. Dempsey punches Spencer in the arm like this is all his fault. Spencer narrows his eyes at me, carefully taking in my words.

"We see you now, speedy," Spencer says. "You're one of us."

I feel the power of his words. He doesn't even know I'm in a relationship—that is what this is, right?—with his uncle, yet here he is claiming me as a friend in their little group. My heart warms at the sense of belonging rushing through me.

"Come on," Gemma says, taking hold of my elbow. "If we don't leave now, Dempsey will start humping your leg."

"Fuck off, womb leech," Dempsey chirps.

"Back at you, genetic garbage can." She laughs and then gives Spencer the finger. "See you idiots at lunch."

They take off in the other direction while me and

Gemma walk toward the science building. Even though she and Dempsey are juniors, I have a couple classes with each of them. My next class is with Gemma.

This is surreal.

The Park family really has welcomed me into their fray.

"I'm sure they told you all about the party, yeah?"

"Yeah," I say slowly. "I'm not sure if I'm going yet or not."

It depends on what Callum says.

I need to get an answer since tomorrow night is the party.

"Your parents controlling gatekeepers too?" Gemma asks as we enter the classroom. "My dad thinks if I go anywhere unattended, I'll get knocked up like Mom did at this age. It's so unfair. Dempsey gets to do whatever he wants."

"That's totally unfair," I agree. "My stepbrother has more freedom too."

Her dark eyebrow arches as we take two seats beside each other. "Levi?"

I cringe at hearing his name. This morning, I was forced to take another ride with him to school. He didn't bother me like the day before, so that was a win in my book. He was probably still gloating over Darren bursting into my room to yell at me last night.

"Totally get you," she continues. "Dempsey is awful. He literally gets detention like every day and guess what. Dad doesn't do anything about it. If I hear that boys will be boys one more time…" She slams her notebook onto the table. "I'm going to go feral."

It's amusing that this flawless, perfect specimen of a young woman could even be capable of going feral. I'm not sure what that would entail, but I think it would be entertaining.

"I'm Willa. Willa Reyes."

She smirks at me. "I know who you are, babe. I know everything about everyone."

Does she know her brother—Callum, not her twin—went down on me last night? I squirm in my chair. Doubtful. Best if we keep it that way too.

"I have a plan," she says, leaning in to whisper. "We'll have a sleepover at your place. Junk food, movies, music. All of it. Then, we can pretend to go to sleep and sneak out. My house is a fortress, so we can't do it there."

Her eyes are glimmering with hope. Like she's actually excited to come hang out with the not-new girl she's never really spoken to until today. Until this week, I've never been one to have sleepovers. It does sound fun, as does the party thereafter, but…

"I have to ask," I murmur. *Your brother.*

"Cry if you have to. I really need this. I have no social life, no boyfriend, nothing. It sucks only being allowed to be friends with your brother and nephew, Willa. It really does."

I can relate to that. Darren thinks I should be besties with his son. As if Levi is the caring big brother type. Gag.

"I'll do my best," I promise.

"It's all going to work out in our favor," she assures me, tossing her long brown hair over one shoulder. "I just know it."

Today, I missed an opportunity to steal a kiss from Callum after my class with him because one of the students was complaining about their grade. I could tell he was pissed to have to deal with them by the way his jaw worked furiously.

Sneaking around to see him is hard.

Thank God for texting.

Because even though I've not been able to touch him or speak to him today, I've still been connected to him. He keeps sending me flirty texts to make me smile. It makes our secret worthwhile.

After the last bell of the day, I get a text from Callum.

Callum: Meet me at the library. I'll pick you up. Tell Levi you have a project in one of your classes.

Me: I'll be there in fifteen.

Callum: Good girl.

I'm still grinning when Levi pops up out of nowhere. His eye is red and swollen like he just got hit. The rage rippling from him sucks the breath out of me.

"Let's go," he spits out, storming toward the exit door. "Now, Willa."

I trot after him, curious as to what has him so angry. "Did you get hurt?"

"One of your buddies sucker punched me." He glowers at me. "Spencer's your new best friend, right?"

"Why did he punch you?" I ask, ignoring his taunts.

"Because he's a dick. Let's go."

"I'm going to the library," I blurt out, voice trembling slightly. "I, uh, have a project I need to work on."

"I'll go with you."

"No," I say too quickly. "I mean, it's boring research. I'll just walk home. It'll be fine."

Levi turns his stare on me, eyes darting all over my face like he can see what I'm hiding. Since he doesn't flip out, I know I'm masking my true intent well.

"Dad said it was okay?"

"Mom did." I give him my best bitchy smile. "Some of us care about our GPA."

"Whatever. I'll drive you there." He motions for his car. "Get in."

Since he's going to leave me at the library, I obey, climbing into his vehicle. Dempsey is sitting on top of his black Range Rover, legs dangling as he calls out to Gemma, who's walking toward them. I duck my head, not wanting them to see me with Levi. I've barely just made friends. I don't need to rub it in their faces that my stepbrother is a major douchebag who fights with their family on the regular.

Levi turns on his music—heavy guitars and pounding drums. It vibrates so hard, it feels like my teeth and bones are rattling. The drive to the library doesn't take long and soon we're pulling into the parking lot. We pass a sleek, silver Audi with dark tinted windows parked up front.

Somehow, I know it's Callum.

Eyes are on me, burning into my flesh and warming me to my core. I fling open the door and don't bother with a goodbye to Levi. It's difficult to walk into the library knowing Callum is watching me and waiting for me.

I barely make it into the building when I hear Levi's tires squealing over the pavement. He guns it down the road, his engine roaring as he goes.

"Oops, I forgot something," I say to the person at the front desk as if they care.

Turning on my heel, I rush back outside. From my vantage point, I recognize the sharp lines of Callum's face, his eyes hidden behind sleek black sunglasses. This hardly seems like real life. He's so hot and interesting and sweet to me.

I open the passenger side door and toss my bag into the

floorboard. Once the door is closed behind me, I lean across the console, eager for a kiss. He's just as needy for one because his large hand slides into my hair, cupping the back of my head, and he pulls me to his mouth.

The crash of his warm lips on mine sends curls of pleasure racing down my spine. This afternoon he tastes like cinnamon. It makes me wonder if he was chewing gum or ate a mint before he kissed me.

"I've been waiting since last night to do that," he breathes against my mouth. "How is it possible to miss you so fucking much?"

"I missed you too." I grin at him. "You taste good." Tugging off his sunglasses, I admire his handsome face. "What are we doing here?"

His blue eyes flash with heat. "Right now, I'm kissing my girl."

"Your girl?" I can't help but preen at his words.

"Mine." He smirks. "You okay with that?"

"All yours."

"Buckle up. I'm taking you somewhere."

"Like on a date?" I sound giddy. Too excited. But I can't help it.

His expression grows stormy for a moment. "I wish I could take you out in public, but—"

"It's fine," I rush out. "I promise."

"Sweetheart…"

"Callum, it's fine. I know what this is. We have to keep it a secret. Going to a restaurant together isn't smart. I'm just happy to get to spend time with you."

He watches me for a beat and then leans forward to press a kiss to my nose. "You really are my sweet, perfect girl."

Publicly dating is overrated.

I'll take our secret rendezvous over a regular date any day of the week.

As long as we get to spend that time together, I'm happy.

For once, I'm truly happy.

CHAPTER FIFTEEN

Callum

I'M A TOTAL PRICK.

Willa, my sweet girl, deserves to be taken around and shown off like the prize that she is. She's adorable and intelligent. If she were even a year older, and not in my class, it probably wouldn't be such a big deal.

But since I'm in a position of power over her and am responsible for teaching her, this could go sour quickly if anyone found out.

Dad would take pride in shaming me for doing, essentially, the same shit he did when I was in high school. Wyatt would fire me on the spot. And Hugo?

Fuck.

That's the worst of it.

My actions directly affect my brother.

"Where are we going?" Willa asks once we're on the road.

With my fingers threaded with hers and resting on her thigh, it feels natural. Like we've been together a lot longer than a few days. It's a little terrifying how hard I'm falling for this girl. To my defense, I've wanted her since she stepped foot into my classroom months and months ago.

"I'm going to take you home and cook for you." I glance over at her. "Is that okay?"

"Yes. I'm excited to see your house."

I give her hand a squeeze and try to ignore the swelling anxiety as I get closer to the turnoff to Park Mountain where we all live. My windows are tinted, but you can still see in the front windshield if you're looking hard enough. I'm hoping Dad isn't home and that Jamie is busy doing whatever it is Jamie does all day.

"Most of my family lives on this road," I explain as I turn. "That's where my dad lives with Dempsey and Gemma, and their mother."

"Your stepmom?"

I flinch at the term—one that's bothered me for the past eighteen years or so. "She's not my anything."

The icy bite of my words isn't meant for Willa, but she feels the sting anyway. She goes quiet, slightly fidgeting in her seat. I feel like a total asshole.

"That's my brother Hugo's house," I mumble, trying to change the subject. "He lives there with Spencer. His second wife, Neena, recently pulled a disappearing act on him."

She nods but doesn't say anything. I know she's feeling confused about my lashing out. I owe her an explanation.

"Jamie. Her name's Jamie." I let out a heavy sigh. "My dad's wife."

"Okay," she murmurs. "And you don't like her?"

Not in the least. There was a time when I thought I loved her, but if she could forge a secret relationship with my father behind my back, then love was never a part of our equation.

"She's my ex-girlfriend."

This gets her attention. Her head snaps my way. "What?"

"I really, really liked her," I say as we turn into my driveway, "but she was seeing my dad. It all blew up in a messy as fuck way when she turned up pregnant. She wasn't even eighteen yet."

"Wow," she breathes. "I'm sorry."

I pull into the garage and hit the button to close us inside. Once the car is turned off, I glance over at her.

"I'm sorry I snapped at you. It's just a touchy subject with me. My dad…" My voice breaks off as anger seeps in.

"He betrayed you." She brings my hand to her lips and kisses it. "You didn't deserve that. You were just a kid."

Her words are a salve to my heart, softening the edge of the painful bite. Besides my brothers, I've spent a lifetime shutting people out. Letting someone—not just anyone, but her—in, feels right.

"Come on. Leave your bag in the car. I'll show you around and then cook us a couple of steaks."

We climb out of the vehicle and head inside. She marvels over the décor, smiling as she takes it all in. I know my house is nice, but I don't ever take the time to appreciate it. Willa takes the time, slowly roving her gaze over every detail.

While I give her a tour of my house, I add in the generic bits about my family history. How the Parks were some of the first settlers in this area long ago and commandeered most of the property, including Park Mountain and the surrounding acreage. I tell her about Grandpa and Jude, Hugo and Spencer, my uncle Theo, and of course the twins. I even tell her about my mother and the gaping hole her death left inside each of us.

"So you have three brothers and one sister?" She stops, pausing to look at a painted family portrait. "Him?"

It's a picture of all of us when we were kids. When Mom was still alive and Jude wasn't so…destroyed. Jude actually smiles in the picture even though we were supposed to look serious. I'm not sure he's smiled since Mom died.

"The picture you showed me on your desk in your home office just had you, the twins, and Hugo. Why wasn't Jude in that picture?"

"You can barely get Jude out of the house once a week for Sunday dinner at Dad's. A picture is an impossibility. He's not exactly happy with the way he looks."

She frowns at me. "What's wrong with the way he looks? He's a cute little boy in this painting."

"That night," I say softly, "when Mom died, Jude had been the one to try and save her."

"How did she die?" She flinches. "I shouldn't ask that."

I take her hands in mine, peering down at her. "You can ask me anything. I want to open up to you, sweetheart. Just because it's not easy doesn't mean I don't want to."

Her smile is breathtaking. "I like learning about you and your life."

Dipping down, I press a kiss to her supple lips. "Then I'll tell you everything. Let's get dinner started first."

Willa moves around my kitchen like she belongs there. While I season the steaks, she starts pulling out vegetables to prepare a salad. A deep ache forms inside my chest. I like having her here. This thing between us feels so damn right, despite how it'd seem to everyone else.

"I think Mom tried to burn the house down with herself inside," I grit out, unable to meet Willa's stare. "She and Dad had already split up, but after learning how he'd gotten my girlfriend pregnant, I think it was too much."

"That had to be awful for everyone."

"The fire department ruled it as a kitchen grease fire. They claim she didn't do it on purpose." I close my eyes, remembering the smell of smoke that stayed with me for months after. "Her body would have completely burned up in the fire, but Jude happened to be skipping school and was at Park Mountain Lodge. He saw the smoke. By the time he made it to the house, it was engulfed."

"Oh no," she murmurs. "He went inside?"

"He did." I swallow down the ball of emotion in my throat. "The firefighters found him passed out from smoke inhalation. He'd been dragging Mom's body away from the kitchen, trying to get her outside, when he succumbed to the smoke."

"That's so awful."

"He won't talk about what he saw, but I know he feels guilty for not rescuing her." I turn my back to her to focus on cooking the steaks. "He never leaves the house. A total hermit aside from our family dinners. That fire completely fucked him up."

Willa hugs me from behind. "That's so sad, Callum. I'm sorry your family has had to go through this."

It feels nice being comforted by my girl. Hugo likes to pretend nothing bad ever happened to our family, while Jude lives with the pain every day. I fall somewhere in between—trying to mostly forget, but constantly reminded of what we lost.

By the time we finish dinner, I'm done talking about sad shit. I learn from Willa that she's obsessed with the Discovery Channel, hates bugs with a passion, and can't wait until she's graduated so she can get the hell out of that house. I certainly don't blame her.

"I like having you here," I say after we clean up. "I wish I could keep you."

"Me too." She rests her cheek on my chest. "But my stepdad will be looking for me soon."

Neither of us moves.

"Soon, but what about now? Do we have a little time?"

She laughs. "Yeah, we have a little time."

I guide her over to my sofa and then sit down, pulling her into my lap. She lays her head on my shoulder, inhaling my neck and pressing a kiss to the flesh there.

"I want to take things slow with you," I whisper, "but sometimes I don't think I have it in me."

"Maybe I don't want you to go slow." She nips at my skin. "Maybe I want you to hurry up and have your way with me."

Her bold words make my cock thicken. "You're a bad girl."

This seems to spur her on because she sits up and repositions herself, straddling my lap. With her palms on my shoulders, she shoots me a fiery-hot grin.

"I think I like being your bad girl too."

"Is that so?" I clutch a handful of her ass over her jeans, pulling her closer and simultaneously having her rub against my cock.

"You get a scary look on your face," she says, chuckling. "Yeah, that one. It makes me think you want to eat me alive."

I lick my lips and raise a brow. "You taste fucking amazing, sweetheart. I can't stop thinking about having my tongue inside you."

She tugs her hands from my shoulders and then peels off her sweater, revealing to me her nice, perky tits, held up in a black, lacy bra. I reach up to thumb her hardened nipple over the lace.

"God, you're beautiful," I rumble. "So beautiful and mine."

"Yes," she breathes. "Yours."

I use my thumb to push away the lace, revealing her rosy nipple to me. "Sit up. I want this in my mouth."

Her lips part as she sits up on her knees. I help her peel back the cups to allow her tits to escape. Leaning forward, I run the tip of my tongue in a circle around one of the hardened peaks.

"Oh," she hisses. "Ohhh."

I grin before sucking her nipple into my mouth. Her fingers latch onto my hair and she shudders wildly. It's when I bite her sensitive flesh that she moans. So fucking sexy.

"You're wrecking my goddamn mind, sweetheart. I'm so addicted to you."

"Same," she chokes out. "Do the other one."

Grinning, I trail kisses over to her other nipple. I give it the same attention, making sure to suck and bite on the nub there too.

"I want this bra off," I murmur, easily unhooking it from behind. "I need to see all of what's mine."

I toss the bra across the room. We both laugh when it knocks something over with a clatter. Her humor fades to moans when I get back to kissing her young tits.

"Callum, I want to…I want us…"

Us.

She wants us.

Having sex with her should wait, but it's hard to deny

either of us when she's writhing in my lap and moaning my name.

"You want me inside your?" I rumble as I unhook the button on her jeans. "Hmm?"

"Yesss."

I drag down the zipper of her jeans, my thumb teasing the bare skin on her stomach. I'm going to need to scoop her up and carry her to my bed so I can enjoy every second of her.

"Callum, please." She tugs at the knot of my tie. "I need you."

Sliding a palm down the back of her pants under her jeans, I rub along her ass crack, seeking her pussy from behind. Since my hand is so big and her jeans are tight, I don't get nearly as far as I want.

"Take these off."

And then I hear the vibration of my garage door opening.

Fuck.

"Shit, hide!"

She scrambles off my lap, snags her sweater, and rushes down the hallway just as some idiot from my family waltzes into my kitchen like I don't get to have one second of privacy.

Who the fuck is even here?

I'm going to kill them. That much is for sure.

CHAPTER SIXTEEN

Willa

I'VE JUST DUCKED INTO CALLUM'S OFFICE WHEN I HEAR the door to the house open. Female voices chatter as they enter the space. My blood runs cold as I clumsily pull my sweater over my body.

Without my bra.

Great.

"Callum, you have to convince Dad, please!"

Gemma?

I stand near the door to get a better listen. Another voice joins in. Female.

"Did we interrupt something?" the woman asks.

Gemma shrieks. "Oh my God. Is that a bra? Mom, he has a chick over!"

Humiliation races over my skin, turning it crimson. I'm not just any chick. I'm his. At least I got my answer as to who the other woman was.

Jamie.

Callum's ex and now stepmom.

I hate her instantly.

"In case you two forgot, this is my house. Occasionally, I have guests over. And, because of your interruption, my girlfriend is hiding out half-naked."

Girlfriend?

I try not to swoon.

"Oh, Callum," Jamie says cheerfully, "this is great news. You should bring your girlfriend over on Sunday. Let her meet everyone."

My stomach clenches at that idea.

"I'll think about it," Callum grinds out. "What am I trying to convince my father to do?"

"I have a new friend," Gemma states proudly. "We want to have a sleepover on Friday night. Dad never lets me do anything."

"A new friend?" Callum asks.

"Her name's Willa."

I can almost picture his face, brows furling in surprise. Guilt rises inside me. Should I have told him about Gemma? We didn't exactly have an opportunity.

"Would this be Willa Reyes?"

"Yeah," Gemma says, the smile in her voice evident. "You know her?"

"She's one of my students," Callum says quickly. "I didn't realize you two were friends."

One of my students.

I don't know why, considering our secret arrangement I've been perfectly fine with until now, but calling me one of his students rather than his girlfriend stings.

A lot.

"We are. We've been trying to plan this sleepover all day." Gemma makes a sound of disgust. "Why is your girlfriend's bra way over here?"

"Do I know her?" Jamie asks.

"No," Callum clips out, ignoring Gemma's question altogether. "My girlfriend just moved here."

Lies.

I'm almost jealous of this imaginary girlfriend.

"Does your girlfriend have a name?" Jamie implores. "You're being so cryptic."

"I'll talk to Dad," Callum barks out. "Just go already. Please."

"We're going," Jamie assures him. "Bring Miss Mysterious by the house on Sunday so we can all meet her. I'm really happy for you."

She sounds sincere, but based on Callum's icily muttered retort, I'd say he doesn't believe it. Gemma chatters about how much fun we're going to have. Lays it on thick, too. Makeovers, movies, lots and lots of candy. She, for obvious reasons, fails to mention her brother or Spencer, nor does she mention the party.

Crap.

"They're gone."

Callum's deep voice in the doorway to his office makes me squeak in shock. I rush over to him, flinging my arms around his neck.

"That was so awkward," I groan, hiding my face against his skin.

"Friends with Gemma, huh?"

There's a hint of hurt in his tone, which makes me feel horrible. "It's a new thing. Like today. I was going to tell you, I swear."

He pulls back, studying me. "I'm not mad, sweetheart. It just took me off guard."

"She kind of forced me into it," I admit. "I like her, though. She seems sweet."

His nostrils flare. "Gemma is anything but sweet." He grows serious. "You know you can't tell her about us, right?"

"I know." My tone is slightly shrill. "I know what's at stake here."

He relaxes. "Good, because I can't lose you. Gemma has a big mouth and she'll run her head to everyone, including Dad."

"I haven't even made sure it's okay yet with my mom." I frown at him. "It might not even happen."

I'll have to keep the fact that she's also a Park from Mom so that it doesn't get back to Darren since I'm not allowed to hang out with them. Darren won't recognize her, but Levi certainly would and then rat me out. Sneaking her past Levi will be a challenge but necessary to keep my secret. It's a lot of work and risk involved. However, the idea of having a friend over is exhilarating enough that I don't worry too much about the what-ifs.

"Let's hope that it does," Callum says with a smile, "because then I won't feel so bad about telling you no about the party."

"You were going to say no?"

"It's a party. With boys."

"Your family invited me," I remind him.

"And they're both little shits. I promise, this is for the best."

I want to push the matter, but his lips find mine, quickly chasing away my words. Soon, I'm swept up in his scent and touch. His palms find my ass and he picks me up. Wrapping my legs around his waist, I hold on as he carries me to his room.

Are we really going to do this?

"We're having sex?" I ask, breathless from our kiss.

"Yeah, sweetheart, we are. Unless you don't want to."

"I do," I say quickly. "I'm just…"

"Nervous?"

"A little."

"You can trust me," he vows. "I'd never hurt you."

"I know."

He sets me to my feet and then rips off my sweater like it offends him. I can't smother a giggle that escapes me.

"Take off your clothes, beautiful. I want to see you naked and waiting on my bed."

His words have desire coiling in the pit of my stomach. Slowly, I strip out of my jeans and panties, shivering at the ravenous way he watches me.

"Open that drawer," he instructs. "We're going to need lube and a condom."

I'm glad he knows what he's doing because I sure as heck don't. Obviously I know what sex is and the supplies you need to make it a success, but in the moment, my brain doesn't seem to want to work. I prefer when he instructs me on what to do.

He moves like a panther—seductive, slow—as he undresses. I'm nearly giddy at the idea of seeing all of him. Every naked inch. With my teeth gnawing into my bottom lip, I watch as he sheds his coat and tie. The white fabric of his shirt barely contains his sculpted muscles. My mouth waters when he begins unbuttoning his dress shirt, revealing his undershirt. He pulls off the dress shirt and I'm dazzled by the way his undershirt strains over his body. His bicep bulges as he reaches behind his neck to yank his undershirt off. I follow the fabric as it tugs free of his slacks and reveals tanned, chiseled abs with a dark happy trail beneath his belly button.

"Say something," he commands. "I can't tell if you like what you see or if you're terrified."

My eyes snap to his. "A little of both. Mostly turned on. A little scared you might vanish and this is all a cruel dream."

He chuckles, low and deep, tossing away his undershirt. "I'm not going anywhere, sweetheart. Not with the most beautiful girl lying on my bed looking like a fucking vision."

I flush at his words. He undoes his belt and then unfastens his slacks. I'm enraptured at the teasing reveal of his masculine form hiding beneath his pants. Black boxers are tight around his bulging erection, giving me a preview of what lies beneath.

I clench my thighs together, wondering how this is going to work. He couldn't get two fingers in last night, but I'm somehow supposed to take his cock, which is much, much thicker than a couple of fingers. He's going to split me in half with that thing.

I don't even care at this point.

I just want it—him.

He pushes down his boxers and his cock bobs heavily, jutting toward me. The tip glistens with pre-cum. His electric blue eyes pin me to the mattress as he takes his thickness in his hand. Slowly, he strokes over the hard flesh, squeezing at the tip, making the cum drip down over his finger.

I want to taste him.

"Can I touch you?" I murmur, sitting up on my elbows.

"You can do whatever you want, beautiful. I want this to be good for you. Your first time should be special."

My heart flutters. Who knew my statistics teacher could be such a romantic?

"I want to taste you," I whisper. "But I don't want to do it wrong."

His smile is sexy and wicked. "You could never do anything wrong as far as I'm concerned. I have an idea." He lies down on the bed on his back. "Come sit on my face."

I must be gaping at him in confusion because his boyish laughter rumbles the bed. Feeling playful myself, I stick my tongue out at him. He grabs my hips, hauling me over him and positioning me right where he wants me.

"Callum," I choke out, voice shaking.

"Just lick and suck on it. You'll get the hang of it. Besides, I'm going to distract you so you don't worry your pretty little head off."

The heat of his mouth on my pussy has me groaning. He licks me from my clit all the way to my asshole, his fingers digging into my hips. I'm momentarily blinded by bliss.

"Told you," he says, words hot against my flesh. "See if you can drive me just as crazy as I'm about to drive you."

Emboldened, I take his engorged cock in my small hand. I attempt to make my fingers touch, but he's too thick. I'm amazed and simultaneously worried about how this thing is supposed to fit inside my body. With a flick of my tongue, I tentatively lick at the glistening pre-cum, tasting his salty seed. His groan is downright feral.

"You're going to fucking kill me," he rasps out. "My sweet, sweet darling girl."

I melt at his praise and throw myself into the task of making him feel good. I've never given head before, but it can't be that hard. I know the logistics of it. Kind of like kissing, but with more sucking and less biting.

Bliss explodes inside me. Speaking of biting, he's nibbling on my clit. It's incredibly distracting, but it also motivates me to do the same to him. I moan around his crown, laving my tongue over his slit. This move has his hips bucking up, pushing his thickness deeper into my mouth. Because he's so massive, I can't take him very far without my teeth interfering. He doesn't seem bothered by the scrape along his sensitive flesh because he's slowly fucking my mouth like he can't help himself.

I love the way his cock feels in my hand, throbbing and hot, now slick with my saliva. His hair at the base is dark and trimmed short. It makes me wonder if it'll feel similar to the way his face scruff feels between my thighs. Will he rub me raw with it?

His thumb pushes inside me, causing me to gasp in surprise. I find myself rocking against it, needing to feel him deeper.

"This pussy is so fucking perfect," he rumbles. "Come on my tongue, beautiful, so I can finally put my cock inside you."

I moan, licking and sucking at his crown, letting his words intoxicate me. It doesn't take much more of his sloppy, wet attention on my pussy for me to come undone. I cry out around his cock as my legs shake so hard, the bed vibrates beneath us.

"Good girl," he growls and smacks my ass. "Now lie down on the bed."

Dizzied by the pleasure, I follow his command, collapsing onto the bed beside him. With hooded eyes, I watch as he sits up on his haunches and grabs for the lube. He drenches his fingers and then edges closer to me.

"Spread your legs, sweetheart. I need to get you ready for me."

I want him to just fuck me already, but I also don't want it to hurt. I've had his cock in my mouth. From the dicks I've seen on the internet, his is much, much bigger in comparison.

He slides his middle finger inside me, fucking my hole slowly, with a heated expression on his face. I get sucked into staring at his eyes, nose, and parted lips. God, he's so handsome.

"More," I urge, fisting the sheets, unsure what to do with my hands. "Please."

His lips curl into a devious grin. "Happy to."

My eyes flutter closed as he pushes another finger inside me. The way he moves now is with purpose, as though he's stretching me with his fingers, scissoring them with each dive. I'm lost to the sensations, completely blissed out, when sharp pain alerts me to the fact he's pushing another finger inside. It feels like too much.

"Ahhh," I whimper. "It hurts."

He pulls his fingers out, pours another generous amount of lube on them, and then goes back to his efforts. This time, the third finger doesn't burn so much.

"I want you," I plead. "No more fingers. Just you."

"You sure?"

"Yes. Please."

He slides his fingers out of me, leaving me feeling empty, before fumbling with a condom. I watch, captivated by the sexiness of it, as he rips the foil wrapper away and rolls the rubber onto his enormous cock. It stretches over him, looking almost painful.

"Does that hurt?"

He chuckles. "Nope. And it's about to feel really, really good."

"Would it feel better without it?"

"Fuck. Don't tempt me, sweetheart. The way I'm feeling right now, I want to fuck you raw and get you pregnant. That way, you'll be mine forever, no matter what happens."

His words are crazy and unrealistic, but I like them. No, I love them.

"I want that," I purr.

He shakes his head. "No, beautiful. I'm going to take care of you like I promised. Knocking you up the first time we have sex isn't very responsible of me. Trust me. We'll have our chance."

Since I do trust him, I nod. "I trust you."

"Good girl." He smiles at me. "Relax and let me make love to you, baby."

Our mouths meet for a heated kiss, his tongue teasing and dancing with mine. I'm dizzied by the sensations he's offering both physically and emotionally, that I almost miss when he starts trying to enter me. At first, it feels as though my body is a wall and he's attempting to crash through it. I clench every muscle in anticipation.

"No, Willa," he growls. "Not like that."

Our eyes meet and his are full of fire.

"Relax. If you don't, it'll hurt, and I refuse to hurt you."

I focus on releasing the tension that has me seized up, but fail miserably. My muscles burn and now my eyes do too.

"I can't relax," I whimper. "I'm too nervous. I'm sorry I'm messing it all up."

"Hey," he murmurs, lips against mine, "you're not

messing anything up. You just haven't learned how to let go yet. I'm going to teach you."

He trails kisses along my jaw to my neck. It feels so good to have the heat of his breath and the slickness of his tongue on my sensitive flesh. A moan rattles out of me and my eyes flutter closed.

"There you go. Such a perfect girl."

His cock is slowly easing into my body, stretching and filling me with each breath we take. I'm overwhelmed by him and us and what we're doing. It's painful and amazing and beautiful and sexy. Too much and yet not enough.

The burn is intense and the stab of him inside me feels like it could leave a bruise, but that's not what has tears forming in my eyes.

It's him.

He's so caring and gentle and attentive.

And he wants me.

Needs me.

Willing to risk everything to be with me.

I've never had anyone go all in with me like this. It's the words he says, the things he does, the way he makes me feel, both mentally and physically.

"Perfect fit," he murmurs against my neck. "Feel me deep inside you?"

"Y-yes."

"I won't last long. Not with how tight you are. Fuck, it's like being a teenager all over again."

"I feel good?"

"You feel fucking amazing."

"Will you kiss me?"

He doesn't answer. Instead, his lips find mine. His hips

thrust and I'm knocked into oblivion. I claw at his skin—neck, shoulders, biceps—all to feel closer to him. The next few seconds or minutes or eons go by in a blur. He slides a finger between my pussy lips, seeking out my clit, when his thrusting goes quicker and quicker. I feel like he's close and he wants me to come at the same time. With him massaging my clit relentlessly, it doesn't take long before my back arches and I cry out something unintelligible.

"Fuck, fuck, fuck," he chants, mouth hovering over mine.

His cock swells and he tenses. I can feel him pumping and pumping. I'm struck with sadness because the condom will keep his cum from filling me up. Now that he's mentioned what he wants to do but won't because he's trying to be responsible, it's all I want too.

He slides out of me and lifts up so he can look at me. His brows pinch together, worry glittering in his electric blue eyes.

"How do you feel?"

"Boneless. Happy. Exhausted."

"Do you feel like you really belong to me now?"

"Only you."

"Good girl."

I don't think my heart can get any fuller without bursting.

CHAPTER SEVENTEEN

Callum

I WANT TO KEEP HER.

On my bed. Locked in my arms. Safe. By my side. Forever.

The thoughts running through my mind are maddening. Completely out of control. I don't understand how you can essentially embark on something new with someone and immediately drown in them.

Yet...it's happened.

I can't breathe.

She sucks the air from my lungs and keeps it all for herself.

At the rate we're going, I won't recognize myself by the end of it.

End?

The thought of ending this thing between us not only sounds ridiculous, but quite frankly, infuriating. I want to wrap us up in a blanket that keeps the world around us out.

Just me and her.

Naked and kissing and fucking and loving.

What more do we need?

"I hear my phone vibrating," Willa murmurs, her face nuzzled against my neck. "Someone in my family is probably looking for me."

As they should be.

I've accosted this girl, brought her into my domain, fucked her into oblivion, and watched twilight darken the room all in the span of a few hours.

She's missing from their lives because I've imbedded her in mine.

It's where she belongs. I feel it deep in my soul, unlike anything I've ever encountered before. If I could, I'd carve a hole in my chest and dig out my insides, just to give her a safe, warm place to call home.

I'm her home.

"Callum," Willa says, once again drawing me from my insane thoughts. "I think you should take me home."

But she feels so good, naked and sated in my arms.

"Five more minutes," I grumble.

"You're stalling."

"Can you blame me?"

She sits up, resting on an elbow. Though I can't see her well in the dark room, I can feel her stare on me. "I would stay if I could."

"You can."

She strokes her fingers over my face. "I can't. You're thinking like a caveman and not like a functioning man of a civilized society."

"Woman. Mine. Rawr."

Her giggle is music. Sweet, melodic music. Like tingling bells. "Stop. You're too much."

Sliding a hand into her hair, I pull her close. Her lips press to mine and she kisses me. Differently now that we've had sex. It's almost as though she's surer of herself. I love it.

"I'm addicted to you, sweetheart. I don't want you out of my sight."

"Luckily, you're my teacher, so you get to see me every day." She smiles against my lips. "And this weekend, I'll find a way to be with you."

"Tomorrow night will be torture. I can't exactly sneak over and see you with my sister staying the night."

Though I'm slightly annoyed Gemma has injected herself into Willa's life and ruined my plans with her, I'm happy she's saving her from that party. Dempsey is a troublemaker who'll fuck anything that moves, while Spencer is a lot more devious. My nephew is much less obvious about his wicked ways. Willa can see them at school, but outside of it, I'm worried I won't be able to protect her from them.

"What's wrong?" she asks. "You're suddenly tense."

"Had a terrible thought of someone taking you away from me."

"I'm not her," she murmurs. "I don't want anyone else but you. No one can take me away from you."

"I know."

"Do you, though?" Her voice hardens. "I want you to trust me."

Trust isn't exactly my favorite thing to do, but Willa makes it easy.

"I trust you, sweetheart." I nip her bottom lip. "And you're right. I need to get you home before they send out a search party."

We manage to peel ourselves apart long enough for us to both dress and for her to check her phone. I can't take my eyes off her. Tomorrow, in class, it's going to be nearly impossible to not look at her knowing that my dick's been inside her mouth and her pussy.

Once we're in my car and driving along the dark road, I feel tendrils of anxiety trailing through me. The farther we get from my house and my bed to the library, the more dread sinks in. Time ticks by all too fast, bringing me nearer to the time when we'll have to part ways.

I clutch onto her hand, bringing it to rest on my thigh. My eyes are on the road, but I can tell hers are on me. It makes me wonder what she sees.

Do I look like some guy who has my shit together?

Or do I look like a guy who's close to losing his shit altogether?

I hope she sees the former, though I'm one hundred percent the latter.

"Who called earlier?" I ask, glancing over at her.

She stiffens. "Mom."

"Did she leave a message?"

"No. She never does. There was a text, though, that said she wants to talk about my behavior lately."

I bristle at anyone thinking Willa is anything but a sweet, good girl. "Your behavior? Has she lost her mind?"

"To Darren," she spits out bitterly. "Sorry. She just makes me angry sometimes."

Bringing our conjoined hands to my lips, I kiss one of her knuckles. "I'm the king of being angry at a parent. I get it."

"She's just so up and down." She sighs heavily. "I'm tired of always being the one to try, you know?"

"I'm sorry things are rough at home."

"I could leave," she murmurs. "I think about it a lot."

"But you'll miss her."

"I don't trust Darren not to completely drown my mother. Not literally. I just feel like she's held on this long, for me, but he's winning. She's a shell of the woman I adored when I was young."

We pull into the library and I turn off the car. Since the library is open until nine, the parking lot is still fairly full, being that it's only seven.

"Is someone picking you up from here?" I ask her.

"No. I'll walk home."

"Not in the dark and alone you won't."

She leans over the console and I go to her, her magnetism drawing me in. Our mouths meet for a kiss that feels like one of the last few I'll get tonight. The thought is sobering and causes my stomach to sour.

It's a damn shame I can't keep her at my house and in my bed all night.

"Callum?"

"Mmm?" I nip at her bottom lip.

"I've never really dated anyone before. Is this, uh, is this how it always is?"

"What?"

"This feeling," she murmurs. "Wanting the other person so badly it physically aches."

"Like the time you have with them is limited and never enough?"

"Exactly."

"It's never been this consuming for me," I admit. "I can't think about shit, sweetheart. Only being with you."

"At least I'm not alone." She sighs. "You can drive me home, but we have to be careful. If Darren or Levi are home and see you, this could be bad for us."

I understand the risks.

Willa Reyes is worth every goddamn one of them.

Dropping Willa off three houses from hers and having to watch her walk away from me, was by far the most difficult thing I'd done this week. Since we slept together, it's like she's in my bloodstream. I can't function without her.

I need some distance.

Some perspective.

A thump to my moral compass that seems to be spinning out of control.

"In here," Hugo calls out.

I close the front door behind me, sweeping my gaze over Hugo's living room. It's normally tidy, but since Neena isn't around, Hugo and Spencer haven't quite kept things clean. I follow the sound of Hugo's cursing to find him in the kitchen, sitting on his ass in front of two open cabinet doors beneath the sink.

"Law firm not paying you enough?"

He grunts, glancing at me over my shoulder. "I wanted to see if I could fix it before I called a plumber."

"Since when do you tinker on your own plumbing?"

"Since I'm now running for AG and the last thing I need is someone calling me a worthless rich prick who can't fix his own pipes."

"But you are a worthless rich prick who can't fix his own pipes..."

He flips me off. "But they don't know that."

We sit in relaxed quiet as he fucks around some more. Eventually, he gives up and stands up, defeated and annoyed that he's been defeated. My brother likes to win. It's a family trait.

"So what brings you here so late and smelling like pussy?"

I stiffen and glower at him. "What?"

"I'm kidding, man. You don't smell like pussy. I got a text from Dad, though, that you had a woman over. And to talk with you so you understand who you date now reflects on me." He shakes his head and walks over to a cabinet where he keeps a bottle of whiskey hidden behind flour and sugar. "I didn't know you were dating anyone."

I scrub a palm over my face in frustration. "Gemma and Jamie just really can't keep their mouths shut, can they?"

"Jamie tells Dad everything. Always has."

"It's just some girl, er, woman."

Hugo lifts a brow and smirks. "Hope she's not too young for your old ass."

"She's not," I lie.

"Dad says we'll get to meet her on Sunday for dinner."

"Dad's wrong," I growl. "It's not even that serious."

The bitter taste of my lies sits on my tongue, burning with the need to tell him the truth. Of course I don't. I can't. He'd lose his shit.

"You brought her home," Hugo says, brows furling as he goes into lawyer mode. "That's something. You don't ever bring women home."

"Maybe because every time I do, someone in my family steals them away!"

Hugo's eyes narrow. "You slept with Neena once. You told me you didn't even like her."

"I didn't. Jesus. I didn't mean it that way." I spear my fingers through my hair, messing it up. "You dating Neena after

I was done with her is not the same thing as Dad stealing my girlfriend. Fuck. I know it's different. I'm just in a pissy mood, unfairly taking it out on you."

He relaxes and nods. "I'd be pissy too if those two showed up while I was getting laid. What a buzzkill."

"You have no idea." I gesture in the air. "Where's Spencer?"

"Who the hell knows. We got into an argument earlier about Neena, actually."

"She finally called?"

"No. Her cell is still turned off. I accused Spencer of running her off."

"Well, he did, didn't he?"

"That's beside the point. Neena left. Whether Spencer was the catalyst or not doesn't matter. He's still here with me and I took her side."

"Have you contacted her ex-husband or Aubrey?"

"I haven't spoken to Aubrey since she left to go live with her dad. And me and Tony aren't exactly on speaking terms."

"Does he even know his ex-wife is missing?"

"She's not missing," Hugo growls. "She's just throwing a tantrum."

Neena is known for trying to manipulate those around her. Hence why I fucked her once years ago and wasn't interested in a round two. Somehow, she got her claws in Hugo after that and got him to put a ring on her finger.

"What if she's hurt?"

Hugo laughs. "Her credit cards aren't hurt. She's been buying shit left and right. If I didn't have a daily bill from Neiman Marcus, I'd be worried."

"You know you're going to have to square things away

with your wife before this town gets wind of it. If they know you two are separated, it'll taint your campaign. Worse if they think she's hurt or missing and you're doing nothing about it."

"I know. I'll fix it. I always do. Just…keep Dad happy. If this chick is just a piece of ass, then be more discreet. Our family likes to meddle, but soon, we'll have the entire town meddling in our affairs. The last thing we need for the campaign is for it to get out that my brother, the friendly neighborhood high school statistics teacher, is a manwhore."

She is so much more than a piece of ass, but I can't tell him that. I'd come here, wanting to speak to my brother and get some advice. Instead, I'm meeting with Political Park. Anything I admit at this point will be twisted into me trying to sabotage his campaign.

"I'll be more discreet," I assure him.

"What did you need, anyway? Did Gemma and Jamie rattle you that much?"

"Nothing. Just wanted to vent. I'm good now."

"You sure?"

"Yeah, man. Can I ask you a question, though?"

"Always."

"How did you know with Cassidy?"

"That I wanted to marry her and have her demon spawn?"

I chuckle. "Yeah, that."

"It was love at first fuck. I felt like I might die if I wasn't with her. Her pussy was magic."

"You were hypnotized by pussy?"

"Absolutely."

"It didn't last very long," I remind him. "How long did it take for the spell to wear off?"

"She left me for Guy Sellers. The dude has a comb-over."

"Sellers is also fucking loaded."

"All it took was seeing his white, hairy *rich* ass in my bed. Spell officially broken."

The Park men are cursed when it comes to love. I'm pretty sure of that.

"A lot of questions for someone 'not serious,'" Hugo says, a knowing glint in his eyes. "Sounds like your woman has a bit of the pussy magic, too."

He has no idea.

"I took her virginity tonight," I admit. "It was pretty goddamn magical."

His brow hikes. "A virgin? Seems like you got yourself a young one, too."

I shrug off his imploring gaze, not willing to admit anything on that front.

"For fuck's sake," he mutters. "You should see your face right now. You *are* in love."

I don't confirm or deny it.

I've already said too much.

CHAPTER EIGHTEEN

Willa

THE HOUSE IS QUIET WHEN I ARRIVE. I'M NOT SURE what I'd expected, but this wasn't it. Not complete silence and a dark house.

I'm alone.

Again.

A shot of anger shoots up my spine and makes my head grow hot. If Mom cares so much about my well-being and where I'm at, why isn't she here now?

She wants to talk about my "behavior" according to her text. As if that statement didn't come directly from Darren's mouth. I hate how he's turned her into a robot.

I should have stayed at Callum's. At least then, Mom would have something to worry about. My heart clenches at the thought of him.

God.

Tonight was perfect. *He* was perfect.

Like any girl, I imagined my first time with a man and how it would go. In my fantasies, the man was gentle and loving. Callum was more than I could have ever dreamed of. He not only gave me incredible pleasure, but he took care of me every step of the way.

I've never felt so wanted or needed by anyone.

For once, I felt like I held power over my life.

I let out a heavy sigh and then make my way to my bedroom. After shedding my clothes, I start the shower and step under the hot spray. I'm not exactly eager to wash Callum off my body, but it's a cruel reminder of what I had to leave in order to be here.

I'm so sore.

I still can't believe we had sex.

This whole thing doesn't even seem real. If you told me a week ago that tonight I would sleep with my statistics teacher, I'd think you were insane. Now, I can't ever imagine myself being with anyone else.

After an entirely too long shower where I replayed every second in Callum's bed in my mind, I turn off the shower and grab a towel. I've barely wrapped the towel around my body and tied it so it'll stay on when I get the creepy sensation that I'm not alone.

The hairs on my arms stand on end and my heart ricochets inside my chest.

"Hello?" I call out, voice hoarse. "Anyone here?"

Complete silence.

I swallow down my nerves and walk over to my dresser. Again, I get the unnerving feeling that someone is watching me.

"You're fucking Park."

A squeak escapes me as I whirl around to face the voice. Levi is sitting on the floor on the far side of my bed, back against the wall. How long has he been sitting there?

"Get out of my room!" I shriek, clutching onto the towel and pointing at the door. "Now!"

He roams his gaze down my body and then licks his lips. "Don't be like that, sis."

Gross. I could vomit. I hate him so much.

"Now, Levi."

"That's where you were, right? Because you weren't at the library like you claim. I went back to see and you were gone."

"It's not my fault if you don't know how to navigate a library. I was there."

"Liar."

"I don't know what you want me to say," I hiss, yanking underwear and pajamas from my drawer. "I was there."

Since he won't leave, I storm to the bathroom to dress in peace. I don't get the door closed before he's muscling his way inside. He grabs hold of my jaw and pushes me against the cabinet door. I cry out in surprise.

"You weren't." He cocks his head to the side. "Was it Dempsey or Spencer? Or both?"

"Fuck you."

He pushes his knee between my thighs and brings his nose to mine. "You can lie all you want, but I know you weren't there."

Fear has my voice locked up and tears burning in my eyes. I was careless in thinking I was alone. Levi is always lurking nearby. I should have known better.

"I'm going to find out which one," Levi says, eyes narrowing. "Either way, you're fucked when Dad finds out."

"There's nothing to find out."

"I'm not an idiot, Willa. I know they invited you to their party."

"I'm not going."

"I'll believe that when I see it."

Lifting my chin, I meet his stare. "I'm not. I have a friend staying over."

His brow lifts. "You don't have friends, aside from the ones you're fucking."

"Gemma." I blurt it out before I can stop myself. "Gemma is staying over."

Crap. So much for keeping it a secret.

He gapes at me, and for a moment, I'm awarded a high for catching him off guard. It only lasts a second before his lips curl into a sinister smile. "Dad is going to flip his shit."

"What? Why?"

"You really are clueless," he says in a mocking tone. "She's still a Park. I wouldn't let Dad know which family she comes from if I were you. You're already on his shit list."

"What's up with this lawsuit anyway?"

"Dad's representing someone suing Theo Park. Something to do with Park Mountain Lodge. I don't know the details, but he's going to be pissed if you bring one of them into this house. It could jeopardize his case. Conflict of interest and all that."

"Might as well tattle on me now," I spit out.

"Tattle?" He laughs. "Nah, I like having this information to hold against you. Who knows what I could make you do in exchange for my silence?"

"Are you done being an asshole? I'd like to shower. Again. Because you disgust me."

He steps back but doesn't release my jaw. Almost like a lover would do, he caresses my bottom lip with his thumb. I'm inclined to bite it, but I'm not looking to get rabies since he's a vile dog.

"I have my eye on you, little sis. Always."

"I'm not your sister and go fuck yourself."

His grin is wolfish. "I will go fuck myself. Maybe I'll go

watch one of the videos where I had my fingers in you as you slept. That never ceases to get me hard."

I think he's bluffing, but I still shudder in horror. "Get the hell away from me."

Finally, he leaves, taking his cloying cloud of smugness with him. I slam the bathroom door shut behind him and lock it. Falling to my ass, I hug my knees to my chest and let loose a sob.

You're going to be okay, Willa.

You're not alone this time.

Images of Callum flitter through my mind, giving me the safe place I need until I can gather my strength to stand again.

One day, I can leave.

It won't be soon enough.

Me: Black.

Callum: Your favorite color is Black?

Me: Stop giving me crap and pay attention in class.

Callum: The student is now the teacher?

Me: Yes. Obey me.

I stifle a giggle, trying to imagine the look on Callum's face as he reads those words.

Callum: I really, really want to punish you for that comment.

Me: Punish? Do tell.

Callum: I should keep you after class when I see you later, but I don't know if I can wait that long.

My heart rate quickens.

Me: Do you want to meet in the bathroom?

Callum: So eager to get spanked…

Me: I think I can use my mouth to get out of my punishment. Maybe that's what I'm so eager for.

Callum: My cock is hard as a rock right now. I'm lecturing from my desk because of you.

Me: How can you lecture and text at the same time?

Callum: I'm a man of many talents. You know this. You've had your pussy on my face.

Heat floods through me. Sexting with Callum Park is so hot. Too hot to be doing while at school. I'm not sure how he's managing during his lecture.

Me: I don't know that I can wait until later to see you.

It's the truth. And more than just sexual. I've been wanting to tell him about Levi. Ever since last night when he showed up in my bedroom, I've been anxious. He grows more and more brazen as time passes.

Callum: Meet me in the copy room.

Me: Now?

Callum: Yes. I have copies to make. I'm giving the class busy work.

Me: See you in five.

I walk to the front of the classroom and excuse myself from class. Since I never leave class, the teacher barely bats an eyelash. The halls are empty and my shoes squeak loudly on the linoleum. My heart is in my throat. It feels reckless to be meeting up with Callum in the middle of the day, but I need to see him.

The copy room is empty when I peek inside. I make sure no one is coming before slipping inside. Leaning against the machine, I cross my arms over my chest, waiting for my man to arrive.

My man.

A silly grin teases my lips.

The doorknob twists and I suck in a deep breath. My stomach clenches. What if it's not him? How will I explain being in here? I exhale with a swoosh when Callum enters the small room. He's so much larger in this tiny space.

"Callum," I murmur before flinging myself into his arms.

His palms find my ass and he lifts me up. I wrap my legs around his waist and crash my lips to his. He tastes like cinnamon.

"Fuck, I've missed you," he growls against my mouth. "So much."

I finger the hair at his nape and nod. "Missed you too."

He swivels us around and presses my back to the door, settling his hard cock against my pussy. I dig my heels into his ass so I can control the movement of my body, doing my best to grind against him.

"Quit that," he commands. "Or I'm going to come right now."

"Maybe I want you to come."

"We're here for punishment, not fun."

My heart trips over itself. I'm such a sucker for his brand of punishment.

"What are you going to do to me?" I ask, voice breathy and lust-filled.

"Spank you, of course." He eases me to my feet. "Turn around and push your jeans down to your knees."

A thrill of pleasure shoots through me. "This is so inappropriate, Mr. Park. Shouldn't you just give me detention?"

His nostrils flare. "I'll do as I goddamn well please, Miss Reyes. Now show me your pretty peach."

I turn around and fumble with my button. I'm nearly desperate to get my jeans down. I start to pull my panties down too, but he swats at my hand.

"Leave them on. I don't want you getting any funny ideas," he rumbles. "Like that your teacher might get distracted and fuck you. This is pure punishment."

"You could be quick," I taunt. "No one would even know if you did it."

He grabs hold of the material and tugs them upward. My panties are dragged between my ass cheeks nearly to the point of pain. He palms one of the bare cheeks before giving it a hard smack.

"You're not in charge here, Miss Reyes. I am. Keep your dick sucking lips closed or I'll be forced to punish those as well."

I lean my cheek against the door and push my ass toward him. He rewards me with smack after smack. They're not painful, but over and over again, the flesh begins to burn. Just when I don't think I can take any more, he slides a hand to my front, seeking out my clit. The pleasure is dizzying. I bite down on my bottom lip, barely suppressing a moan. His lips find the side of my neck and he sucks me hard while he fingers me into oblivion.

"Oh, God," I whimper. "That feels so..."

My words trail off as my orgasm nearly sweeps me off my

feet. The world tilts and whirls around me. He waits until I've come down from my high before he pulls his fingers away. I'm a boneless mess, satisfied to let him right my underwear and pull up my jeans. Once I'm put back together again, he turns me around and plants a wet kiss on my lips.

"You're the most perfect goddamn girl on the planet, sweetheart. I'm going insane for you and I don't give a damn." He leans his forehead against mine. "Keep it up and I'm going to keep you forever."

"Promise?"

He kisses me hard, letting me feel the promise in his unspoken word. Callum Park wants me. Really, really wants me. Not for some quick fuck, but forever.

"I have to tell you something," I murmur. "It's probably stupid, but I don't have anyone else to share these things with."

"Oh no, did you get a B in one of your classes?"

His teasing is so youthful and sweet, I nearly give in and ignore what I wanted to tell him in order to preserve his good mood.

"It's about Levi," I admit.

This sobers him up. He transforms from playfully smiling to glaring. "Did he hurt you?"

"Not exactly, no. He just scared me."

Callum's teeth grind together noisily. If he keeps it up, he's going to crack them. "Go on."

So, I tell him the story of him waiting in my room after my shower, his hunting me down at the library, and then the manhandling. By the time I finish, Callum is seething.

"I'm going to fucking kill that piece of shit."

I grab hold of his tie, pulling him closer to me. "You can't. He's seventeen. You're his teacher. I can handle him for now."

"For now," he growls. "But what happens when you no longer can?"

It's on the tip of my tongue to ask if I can come live with him and then I wouldn't have to worry about Levi anymore. But then I think about Mom. All alone with those two freaks.

"I'll let you know if he does it again," I promise. "We can decide what to do then."

"You'll tell me if he so much as looks at you wrong?"

"Yes. No secrets between us. You're my..."

The fury fades and he smirks. "Your what?"

"Boyfriend." My face blazes with heat, a sudden unsureness settling in my bones. "Right?"

He kisses me sweetly on the lips. "Yeah, sweetheart, I'm your boyfriend if you want to get technical. And you? You're my everything."

His everything.

When he puts it that way, I don't feel so alone in this world. I have a partner. Someone to count on and spend time with. Someone to sneak kisses with and trade orgasms in dark closets.

You're my everything too, Callum Park.

CHAPTER NINETEEN

Callum

IT'S DISTRACTING AS FUCK HAVING WILLA IN MY CLASS. I barely made it through the damn period without being overly obvious that my attention was solely on her. What was even more maddening was having to ignore that dipshit of a stepbrother of hers. After what she told me earlier today in the copy room, I'd wanted to beat the shit out of him.

Somehow, by some goddamn miracle, I survived the class period with both of them.

Now I have more shit to deal with.

Like my annoying little sister.

"Did you talk to Dad?" Gemma bounds into my classroom without so much as a hello.

Groaning, I close my laptop where I'd been grading assignments during my planning period and look up at my sister. Sometimes she reminds me exactly of Jamie at her age. It's probably why I'm not as close to her as I am with my brothers. She's a never-ending reminder.

"Yep."

Her hands go to her hips and her brows hike up. "And?"

And it fucking cost me.

"I told him the girl you want to stay the night with is a good student and that you'll be safe." I grit my teeth. "And now we're having dinner tonight together."

She squeals happily, not at all concerned with the fact I've taken a proverbial bullet for her. "Thank you, Cal. You're my favorite brother. No lie. I owe you big for this."

I lean back in my chair and it creaks. "Don't corrupt my student." *My girlfriend.*

"I'm a good girl," Gemma says, with a wicked gleam in her eyes. "We're just going to watch movies and eat snacks."

"Stay away from her stepbrother."

Her lip curls up. "Levi? Spencer and Dempsey would freak if I even talked to him."

"I'll freak too," I grumble. "Seriously. He's a dick and not exactly nice to his sister."

"I won't talk to him."

"Good. Now go to class already."

"I'm late now. Write me a note."

I grumble but rip off a piece of paper from my notebook and scribble out an excuse for her being late.

"Have fun at dinner with Dad," Gemma says sweetly. "Who knows...maybe you two will finally patch things up."

Doubtful.

"Maybe," I allow. "Later, twerp."

She flips me off but is all smiles as she leaves my classroom. As soon as she's gone, the reality of my situation hits me in the gut. Tonight I'm having dinner with Dad. Just the two of us. While my bratty sister spends the night with my girlfriend. So fucking unfair.

Wilde Eats is Park Mountain's most beloved restaurant. It's been around longer than I've been alive and has seen multiple renovations as the times change. Recently, it's undergone a modern upgrade with sleek metals and warm woods. Despite the high-end feel to it, Wilde Eats still boasts the same menu it's had since its inception. Juicy, tender steaks, savory seasonal casseroles, and secret-recipe pies that lure in tourists from sea to shining sea.

It was also Mom's favorite place to eat.

We all frequent Wilde Eats. Well, everyone except Jude. Mom's death haunts him the worst.

"Hey, Mr. Park," a friendly, young voice chirps. "Your dad's already waiting for you."

I recognize the student from a couple years ago who's since graduated—a freckle-faced girl who spent every class cheek down on the desk and drooling.

"Miss Thompson," I greet with a nod. "Hope you're doing well."

She grins and wiggles a hand at me that reveals a thin gold band with a speck of a diamond. "Mrs. Wendell now."

"As in Josh Wendell?"

"Got pregnant after high school and he made an honest woman out of me."

"Congratulations."

I leave her at the hostess stand and wonder if Josh is still a loser. The kid barely ever came to class. He failed statistics miserably. But people change. For their sake and the kid's, I hope he did.

Dad sits in a booth by one of the big windows that offers a picturesque view of Park Mountain. The lodge, twinkling and massive, can be seen in the distance beyond the thick trees that blanket the mountain. He's dressed impeccably in a three-piece suit, having come straight from the office. I'm made aware of the fact we're wearing an eerily similar suit, which makes my skin crawl.

I am not like him.

"Dad," I greet, voice flat and emotionless.

He turns his attention from the window to take my presence in. His icy blue eyes skate over me and then, in a dismissive way, he picks up his wine glass and brings it to his lips.

I slide into the booth and roll my head over my shoulders, attempting to force my tense muscles to relax. Being near Dad never fails to keep me wound the fuck up.

"I see Gemma has you doing her bidding," Dad says as he pours me a glass of wine from the bottle on the table. "How'd she manage that?"

"She's a good kid." I shrug and pick up my glass. "Plus, she's really good at begging until you give in."

Dad smiles in a warm, fond way that irritates me. The twins, even Dempsey's bad ass, have always been his favorites. Even over Hugo, which is quite a feat since my older brother literally does everything in his power to please Dad.

The waiter stops by to take our order and once he's gone, Dad launches into campaign talk. I pretend to listen intently, but mostly, I think about Willa.

Sweet, sexy Willa.

Dad's phone rings and he takes the call, voice slipping into something far more jovial than I'm accustomed to from him. He's a master when it comes to schmoozing. I take the opportunity to check in with Willa.

Me: I miss you, sweetheart.

Willa: I miss you too. Having fun at dinner?

Me: I'd be having a lot more fun if I were at home with you in my bed.

Willa: Sounds like heaven.

Me: More fun than a sleepover with my sister?

Willa: You make me come, soooo, yeah.

Me: Filthy girl. You enjoy getting me riled up.

Willa: Makes me feel powerful.

Me: You're the only woman who's been able to make me lose my fucking mind. Use your power for good, babe, not evil.

Willa: So I shouldn't tell you I'm not wearing any panties?

My cock stiffens. This fucking girl.

Me: You had some on earlier…

Willa: I took them off.

Me: Show me.

A few seconds later, she sends a selfie taken from an angle above her head that reveals her smooth, silky skin beneath the zipper of her jeans.

Me: Where's my sister?

Willa: Putting on a movie for us. I'm taking a bathroom break.

I glance up as the server brings us our food. Dad is still yapping on the phone, so I smile at the server before turning my attention back to Willa.

Me: Pull your jeans down and let me see your sweet pussy.

My dick is straining in my slacks, but my napkin and the dark atmosphere hide it for the most part.

She sends me a picture that has my skin burning with need.

Me: More. Pull your lips apart and let me see your hole. I bet you're dripping, baby.

Without hesitation, she obeys me, sending me my requested picture. Her lips are pink and slick. My mouth waters. I wish I were eating her for dinner instead of the filet right in front of me.

Willa: I should go back into my room. Gemma's probably worried.

Me: Way to kill my boner.

Willa: You shouldn't have one at dinner with your dad.

Me: Put your finger inside yourself.

"Something wrong with your steak?" Dad asks, his deep voice cutting through me and killing my erection completely.

I clear my throat and set my phone down in my lap before picking up my utensils. "Sorry. Work stuff."

My phone buzzes against my cock, vibrating it back to life. I know a picture of Willa is waiting for me and it's almost too tempting to ignore.

"Jamie wants to do something with the twins for spring break," Dad says around a mouthful of steak. "It's not an ideal time for us to leave, but you know I can't tell that woman no."

I bristle at the reminder. I'd always wondered who came onto whom. Exactly how my relationship with Jamie deteriorated to the point she was able to slip away and fuck my dad enough times to fall in love with him. Was she the one who pursued him? And he couldn't tell her no?

Looking down into my lap, I flip my phone and find the picture waiting for me along with a voice message. Pink lips, glistening with arousal, seem to be wrapped around her finger. Like a kiss or a mouth around a dick.

Goddamn, she's hot.

And mine.

No one's going to be taking her away from me.

Not Dad. Not Levi. Not anyone.

I'm forced to pull my attention from the picture to listen to Dad discuss possible nearby vacation spots for them to go to.

"Of course the invitation always stands for you boys to join us. We're a family."

A family.

Because normal families have our fucked up dynamics.

Nice try, Dad.

"I'm sure you can convince Hugo and Spencer to go," I murmur before lifting my phone to play the voicemail. "Excuse me."

Dad's lips purse together as though he's annoyed with being blown off, but I don't give a shit. I need to hear her voice.

"Hey." A pause. "I have to go back in there, but I can't wait to see you again." A ragged breath. "We're going to binge-watch *Riverdale* probably. I'll call you later if I can after Gemma goes to sleep. Miss you."

I replay the message just to hear her soft, breathy voice again. Tonight is going to be the longest night ever.

"More work stuff?"

"Work has really consumed me lately," I admit.

"Shaping Park Mountain's youth. Admirable career, Son."

The sarcasm is thicker than my juicy filet. I know he hates my job, hence why I took it in the first place. Any jab against Dad I can sneak in, the better.

He brings the subject back to potential vacation spots, though he's leaning toward Vancouver. I stare at my father, still wondering how he managed to wreck my life when I was a teenager.

After all these years, I should be over his betrayal. And, maybe, I could have gotten over it had he not married my girlfriend and had children with her. They live two houses down from me, for fuck's sake. There's no forgetting or moving past it. It's a constant reminder every damn day. Every time I see Gemma—a spitting image of her mother. Every Sunday when I see Jamie as she flits about the kitchen, happy in her role of the beloved wife of Nathan Park.

But things are changing.

I have Willa now. She's the distraction I've needed. The push in the right direction so I can heal my heart of all this hatred for my father and Jamie. Willa is innocent and sweet. Loving and kind. She doesn't have a mean bone in her body.

Simply put, she's not capable of hurting me.

She wouldn't.

She just wouldn't.

Relief floods through me because I know it to be true. Willa's not like Jamie. It's time to acknowledge that and believe in it. Hope curls around my heart and tugs.

With Willa, I can move past all this shit.

Finally be happy.

As Dad prattles on about how expensive his wife is, I find that I'm not boiling over with rage like usual. A wave of calm washes over me.

It doesn't matter anymore. This thing with Willa is already so powerful. Life-changing. I can feel it from my head all the way down to my toes.

She's quickly becoming my everything.

And my past, in comparison, is absolutely nothing.

Fucking nothing.

CHAPTER TWENTY

Willa

"…AND THEN HE ASKED ME OUT, BUT I TOLD HIM NO. I HAD to do it, right? Right?"

I blink away my Callum daze and meet Gemma's questioning stare. She gnaws on her plump bottom lip as though she's second-guessing everything.

"Um, right," I say, though I have no idea if it's the right thing to say or not.

She sighs heavily and relaxes. "Not only would Dempsey give him shit, but my dad wouldn't allow it."

"Your dad seems strict."

"You have no idea. Mom is really cool and if it were up to her, she'd let me do more stuff. But it's Dad who keeps me under his thumb. I hate it. It's so unfair."

I reach over and take her hand. "You got to come here and have a sleepover."

"Freedom. Finally." She grins in a slightly wicked way that reminds me of Callum.

She flips through the apps on my television, searching for another movie to watch, and continues her babbling. It's nearly midnight, but I'm still buzzing with energy from the text exchange me and Callum shared earlier. I'll need to come off this high if I ever have a hope of falling asleep. I've blocked the door from any unwanted intruders, but I still can't believe

Levi hasn't tried to peek in on what I'm doing. I'm grateful but wary.

"Did you hear that?"

Gemma puts a finger to her lips, eyes wide and dancing with mischief. I listen for the door, but there aren't any sounds coming from that direction. Before I can relax, I hear the sound too. At the window.

For a split second, my heart thunders so hard in my chest I can feel it in my ears. I have an awkward encounter already playing in my head of Gemma discovering her much older brother is coming to the window of her new friend.

He won't.

He knows better.

Gemma tosses the remote control onto the bed before climbing off and sauntering over to the window. She pulls the curtain aside. Two figures loom in the darkness.

Levi? Darren?

But it's not them.

It's more of the strikingly beautiful Park family. Not the Park I want to see, but lovely to look at nevertheless. Spencer steps closer, smirking, and Dempsey waves, grinning.

I've never had friends like this. Sure, there's been a person or two I've talked to or even liked, but never this. Friends showing up at the window at midnight and one of them staying the night.

"Hold on," Gemma whispers. "We'll open the window."

As soon as the window is up, Dempsey climbs through first. I get a whiff of weed coming off him. He's dressed in a black hoodie, black jeans, and black boots. Typical Dempsey. It's Spencer who doesn't look like his usual preppy self. He's also wearing a black hoodie, dark jeans, and black boots.

They're closer to looking like twins tonight than Dempsey and Gemma.

"Speedy," Spencer says to me, eyes flashing with amusement. "Cool room."

I follow his gaze to the K-pop posters on the wall. My cheeks burn hot, but I shrug it off.

"What are you two doing here? How did you find my house?" I ask, changing the subject. "Stalkers much?"

Dempsey holds up his phone. "I can track Gemma."

Gemma rolls her eyes. "Total stalkers. My whole family is."

"You guys gonna get ready or what?" Spencer asks. "Or do you want to party in your pajamas?"

Crap.

The party.

"I don't have anything to wear," I mutter. It's not a lie.

Gemma's eyes twinkle. "Don't worry, babe, I got you covered." She motions for her bag on the floor. "I brought us lots of options."

Dempsey plops down on my bed and stretches out. Heat burns over my flesh as I remember having Callum between my thighs in that very same spot.

"Don't mind us," Spencer says as he walks over to one of the posters and studies it like it's art in a museum. "We'll just poke around and get to know you better."

"Just be quiet," I warn. "My stepdad will freak if he finds you two in here."

And for a myriad of reasons.

Mainly because they're Parks and I have three of them in my room.

"Come on," Gemma says after she scoops up her bag. "Let's get ready."

We spend the next half hour trying on outfits and putting on makeup. Even though this isn't my normal thing, I'm having fun. Gemma is funny and is amazing when it comes to artfully putting on makeup. I hardly recognize myself by the time we're through.

"I don't know if I can go out there," I mumble, tugging at the hem of the tiny black shorts I'm wearing. "This outfit is a little much."

More like not enough.

I really should change.

"All the guys are going to be tripping over themselves to talk to you tonight," Gemma says, eyeing me in the mirror as she paints mascara onto her lashes. "Ignore them all because if they haven't noticed you until tonight, they don't deserve you."

My cheeks turn pink in the reflection. I don't want guys falling all over me. In fact, I just want Callum. I have Callum.

I wonder if he'd like this look.

I'm tempted to take a picture and send it to him, but my phone is in the other room. I know he'd said he didn't want me going to the party, but he'll understand my going. I'm basically being ambushed by his family. The peer pressure is strong with these three.

If I can do it without anyone noticing, I'll give him a quick heads-up and let him know where I'll be at.

I wish he could meet me there. That we could sneak off to some quiet place and kiss until dawn. Whenever I'm in his arms, the world seems to pause, no longer spinning on its axis. It's just me and him.

"You sure you don't want to wear the orange crop top?" Gemma asks after she caps the mascara. "It really makes your tits look good."

I tug at the off-the-shoulder glittery red top she loaned me. It covered the most skin, therefore was my favorite. I'm barely over the idea of wearing these itty bitty shorts, much less baring my stomach for all to see.

"Pass," I tell her. "I like this top best."

She makes a motion for me to spin around, so I do. A satisfied hum leaves her.

"You're right. With that ass on full display," Gemma says with a knowing smirk, "no one will be looking at your tits."

When we're finally finished, I exit the bathroom to find Spencer thumbing through a book from my desk, while Dempsey flips through the apps on my TV. At the sound of the door opening, both guys look our way. They go from seemingly bored to wide-eyed, mouths gaping.

"She looks hot," Gemma chirps in a smug tone. "Am I right?"

Dempsey sits up quickly on the bed, sweeping his tongue across his bottom lip like he's craving a taste. Spencer abandons the book and prowls my way. His eyes narrow in a predatory way that makes me shiver.

I'm definitely not used to this kind of attention from guys.

"Thank fuck you're going with us and not alone," Dempsey rumbles as he climbs off the bed. "Everyone will know you're Park property."

Park property?

I want to argue, but I like being Callum's.

"Don't be gross," Gemma grumbles. "She's no one's

property. But you can keep the animals away. We're just going to have fun, drink, and get our dance on. I won't have some douchebags ruin my only night out."

Spencer's stare never leaves me. He's studying me with an intensity that makes me want to fidget. Like he's discovered something really cool and he wants to lay claim to it for bragging rights or something. Whatever it is, I'm not entirely fond of the feeling. It makes me miss Callum.

I want to text him, but it'd be super obvious if I did that now.

"Come on," Dempsey says. "I'm ready to get shit-faced."

For the first time in my life, I sneak out to go to a party with the most popular kids from my school. This week I've gone from a nobody who fades into the background to this girl who sleeps with her teacher and behaves badly with her new friends.

I'm kind of liking this new me.

I'm liking her a whole lot.

Park Mountain Lodge, while rustic and having been around for as long as I can remember, is stunning. The monolith sits on Park Mountain, a massive, log cabin style structure, looming over our town as if looking down its nose at everyone.

And it has every reason to be that way.

This place is not only gorgeous, but it's owned by the wealthy Parks, three of which I'm attending with.

"Will you get in trouble for partying here?" I ask as we roll into a parking spot.

"If we get caught," Dempsey says from the front seat beside Spencer. "We're going in through the side."

We all climb out of the vehicle and make a beeline for the side of the lodge. There's a guy sitting on the concrete step, smoking. When he sees us, he gives us a chin lift in greeting. Spencer pulls some cash from his pocket and smacks it into the guy's hand.

"Room thirty-seven," the guy says. "The place is already full. Not sure if you want to let any more in."

"Nah," Spencer tells him. "We're good. Anyone else shows up, send them away."

Spencer opens the door and holds it for us to pass through. His stare is on me again as I enter the lodge. I'm quickly distracted by the scent of oranges and cloves. It's a warm, cozy smell that has me relaxing.

"This way," Spencer says, taking hold of my wrist and tugging me toward a stairwell. "Stay quiet."

My instinct is to jerk my arm from his grip, but I don't. He's not hurting me and not being creepy. I'm just jaded from having to deal with stupid Levi all the time.

I allow Spencer to guide me to the third floor. As soon as we push through the door, he lets go of my wrist. He saunters ahead to room thirty-seven and we follow. I can hear the soft thumping of music from beyond the door. It's not so loud as to get reported, but it's there if you're listening for it.

"I booked the rooms on either side and the one below," Spencer says, flashing me a wolfish grin. "The last thing I need is someone telling my fucking dad."

The music grows louder once the door is opened. It's already packed with familiar faces from school. A heady scent of weed hangs in the air. Red plastic cups litter the room and several bottles of hard liquor line the dresser beside the TV. Dempsey makes a beeline over to the liquor.

Gemma leans in and points a discreet finger at one of the beds where two people are making out. The guy has his hand beneath the girl's dress, clearly fingering her in front of thirty or forty people.

"To think I almost said yes to going out with him," Gemma hisses. "What a pig."

I quickly put together that the guy on the bed is the one who asked her out. Gross.

"You can do better," I assure her. "Guys our age are all immature assholes."

She flashes me a grateful smile. "Right? We should totally date someone older. You think any college guys are here?"

There are a few unfamiliar faces, so it's likely. I notice a cute guy wearing a PMU T-shirt that molds to his muscular shoulders and chest.

"Like him?" I ask, nodding his way.

Gemma quickly glances over at him and then her eyes widen when she looks at me. "That's Justin Fairbanks. God, he's so hot. He's a senior at PMU. I doubt he'd even look twice at me."

"So we'll make him," I say with a grin. "Come on."

I drag her close to where he's drinking with a couple of guys. She bites on her bottom lip as though she's nervous. It's crazy to me that someone like Gemma Park could ever be nervous. She's perfect and popular and mega rich. But if her dad is as strict as she claims, she probably doesn't get out all that much. It's oddly satisfying to know that I'm not the only one who's new to this sort of thing.

We begin dancing together. Dempsey shows up with two red cups and a devious grin tugging at his lips. I take my glass and mouth my thanks to him. At the first sip of whatever he brought me, I nearly spit it out. It tastes like fire and gasoline. So gross.

"Holy shit," Gemma croaks. "This is so strong. I knew I should have made our drinks. Dempsey is a fucking idiot."

The next sip isn't as bad and by my second glass, not too much later, I decide it's actually pretty tasty, whatever it is. The alcohol loosens both me and Gemma up, both of us giggling as we get more and more risqué with our dance moves.

Justin, now well aware of Gemma, approaches and dips to say something into her ear. She nods at him and then turns to look at me with wide eyes before mouthing, "Oh my God."

I laugh and give her a thumbs-up before they both walk away. I'm left with a few others dancing. Even though Gemma is gone, I don't feel alone. I came here with my friends.

I have friends.

Warmth blooms in my stomach. I wish I didn't leave my phone back at the house because I'd be incredibly tempted to find a dark corner and call Callum. Since Gemma left her phone so no one would track her to the party, I figured it was a good idea in case Darren got any crazy ideas.

"Everyone's eyes are on your ass," a deep voice says in my ear. "I guess I should protect you from those horny fucks."

I shudder at the touch of Spencer's hands on my waist. His body is so close to mine I can feel the heat of his chest on my back.

Dempsey shows up, flashing me an evil grin. "No fair, cuz. You don't get all the fun."

Spencer's fingers dig slightly into my hips as Dempsey starts dancing in front of me. They've sandwiched me.

"I have a boyfriend," I blurt out loud enough for both of them to hear.

Spencer chuckles. “Liar.”

“I do,” I argue, turning my head to look at him. “I’m not lying. So don’t try anything.”

“Yeah, she does,” Dempsey says, the heat of his breath close to my neck. “Me.”

“Relax,” Spencer teases. “We’re just dancing. You can tell your *boyfriend* all about it later.”

Since neither of them is touching me beyond the basics of dancing, I decide I can trust them. I’ve let them know I’m off-limits. If they go further, I’ll kick them in the nuts.

The song changes to one I love and I do let myself relax.

This is fun.

A lot of fun.

I can’t wait to tell Callum all about it.

CHAPTER TWENTY-ONE

Callum

HOW LONG WILL WE HAVE TO HIDE OUR relationship?

The question has been plaguing me since I took the plunge with Willa. I wish I could tell everyone to fuck off and proudly parade her around town on my arm. She's legal. It's not a crime.

But this isn't a question of legalities.

It's a moral one.

The people of Park Mountain, Washington, are judgmental as fuck. Nosey, too. As soon as they get wind that one of the high school teachers is sleeping with his student, they'll be relentless. The spotlight will be on me and my family as they dissect every aspect of my personal life.

First off, they'll want to know how long this has been going on for. I'll be accused of being a pedo piece of shit. They'll say I groomed her. It'll be frustrating and humiliating, but nothing I can't handle. And it's not true.

The problem isn't that I can't take the heat.

Because I can.

And I'd gladly welcome hopping into the frying pan if it meant I'd be able to keep Willa at my side. It's a no-brainer.

It's Hugo.

Not that my brother will give a fuck who I sleep with.

He won't care. But what he will care about is his campaign. If it comes out that I've deflowered an innocent girl from my class, the press and people of this town won't come after me. No, they'll go after him.

Politics are so fucked up. Why Hugo wants to dive into it is beyond me.

There's no easy way around this situation that's littered with moral and ethical landmines. No matter which way I step, my relationship with Willa threatens to explode, injuring everyone around me, the worst of it hitting Hugo.

Then there's Willa.

The press will pick apart her life, uncovering any and all parts of her that she's chosen to keep hidden. They'll find out about her mom's neglect, her stepfather's shady dealings, and her pervy stepbrother. Even though she's the sweetest girl on the planet, they'll brand her as equal parts victim and whore.

My blood boils at the thought of anyone touching her, even with their condescending words.

She deserves so much better than that.

Which is why there will be no walking around town with her hand in mine, proudly showing everyone we're a couple. We'll keep this thing between us quiet and hidden. Our precious little secret. One day, when the campaign is over or at least when she's out of school, we can be more open about us.

My chest aches with the need to see her or talk to her. As much as it drives me insane that Gemma is staying with Willa tonight, which means, I can't see Willa, I'm not all that bothered by it. Dad does keep Gemma pressed under his thumb more so than Dempsey. It's not really fair that Dempsey is allowed to run the town and get into heaps of trouble, but it takes an act of Congress for Gemma to be able to spend the night out.

I pull my phone from my pocket and text Jude. Anything to get my mind off Willa since it's doing nothing but make my mind race.

Me: Any news?

Jude: A few leads. Nothing solid.

I'm half tempted to take the long jaunt from my front doorstep to Jude's, if only to keep my thoughts on something else, but take to stalking Gemma's Instagram instead.

Sometimes it hurts to look at Gemma. She closely resembles Jamie when she was that age. Her Instagram is nothing but perfect selfies, highlighting her best angles all the time without fail. I'm disappointed, though not surprised, to not find any pictures of Willa. Gemma hasn't posted any pictures tonight.

I'm about to close the app and head for bed when someone tags me in a picture. Since I barely use the app for posting anything and just for stalking people, I frown at the tag. It's from a kid in one of my classes. Tommy Baker.

"Who knew a Park sandwich could be so hot?"

A Park sandwich?

I open the picture and try to figure out why the fuck I was tagged in it. Two guys are dancing with a scantily dressed chick between them. It takes all of two seconds to realize the guy behind the girl is Spencer and the one in front of her is Dempsey. This wouldn't be the first time I was accidentally tagged in my family's bullshit.

They're obviously at the party Willa was thinking about going to. I'm thankful as fuck she didn't go because instead of the girl between those two, it'd be her. I can almost promise that.

Though, something about the girl feels familiar.

I travel my gaze up her smooth legs and to her hips, where Spencer is holding on to her tightly, and begin to realize I know this body. Quickly, I snap my eyes to her face that's partially shrouded in her messy hair. Plump, parted lips peek out behind a few strands.

Lips I know very, very well.

My cock is already filling with blood, thickening and bulging against my boxers. For a split second, I'm half tempted to rub one out just looking at her mouth.

But then it hits me.

A painful blow to the gut.

It's Willa.

My Willa.

Willa, who's supposed to be tucked into bed with my sister, far away from parties and my horny family, is sandwiched between my brother and nephew. Not only is she dancing with them, but their hands are on her. She's allowing this. She's allowing all of this.

My stomach lurches and bile creeps up my throat.

I'm mistaken.

But after reading a few comments asking who the girl was and receiving my answer, I realize what I'm seeing is the truth.

Willa lied to me.

She told me she wouldn't go to the party and yet...there she is, grinding her ass against Spencer's cock. I squeeze my phone so hard in my grip it makes a cracking sound. Only then do I relax my hold for fear of breaking my only proof of what's happening.

This is Jamie all over again.

I've been fucking duped all because I let my heart cloud my judgment.

Is this my destiny? To have this shit happen over and over again until I die?

Apparently so.

Pain lances through my chest and I swallow hard. Despite the anger simmering in my veins, it's the hurt that's overwhelming me. The more I look at the picture, the more I realize I've been played. I can't even understand it.

Willa was different.

Or so I thought.

She's just another young, confused teenage girl who I have no business being involved with.

I'm hit with a barrage of flashbacks. The horror of discovering Jamie was pregnant by my own fucking father somehow weaves its way into the pain I'm feeling now at Willa's lies and betrayal. I want to crawl into bed with a bottle of cheap whiskey and drown my sorrow and despair.

That's what I should do.

But there's a tiny part of me—okay, massive—that wants to shut down the fun for all of them. They're all underage and probably drinking. God only knows what else.

Before I can second-guess it, I call an old friend.

"Lieutenant Campbell," Sloane greets in a bored tone.

She's Park Mountain's very own cheerleader turned cop. Since she's a local sweetheart, she gets a lot of crap and is never taken seriously, but I consider her a friend of the family. And since she's best friends with my "stepmother," she's really the only person at the station I can trust to keep our family's business out of the news.

"I'd like to report a party. A bunch of students drinking."

Sloane's chuckle is throaty. I always thought she'd be suited for country singing or something with her velvety voice. "Seriously, Callum?"

Though she finds this humorous, I don't. "The twins are there. If this gets out…"

"The twins? As in Gemma too?"

I knew that would grab her attention.

"I saw some pictures on Instagram. It's only a matter of time before it gets back to Dad. And with Hugo's campaign, it's just best if you bring them home."

"I'm on call. If I go get them, I'll have to bring them in to the station first."

Not ideal because of how this town likes to talk, but quite okay in my quest for petty revenge. Willa hurt me, but I'm not some teenage boy like I was when Jamie hurt me. This time, I can hurt back.

"Do whatever you have to do. Just keep it quiet."

She sighs heavily. "I told Jamie she has to let Gemma loose every now and again or it's going to bite her in the ass because she'll rebel in a big way."

"Well, the time has come. Call me when I can come get them."

We hang up and I throw on some clothes. It's hard to fathom that just fifteen minutes ago I was aching over how much I missed Willa. Now, I'm dreading the moment I'll see her. Will she lie to my face? Will she cry and tell me she's sorry like Jamie did all those years ago? Whatever she does, I'll be immune to it. I'm done with putting my heart on the line for someone to utterly destroy it. Fucking done.

Fifteen kids were arrested tonight. Every single one of them is a student of mine. When I'd arrived to pick up my group, all fifteen avoided my icy glare.

Good.

I hope they all feel like shit for getting busted. They don't know I was the snitch, but I'm not opposed to telling them. It's not like they'd expect anything less. I'm not one to put up with bullshit in or out of the classroom.

Sloane, her blond ponytail swinging from side to side as she walks, leads the four I've come for into the station lobby. Since I knew this was coming, I was already waiting when they got here. They spent less than half an hour behind bars before I was able to get them out. Some of these kids will spend the night here as their parents are probably asleep already. Sucks to be them.

"They're all yours," Sloan says, eyes narrowed as she studies each one of them. "Get them out of here before all the other parents start showing up."

I can feel Willa's stare on me, but I ignore it. I'm not about to have this conversation with her with an audience. If I even decide to speak to her to discuss tonight, it'll most certainly be alone. Now that I've seen her true colors, it won't be worth the risk of my career if anyone happens to overhear.

"Get in," I grunt out, motioning for my car that's parked on the curb outside.

The four of them are silent. Spencer takes the passenger seat while Dempsey, Gemma, and Willa all squeeze into the back seat. Once I'm on the road, it's Spencer who's the first to speak.

"Are you going to tell my dad?"

I grind my teeth together. Hugo is the least of Spencer's problems. He was just grinding against my fucking girlfriend. *I'm* his problem. He's a kid, and family, but I want to punch him in his goddamn face.

"He's going to find out," I grumble. "This town's too small for secrets." My eyes cut to the rearview mirror where Willa watches me intently.

"Where are we going?" Gemma asks from the back. "Willa's house is that way. Spencer's car—"

"If you think I'm letting Spencer drive anywhere when he's been drinking, you're insane." I blow out a frustrated huff. "I'm taking all three of you home and then I'll take Willa to her house."

"What about my stuff?" Gemma whines. "It's at Willa's. Please, Callum. Just take me back there. Dad will freak out if I show up in the middle of the night."

"Stay at Spencer's. Stay at my house. I don't give a fuck. You're not going back to Willa's." I grip the steering wheel so tight I wonder if I have the strength to yank it off if I tried. Probably so in this infuriated state. "You can get your shit tomorrow."

Gemma starts to cry in the back seat. Her crocodile tears worked on me when she was a toddler, but I'm immune now.

Dempsey mutters something under his breath.

"What's that?" I growl.

"I said you don't have to be a dick," Dempsey snaps.

"This dick just saved your asses from a media frenzy. This dick just saved your dad's campaign." I poke a finger at Spencer. "The least you four could do was act appreciative."

I hear Willa's thank you muttered softly among Gemma's

crying and Dempsey's huffing. Spencer is quiet, but I can sense his anger in the way he keeps fisting and uncurling his hand. I bet he'd like to punch me in the throat. I'd like to see him try.

As soon as we pull up in front of Dad's house, I make a motion for them to get out of my car. Gemma stomps over to Hugo's house, our brother and Spencer on her heels. I put the car in reverse before Willa can decide to join me up front. With her in the back seat, it's easier to stay pissed at her.

"Callum…"

Her voice is soft and barely reaches me in the front seat. I pretend not to hear. Ignoring her futile attempts to speak to me, I focus on the road and my anger. Not the nervous rushes of her breathing or the occasional sniffle. It'll only weaken me and I need to stay pissed.

I will not beg someone to be loyal to me.

When we're near her house, I put the vehicle into park and drum my fingers on the steering wheel in an impatient way that says, "Get the fuck out of my car already." She doesn't move.

"Callum—"

"Get out."

I meet her eyes in the mirror. They're round, clearly shocked at my words and the venom behind them.

"W-What?"

"I said get out of my fucking car, Miss Reyes."

She leans forward and curls her fingers around my bicep. "Callum, can we talk?"

I jerk my body away from her grip and scowl over my shoulder at her. This close, I'm tempted to get lost in her pretty, innocent features. I crave to kiss her supple lips and pretend this is all a damn nightmare.

"I can't talk to you," I clip out. "Not now. Not…ever."

She sucks in a harsh breath. "What? Why? Because I went to the party?"

I grit my teeth and wince at the pain that shoots through my jaw before relaxing slightly so I don't break my teeth. "Because you're a liar," I snarl. "And a fucking cheater."

A shocked gasp escapes her and then she's scrambling out of the car. The door slams behind her. I can't help but fixate on her barely clothed ass—an ass that Spencer was grinding against this evening. She stops mid-step and then whirls around. Like a storm of fury, she charges my way. She beats her fist on the glass until I lower the window.

"You're an asshole, Callum," she spits out, tears welling but not falling. "You didn't even give me a chance to explain myself."

I scoff and sneer at her. "Explain yourself? The pictures explained it all. I saw how you were five seconds away from a fucking threesome with my goddamn brother and nephew! For fuck's sake, Willa, you had to have known how this would destroy me."

Her bottom lip wobbles and a tear leaks free. She hastily swipes it away and her nostrils flare.

"I'm not *her* and yet you keep comparing me to her," she hisses, reaching into the car and poking me hard on the arm. "I am not like Jamie, and deep down you know it, but you're just too stupid to see it."

"You *lied* to me," I snap, glowering up at her through the open window. "You said you wouldn't go to the party and you went anyway. I didn't even get as much as a courtesy text."

She blinks at me several times, her expressions a constant war of hurt and anger. What the hell does she have to be angry about? I'm the one who was wronged here.

"You clearly don't trust me and probably never will." She tears her gaze from mine to stare up at the sky. "I guess it's not going to work out after all."

She's so damn beautiful with the moonlight shining over her silky hair and highlighting her pretty face. I ache for what could have been between us. Up until tonight, everything felt so real. So perfect. And now it's ruined. Once again, I got lulled into a false sense of security by a beautiful young woman.

An ugly villain in a lovely package.

"Goodbye, Callum," she chokes out before turning on her heel and heading toward her house.

I clamp my lips together to keep from calling out to her. I want to continue to make her feel like shit for how she hurt me. But I also want to pull her close and pretend it never happened. I want to kiss her and make love to her. I want to fucking keep her forever.

The air is chilly tonight, but it doesn't even begin to touch the coldness seeping into my heart. Or what's left of it anyway. What little bit I had just walked away from me and climbed through a window.

Never again.

This is one lesson I refuse to learn a third time. Once sucked, but two is more than I can handle. With a sigh and a hard swallow to keep my emotions at bay, I put my car in drive.

I leave her behind.

As much as I don't want to leave my heart with her, I'm

forced to. My brain speaks logic and the farther away I get, the more my decision makes sense.

It's better this way.

The lie sounds good in my head, even though every cell in my body begs me to turn around.

I don't.

I drive and drive and drive until I'm numb.

Numb feels a lot better than soul-crushing pain.

Numb is the new me.

CHAPTER TWENTY-TWO

Willa

THROB. THROB. THROB.

The pounding inside my head is nauseating. Whoever thought drinking was a good idea must have been a sadist. It's miserable. *I'm* miserable.

If only it were just the alcohol to blame.

The alcohol is more like the icing on top of a shit cake.

Last night was supposed to be fun. Turns out, it was nothing but a giant nightmare. Somehow, while being with my new friends, I managed to lose my boyfriend in the process.

Sun gleams in through the window, attempting to cheer me up, but it's a lost cause. I'm far from happy today.

My stomach roils violently. If I don't put food in my body soon, I'm going to spend the rest of my Saturday hugging the toilet.

Somehow, I find just enough energy to crawl out of bed. As much as I'm dying to text Callum, I avoid my phone and stagger to the bathroom. My room tilts and spins. Saliva fills my mouth. I clutch onto the doorframe of the bathroom, clenching my eyes closed so I don't puke my guts out. Once the wave of nausea has passed, I'm able to pee and brush my teeth, all of which while avoiding my reflection. Eventually, I chance a peek.

I look like death warmed over.

Dark hair is ratty and puffed up on one side. Black smudges remain under my eyes even though I managed to wash my makeup off before falling into bed last night. My eyes are red and swollen from crying. I'm a mess.

Tears burn my eyes, but I quickly blink them back. If I start crying, I'll never leave my room, and if I don't eat something soon, I'll never leave the toilet. With a sharp inhalation, I stagger out of the bathroom to my bedroom door where the nightstand blocks the door. It takes more energy than I possess to move it aside, but I finally get it moved.

Now I somehow need to make it to the kitchen and back without any run-ins with my family. The house is quiet, so I'm hoping everyone is still asleep. I turn the knob and slowly open the door, wincing when the creaking sound echoes down the hall. Before I exit, I pause to listen. Nothing. Good.

I creep my way into the kitchen, doing my best to keep silent. When I see Darren sitting at the kitchen table, I nearly crawl out of my skin. His gaze lifts from his phone and he spots me right away. No retreating now.

"Morning," I croak out, offering him a slight wave as though his presence doesn't bother me.

But it does bother me.

Everything about him and Levi bothers me.

"Morning," he parrots. "You look a little green around the gills. Feeling okay?"

His voice almost sounds sincere, which has alarm bells ringing inside my head, making the hangover headache throb even harder. Darren isn't the caring stepfather he portrays to the outside world. He's a total dick.

"I'm fine," I croak. "Where's Mom?"

"She went into the office." He sets his phone down on the

table with a soft clank. "Want me to make breakfast? Sausage gravy and biscuits perhaps?"

I nearly throw up at the thought, which makes me think that was his intent. With a quick shake of my head, I reach into the cabinet and grab a box of PopTarts. "This will do."

Mom never goes into the office on Saturdays. Usually, on the weekends, she sleeps. A lot. It's when she takes many of her pills. It's like she knows she has to put up with Darren and Levi too, but chooses to check out completely, leaving me on my own to deal with them.

"I should go visit her," I say, not looking at him. "Maybe bring her lunch."

"Don't bother your mother. Besides, she should be home by lunchtime anyway."

I snag a bottle of water from the fridge and am planning to take the whole box of PopTarts with me to my bedroom when I'm stopped by Darren's laugh.

"This is too good to be true," he murmurs, shaking his head with a grin splitting his face. "Unbelievable."

"What's too good to be true?"

He holds up his phone. "It's all over the news this morning. Underage drinking bust at Park Mountain Lodge. Do you know what this means for my lawsuit?" He chuckles again and then glances over at me. "We should go to dinner tonight to celebrate."

If it weren't for my intense desire to leave Darren's presence immediately, I'd have probably thrown up at his words. But I'm desperate to lock myself away in my room away from him.

Callum's family is under scrutiny for last night's party.

This will be bad for the campaign—the whole family really.

"I'm going to lie back down," I murmur. "I'll let you know if I'm feeling well enough for dinner later."

I don't wait for a reply and rush out of the kitchen. Once I'm safely in my room, I set down my stash on my dresser and then start for the door to block it with my nightstand. Just as I reach it, someone pushes inside.

Levi.

"Get out," I hiss over the thunderous roar of my panicked heart.

He ignores me, shutting the door behind him. "Don't be like that, Willa. You shouldn't be mean to your only friend."

His words grate on me. Lifting my chin, I affix him with a heated glare.

"I have friends."

He sniggers. "Once Dad is done running the Park family's name through the mud, those new friends of yours won't want anything to do with you."

I take several steps back when he prowls my way. My eyes flicker over to the window and then the door behind him, counting the distance to my exits. Before I can make my escape, he pounces. His large hands seize my face and he uses his body against mine to press me to the nearest wall. My head thuds against the sheetrock with a loud thunk.

And then his lips are on mine.

I freeze, a shriek of terror lodged in my throat. His mouth isn't gentle as he groans and attempts to get his tongue past my lips. The whimper that escapes me gives him the access he needs. He shoves his tongue into my mouth, making me gag at how deep he goes. My brain catches up with my body and I grab at his T-shirt to push him away. This only seems to embolden him. He bites my bottom lip hard as he slides a hand to my throat, pinning me. His other hand slips down my front and crudely finds its way into my shorts

"Ahh," I cry out, tears filling and spilling from my eyes. "Don't! S-Stop!"

His finger is rough as it probes my pussy, seeking entrance inside me. The dry burn of his thick digit makes me sob as he forces it into my body.

"Fuck, yes," Levi murmurs against my mouth. "So fucking tight."

A door slams against the wall and before I can process what's happening, Levi is being dragged from me, Darren's grip on his ear leading him away. I collapse to the floor, gaping up at the two of them.

"Your mother better deal with your whore ass or I will," Darren snarls at me. "And, Son, you're in a fuck ton of trouble."

The door slams shut behind them, rattling all the windows in the house along with my teeth. The chattering of my teeth doesn't stop as I curl into a ball on my side on the carpet. Shivers ripple through me and I sob silently, both shocked and humiliated at what just happened.

Darren thinks *I'm* the whore?

His son is a monster. He doesn't care. Mom doesn't care. And Callum?

If he cared, he wouldn't have so coldly shut me out last night without letting me explain myself. Levi was right. I'm all alone. I don't have anyone.

Hours pass and I'm unable to move. I've fixated on my discarded shoe from last night that sits on its side a few feet in front of me. If I look at the shoe and focus on it, I won't have to think about how I can still feel Levi's finger inside me.

My eyes burn from being dried out. I cried all my tears earlier. Now all that's left are the hiccups and ragged breathing.

I have to leave this place. I can't stay here any longer because of my love for my mother when my own safety and happiness are at stake. I'm tired of living this way.

In a perfect world, Callum would have saved me from all this. I'd call him and tell him everything that happened. He would make me pack my things and move me into his home—into his bed.

But I live in an imperfect world.

My boyfriend was more of a passing moment than an actual relationship. It almost feels like a dream. A fantasy made real in my mind, but not reality.

Voices can be heard somewhere within the house. It doesn't take long for them to become shouts. One of them is female. A door slams.

"Willa?"

Mom's voice is soft and motherly like I remember. A strangled sound crawls up my throat. I want my mom. I need her.

"Oh my God," she cries out as she pads over to me and kneels. Her fingers slide into my matted hair. "My poor baby girl."

At her words, the dam breaks again. I start to sob as my mother lies down on the floor beside me, curling her body around mine. She strokes my hair and kisses my head, murmuring quiet reassurances I desperately want to believe.

This will never happen again.

I'll protect you from that monster.

I'm going to get you away from this mess.

I let my mother kiss away my worries and hold me tight. When we've both calmed, she leaves me to start a bath. And, like when I was a child, Mom helps me undress and bathes me while singing songs I'd long forgotten.

I needed my mom and now I finally have her.

For how long?

The bitterness rears its ugly head as I sit on the toilet, wrapped in a towel, while Mom brushes out my tangles. She's been clouded by her pills for so long, I'm not sure I can fully believe she'll make good on her promises to keep me safe.

What choice do I have, though?

I don't have anywhere to go. No job or money. No friends. No boyfriend. Just Mom. I have to trust she'll keep her word to fix this mess.

"I love you so much, baby girl," she whispers as she leads me back to my bed. "Just rest."

After she tucks me in, panic rises in my chest, but then she lies down in bed with me, hugging me tight.

I'm safe.

For now.

I wake to the sound of whispered voices. It's dark in my room aside from the light from the bathroom. There are people in my room.

Levi?

"Mom," I whimper.

"I'm right here," Mom says, sitting on the bed behind me. "Gemma's here to pick up the things she left. It's just the three of us."

I can feel Gemma's stare on me, but I can't look at her. Not when she reminds me of Callum. Plus, I don't want to see her pity. She doesn't know her brother broke up with me and I doubt Mom divulged what happened with Levi. All Gemma will see is a pitiful girl who finally made friends with the cool people and went to jail, and now her life is falling apart. I must seem pathetic.

"Call me later?" Gemma whispers, touching my foot. "Your mom said you've caught a bug. Just let me know you're alive."

I manage a nod, but no words come out of me. Gemma squeezes my foot and then releases it, not saying anything else. Mom disappears for a few minutes and then returns. The savory scent of chicken noodle soup fills my nostrils and my stomach growls.

"Time to eat," Mom says gently. "Let Momma take care of you."

As much as I want to scream, "It's about time!", I don't. I sit up, ignore the anger brewing inside me at my mother for years of neglect, and allow her to take care of me.

I may be mad at her and hurt by her actions, but she'll always be my mother.

And right now, I really, really need my mom.

CHAPTER TWENTY-THREE

Callum

WHAT'S THE POINT OF A HEART ANYWAY?

To pump blood? Big fucking deal. My blood can turn to sludge for all I care as long as I don't have to feel this soul-deep ache in my chest. It's never-ending. Completely maddening. All those years of hardening myself against pain like this were a waste. I shattered the protective layer around me and let another wicked girl poison me.

Willa, why?

I want to grab her by her delicate shoulders and shake her until she gives me an explanation that makes sense. I'd thought she was perfect—different—and yet I was so completely wrong.

Alcohol seems like a good way to drown my sorrows, but that would require moving. I haven't left the sofa all day. I've sat in silence, staring up at the ceiling, wondering what it is about me that says: I'm a chump, so fuck me over, please.

Beep-beep-beep-beep.

A groan rattles in my chest. Whoever is walking into my house like they fucking own it is not welcome. I'm pissed at half my family right now, so this meeting won't fare well.

"Callum?" a deep voice calls out. "I've been texting you all damn day. What the hell, man?"

Heavy footsteps thud into the living room, revealing

Hugo's tall form. He's wearing a suit as though he's been at the office on a Saturday. Sometimes he's so much like Dad, I can hardly look at him. Right now, though, it's how much he resembles his son that has my blood boiling.

"Get out," I snap.

Both of his brows rise in surprise at my sharp tone.

"Hangover?" he asks, ignoring my demand for him to leave. He settles into an armchair and sprawls out. "You usually only act this bitchy when your head is pounding."

"What do you want?" I scrub my palm over my face, noting the dark hair along my cheeks has grown in rougher from not having shaved today. "I'm not in the mood for chitchat."

He snorts. "I'm not here to chitchat. I'm here to discuss the bratty twins and my reckless son." A huff escapes him. "I appreciate you bailing them out last night. Spencer is grounded forever. It's still a shit storm because of where the party was, but at least we don't have three more Parks to add to the buzz."

"There's buzz?"

"If you'd stop ignoring my texts," Hugo complains, "you'd know this already."

Guilt trickles through my veins. I'd wanted to break up their fun, not get Hugo and his campaign involved. "I'm sorry."

He studies me intently, blue eyes narrowed and piercing. It's no wonder he's a good attorney. He doesn't miss much.

"It'll pass," he says after a moment. "My campaign manager has some community speaking engagements this week I'll attend in an effort to redirect the focus. Annoying that I even have to do this, but necessary. Now, can we talk about why you look like someone stole your puppy?"

His words are a kick to the nuts.

"You won't go away until I tell you?"

He shakes his head. "Nope. Might as well spill."

Sighing, I sit up on the couch and run my fingers through my messy hair. "I broke up with my girl last night."

His lips curl downward and familiar concern flickers in his eyes. "I knew you were seeing someone who was more than just a fuck buddy because of how you've been acting, but I didn't realize just how much you liked her."

"I don't," I lie, voice like acid. "Not anymore."

He frowns. "She hurt you." Not a question. A statement. "Like Jamie."

For fuck's sake, am I that obvious?

"It's over now, so it doesn't matter." I shrug and avoid his astute stare. "I'll be fine."

"Man, you look like shit. Are you sure you'll be fine? Do I need to lock away all the sharp objects?"

"I'm more likely to become homicidal than suicidal."

"Don't kill Jamie before Sunday dinner. Tomorrow she's making her homemade tortellini." He chuckles. "After is fine, though. I'll even help you bury the body."

This earns a smirk from me. Hugo is one of the few people who can bring me out of one of my dark moods. If it weren't for Hugo back then, when Dad and Jamie nearly destroyed me, I would have gone to a low place and never returned. His annoying ass won't go away until he's sure you're not going to off yourself.

"I really am sorry about your campaign."

"And *I'm* sorry about your breakup." He tilts his head up and stares at the ceiling. "Why God likes to punish us Parks is beyond me."

"I blame Dad. He sold his soul and each of ours upon birth to the devil in order to make more money."

"Sold his soul to the devil?" Hugo grins. "Nah, I think he just married her."

This makes me smile in return. I'm thankful as fuck I can always count on Hugo. The rest of my life may be going to shit, but my brother always has my back and knows just what to say.

"Come on," Hugo barks out, rising to his feet. "Grab a shower and shave your pretty boy face. I'm starving and you need a stiff drink. Let's get out of here and go somewhere where we can shit talk all your exes."

Gemma: I'm worried about Willa. Did she say anything to you when you dropped her off?

My mood, improved by Hugo's company and a steak dinner, sours instantly. He dropped me off not five minutes ago and I'm already back in this deep, dark hole of feeling sorry for myself at just the mention of Willa's name.

Me: She was fine when I dropped her off.

Gemma: I went by to grab my stuff today and she was in bed. Her mom was taking care of her. Said she had a bug, but I don't believe it. Her stepbrother is a prick. I just worry.

As much as I don't want to care, I can't deny that I do. That asshole's smug face pops into my mind.

Me: You're a good friend. If she seems weird in class on Monday, I'll ask her if she's okay.

The thought of talking to her has both a ripple of dread and a slight thrill of desire warring for ownership in my body.

Gemma: You're the best.

She wouldn't be thinking that way if she knew it was me who called the cops on their little party and interrupted their fun.

I flip over to Willa's contact and pull up our text conversation. It takes everything in me not to scroll through the entire thing, reminiscing on a time when everything was blissfully perfect. Before I can talk myself out of it, I shoot her a text.

Me: Gemma is worried about you.

I can't bring myself to tell her I am too.

No response.

I wait for a good five minutes before texting again.

Me: Just let me know you're okay and I'll leave you alone.

Still nothing.

An uneasiness settles in my gut. She doesn't deserve my concern, but it's there anyway. My mind whirls with reasons as to why she's not responding, none of them good.

Me: If you don't answer me back, I will be forced to check for myself.

If she's fucking my little brother or nephew, then surely she'll respond to keep me from showing up.

Five more long minutes pass.

Me: Has Levi done something?

Me: For fuck's sake, Willa. Answer me.

Since she won't reply to my texts, I call her. It rings and

rings before going to voicemail. The unnerving feeling intensifies and worry begins taking over my every thought.

"Fuck this," I grumble, grabbing my keys from the bar.

I stalk out of my house and climb into my car, thankful I didn't get shitfaced at dinner like I'd originally intended. Within minutes, I'm out of my driveway and headed her way.

The entire way there, I check my phone. She hasn't read my messages or attempted to call me back. Dread infects my every cell. I hate that, despite the fact she's hurt me so fucking much, I'm pining over her.

Again, screw having a heart.

It's pointless.

When I arrive at her house, I pass by it and park a little ways down the street. I climb out and prowl through the shadows like the creeper I am until I'm standing outside her window. The curtains are drawn and only a sliver of her room is revealed.

A body lies on the bed, barely illuminated by a lamp.

It's early to be in bed already. Maybe she really does have a bug.

I tap on the window, but she doesn't move. Anxiety crawls over my skin like a thousand angry ants. If I tap any louder, I chance someone in her house hearing. I'm only able to wait patiently for a whole fifteen seconds before I'm attempting to open the window.

Not locked.

Relief floods through me as I slowly lift the glass. Once I've opened it all the way, I push apart the curtains and let myself inside. As quietly as I can, I close the window and then survey the room. It's slightly messy with discarded clothes and shoes on the floor. On the dresser there's an untouched bowl of soup, an unopened box of PopTarts, and a couple bottles of water. Her nightstand is pushed against the door, blocking it.

Somehow, deep in my gut, I know.

That motherfucker hurt her.

I can't explain how I know. I just do. I've gotten pretty good at reading Willa. This is completely out of character for her. Something's wrong.

Against my better judgment, I kick off my shoes and crawl into bed behind her. She stiffens and a whine filled with terror escapes her.

"Shh," I rumble. "It's just me. You're safe."

Her body relaxes and then she sniffles. All my anger and rage have taken a back seat to the desire to comfort her. I wrap an arm around her body, pulling her to my chest, and greedily bury my nose in her hair.

God, I've missed this—missed her.

I shouldn't feel so relieved to have her in my arms like this after all she's done, but I can't help myself. You can't turn off feelings with a snap of your fingers. She's not pushing me away and I certainly don't see Dempsey or Spencer here holding her. We may not be like we were, but she's still hurting, and I can make her feel safe.

"Want me to kill him?" My words are soft, though the threat in them is heavy and laced with intent. "I'd take pleasure in it."

She doesn't reply, and I'd almost take it for rudeness if not for the fact her fingers have found mine, digging into my flesh like she can keep me from ever leaving her again. In this bubble—this frozen moment of time—I can nearly pretend last night didn't happen between us. That things are still perfect. That she didn't betray me and ruin a beautiful, blooming love story.

I let my lips find their way to her neck. Gently, I press a kiss to the warm flesh there. She feels so fucking right in my arms. It's why it's so gutting what she did to me. That wasn't supposed to happen. *We* were supposed to happen.

"When you're able to, I need to know what he did, sweetheart. I'll need to know what I'm going to prison for murder for."

Her fingers relax and she slides them between mine, squeezing. I grip onto her hand like I have the power to drag her back to a few days ago when she was in my bed where she belonged.

Though our mouths don't speak the words, our hearts do it for us. She's clearly upset with me, hence the silent treatment, but needs me.

She may have broken my heart with what she's done to me. However, it doesn't make my feelings for her disappear instantly. I still care about her and her well-being.

It kills me that she's lying in bed so…broken.

All I want to do is hold her until she's whole again.

CHAPTER TWENTY-FOUR

Willa
Two Weeks Later

I DON'T RECOGNIZE MY LIFE ANYMORE.

Everything is a blur. Time passes too quickly and I feel almost groggy when I note just how much time has gone by. All I want to do is sleep.

Sleep and never wake up.

Probably because when I sleep, he's there with me. Every single night.

My heart clenches painfully in my chest. Though we're still not on speaking terms, Callum comes into my room each night since Levi's attack and holds me.

It's so messed up.

All of it.

Though Levi hurt me, and both Darren and Mom know what happened, he's still living under the same roof as me. At school, he follows me like a dark shadow. It's as if he's claimed me somehow and is making sure the whole school knows it.

In Callum's class, I keep waiting for him to notice. To swoop in and save me from the monster in my life. He probably would if I actually talked to him. So badly I want to whisper what Levi did to me whenever Callum has me wrapped in his safe arms, but I always find a reason to bite my tongue.

He hurt me.

Callum really hurt me when he blew up, assuming I did the worst with his brother and nephew, and never let me explain.

"Hey, Willa," Levi says, flashing me a boyish grin as he passes by my desk. "You look pretty today."

His words—his niceness—make my skin crawl. I don't want him to look at me or speak to me. It's bad enough sharing a class and a house with him.

"Take a seat, Mr. Paulson," Callum calls out as he enters the classroom, voice thunderous and commanding. "This isn't social hour, though your grade in my class begs to differ."

The class sniggers. The chill that had settled in my bones is chased away by Callum's warm voice. He doesn't know the story, but he's accurately deduced Levi did something to me. In his subtle way, he's protecting me.

Tears sting at my eyes. This is all such a mess. If Callum cares enough to protect me from Levi, why didn't he care enough to protect our relationship from his past trust issues?

Class goes by in a blur. I take half-ass notes but don't pay attention to much other than Callum's deep voice as he lectures. It's nearly as soothing as his strong arms when he holds me at night. When the bell finally rings, I startle at the unexpected shrill tone.

"Miss Reyes," Callum rumbles. "Can you stay after class?"

I lift my chin, tearing my eyes from my notes to where he sits perched on the edge of his desk. Somewhere during his lecture, he lost his suit jacket. The crisp, white material of his dress shirt stretches to the limits over his broad shoulders and muscular biceps. He's leaned forward, elbows resting on his knees, and his plum tie slightly sways in front of him.

I want to wrap my fist in the silky material and pull him to me. To kiss away the frown on his lips and beg him to take us back to where we were two weeks ago. Before all this…drama.

Instead, I gather up my belongings once the last person has left the room, shoulder my bag, and walk toward the front of the room.

"Set your bag down," Callum instructs when I'm up front.

He slides off the desk and strides over to the classroom door. My eyes follow his ass, barely contained in his charcoal slacks. It's hard not to drool over this man. His body is perfection, his voice is heaven, and his mouth is an addiction I'm desperate for another hit of.

The door clicks shut, effectively silencing the noise in the hallway. Now, all that can be heard, is the dull roar of blood rushing through my ears.

"Come here."

His command is deep and authoritative. It leaves no room for argument. Despite my lingering anger and hurt, I find myself obeying him. Needing to be told what to do.

I slowly walk toward him, my knees slightly wobbly, until I'm two feet away from him. He closes the gap, stepping until we're so close I have to crane my neck to look up at his handsome face.

"Sweetheart, you're breaking my heart."

I swallow at his pained words. Concern etches into his face at the tiny crow's feet near the corners of his eyes and a few lines between his brows. Fierce blue eyes dart over my face, inspecting every detail, every expression.

"Why?" I croak out, swallowing hard.

He lifts a hand, cupping my cheek. My eyes flutter closed

and I lean into his touch. "You're so fucking sad. I can't stand seeing you this way."

Tears fill my lids, but I don't let them spill over, instead blinking several times to chase them away. I attempt to look away—anywhere else—but his thumb presses into my cheek and he clutches my face so I can't. A whimper crawls out of me as his thumb caresses my skin.

"Why won't you talk to me?" His words are filled with the same pain that claws away at my insides. "I *need* you to talk to me."

The desperation in his voice has me lifting my hands and skating them over the front of his chest. I want to comfort him somehow. Make the sadness go far, far away from him. He shudders at my touch and a sound I've never heard him make echoes in the classroom.

Need.

Anguish.

Misery.

I understand his feelings wholeheartedly and want to erase them. It was easier to be angry at him when it felt like he was being a dick, but this is different. He's in pain. Pain I've somehow caused, even by accident.

"I'm sorry," I whisper. "You had it all wrong and I was mad at you for assuming the worst."

His gaze darkens as he swipes away a tear that's escaped down my cheek. "Assuming the worst?"

God, he's such an idiot, but clearly Jamie screwed with his mind. Instead of getting upset, I should have been patient with him. I should have let him cool off and then explain that I'd never betray him like she did.

"It was just a party with my new friends. Nothing more.

I thought about you the whole time. Wished I were with you instead. Everything transpired so quickly with them showing up at my house, so I didn't have an opportunity to let you know what was happening. But I assure you, it was all in fun, and nothing whatsoever romantic. I didn't deceive you intentionally." I bite down on my lip when it wobbles. "I hate that you didn't trust me. You never let me explain, Callum."

"I begged you to talk to me for two weeks," he murmurs. "Why now?"

"Because I'm tired of being apart. I need you—need us. I'm sorry. I should have handled it better."

He dips his head forward, running his nose along mine. "I fucked up." His eyes close and he lets out a ragged sigh. "I overreacted and fucked everything up. Jesus, sweetheart, I'm sorry too."

Before I can even revel in his words I've been aching to hear for two weeks, his mouth descends upon mine. I willingly greet him with parted lips. The kiss starts as something tentative and hopeful but quickly turns ravenous.

Teeth and tongues and slick lips.

He's trying to devour me whole and I love it. I need it. I need him. Our kiss feels like a blissful eternity and then he's pulling away.

"What happened with Levi?"

I want to rewind to two minutes ago when we were making out and making up. Not this. Not the reminder of my stepbrother. I can still feel his finger jamming inside me.

"He assaulted me," I croak out. "The morning after the party."

Callum's teeth grind together. "How?"

"Does it matter?"

"Yes. You can't keep this all to yourself, sweetheart. I can't help unless I know."

"There's nothing to do."

His lips thin at my reply. All I want to do is get back to kissing and touching and—

"Sweetheart," he growls. "Tell me or I'll spank your pretty little ass for disobeying."

A thrill shoots through me. As much as I'd love a spanking from him, I'm aching to go back to being his good girl, even if admitting what Levi did to me is painful.

"He, uh, pinned me, shoved his tongue down my throat, and forced his finger inside me." I shudder at the memory. "And then Darren walked in, stopping it. Levi hasn't touched me since."

"My poor, sweet girl," he croons, peppering kisses on my face. "I'm so fucking sorry."

A sob claws its way out of me. "I just...hate that he's the last thing I remember. No matter how hard I tried to erase it and replace it with you, I couldn't."

He kisses me deeply. I stiffen when I feel his hand slide down my stomach to the button on my jeans. His thumb runs over my skin just beneath my shirt along the top of my jeans.

"Can I touch you? I want to make you feel good. Give you something good to remember when you're all alone with your thoughts and memories."

Could it be that easy for me?

"Y-Yes. I need you, Callum. Only you."

I gasp as the button on my jeans pops from its hole and he runs the zipper down. Then, his large, masculine hand is sliding into my jeans and under my panties. At first, the feel of a finger touching my pussy has me panicking, but then I ground my thoughts and remind myself it's wanted. I want Callum to touch me. His finger finds my clit. He's gentle, slowly massaging it back to life. Fear and apprehension bleed away to desire. His mouth captures mine and he rubs me until I'm dizzy with need.

"I want you to come and then I'm going to slide my dick into your wet, needy pussy. Why, sweetheart? Why am I going to do that?"

"I don't know," I say with a moan, unable to think when he's rubbing me to ecstasy.

"Because you're mine. Because only I belong inside you. I'm going to come inside you. Fill you up to the brim with me. My cum will run out of you for the rest of the day. It's all you'll be able to think about. Is that what you want?"

Callum erasing all the dirty, wrong parts of what Levi did to me? Yes, please.

"I want that," I whisper. "Please. I need you and only you."

He crashes his lips to mine again, intensifying his efforts to make me come. When it finally happens, stars glitter across my eyes, disorienting me. I can feel Callum moving my body and bending me over the desk, and I willingly allow him to mold me to his liking. Cool air kisses my ass as he pushes my panties and jeans down to my knees.

Someone could walk in.

They could see us—him fucking me—and we'd both be ruined. Especially him. This is reckless, yet here we are.

"Get my hand nice and wet," Callum orders, pressing his palm to my mouth. "I don't have lube and I need to take you fast."

I grip his wrist and start licking every inch of his palm. His belt jangles from behind and he shuffles to get his dick out with his other hand. A moan echoes from me when his long, thick erection slides along my ass crack.

I need him inside me.

Badly.

"Callum," I beg. "Please. Hurry."

He pulls his hand from my face and I'm assuming strokes the wetness onto his cock because seconds later, he's pressing the crown of his dick against my opening. It's not as good as lube, but it's wet enough to get the job done. I reach forward to grab hold of the edge of his desk nearest his chair and cling on to keep from getting fucked right off it. He's slow and gentle as he pushes every ridiculously long inch of his erection into me. Then, he eases out before pressing harder into me with a quick thrust.

"Ah!" I cry out.

"Too much?"

"No," I say with a gasp. "More. Faster. Harder."

It still hurts being stretched by his thickness, but it's a good kind of burn. His size is so big that he fills me and stretches me to my limits. It makes me feel like we're a perfect fit—destined to slot together like this.

He caresses both my ass cheeks with his hands, spreading them apart as he quickens his pace. The slapping of flesh and scraping of the desk nudging along the linoleum floor is the background music to my soft moans and his hungry grunts.

"You're so fucking perfect," he growls, "and mine." He punctuates the word "mine" with an almost painful squeeze of my ass cheeks. "Mine, sweetheart. All mine."

I want his fingers to bruise my flesh, marking me as his.

"Yes," I hoarsely agree. "Yes."

He grips onto my hips, lifting my body slightly off the

desk, and continues pumping into me. From this new angle, he glides across my G-spot over and over. I almost black out from sheer pleasure. All I want to do is live in this moment forever. He makes a feral sound that warns me he's close to coming. It unlocks something inside me—something primal—and I give in to the pleasure he's offering me. The orgasm hits me like a storm, decimating me from start to finish. My body shudders wildly as it quakes through me. This must set him off too because he makes a delicious groan of pure bliss before his cock thickens as cum gushes into me. As promised, his cock throbs shot after shot of claiming semen into my body.

"Goddamn, you're so fucking perfect, baby."

His praise washes over me, rinsing away any last dirtiness. I want to stay with him in this protective cocoon of happiness, but his planning period won't last forever. Someone is bound to burst into the classroom and I refuse to lose him over something so stupid.

"I have to go," I say with a pout in my voice. "I don't want to."

"You need to. Your grades have slipped the past two weeks." He slides out of me and cum runs out along with it. "Stay put while I clean you up."

I wait patiently as he grabs tissues from the box on his desk. He cleans away what's already come out of me and then gently pushes the tissue into me.

"This will keep it from soaking into your panties and jeans." He pulls my clothes up and then helps me to my feet. "Keep it there until you can properly clean up."

Once he has me sorted, he pulls me to him for a long kiss. I melt in his arms, no longer worrying about anyone or anything. I'm completely distracted by Callum Park.

I have no idea what's happening with my life right now, but as long as he's a part of it, I'm happy.

"This thing between us," he murmurs, lips brushing over mine. "It's not going anywhere. It's the forever kind of thing. My heart doesn't know any other way with you."

"Aww, Mr. Park," I tease. "I think you just admitted you love me."

His grin is boyish and adorable. "You think you have me all figured out, don't you?"

"Yup."

"Hmm." He pecks my lips. "I suppose you do."

My heart thunders in my chest. Did Callum Park just admit he loves me?

"The feeling's mutual," I assure him. "And I'm not going anywhere. Even if you jump to wild conclusions again."

"Promise?"

"I promise."

"And I'm going to trust you, sweetheart. I have to. I can't lose you. The past two weeks were hell. If my head tries to fuck with me again, you have permission to smack it."

I kiss him again and then let out a giggle when he picks me up, spinning me around. My chest is no longer tight and all the sadness that plagued me is gone.

This is what happiness feels like.

Trapped in Callum Park's arms, locked in his possessive stare, and spoiled with tender kisses.

There's nowhere I'd rather be.

CHAPTER TWENTY-FIVE

Callum

COLD RAIN ASSAULTS ME AS I RUN FROM THE BUILDING toward my car, splashing through puddles, no doubt ruining my leather Dulce & Gabbana calfskin dress shoes. Nothing can ruin my mood, though. Not even destroying an eight-hundred-dollar pair of shoes.

Why?

Because I have my girl back.

Fuck.

I did not come to school today expecting to reconcile things between us. That was the last thing on my mind. Seeing her, though, broken and fading away was too much to bear. The past two weeks have been all for nothing.

She didn't betray me.

Guilt slides around my throat and constricts, choking me. I fucked up because I let my emotional baggage get in the way. What could have been a conversation, where I let her explain, could have meant we could have been happy. I let what Jamie had done to me infect what I had with Willa. It wasn't fair to either of us.

By the time I reach my car, I'm soaked to the bone. I hit the button on my fob and am stopped dead in my tracks when someone pops up from behind an SUV. The other man—or student in this case—is also drenched. His hoodie is pulled up over his head, but I'd recognize that piece of shit face anywhere.

Levi fucking Paulson.

"Mr. Paulson," I bite out in an icy tone. "May I help you?"

He lifts his chin, sneering at me. "Stay the fuck away from Willa."

A burst of fiery wrath surges up inside me, chasing away the chill of the rain. "Watch how you speak to me, kid. We're on school grounds. I can have you expelled for threatening a teacher."

He laughs, cruel and callous. "Nah, Park, I think you'll let me slide this time."

"Doubtful." I prowl toward him, fisting my hands at my sides to keep from smacking the shit out of him. "Go home, asshole."

"Willa is mine," Levi snaps. "Not yours. Fucking mine."

I want to challenge him on this, but that would mean owning up to the fact I'm fucking a student. This prick will only use that information to try to destroy me. I'm well aware I need to tread lightly.

"She's your sister. Don't be disgusting."

His nostrils flare and violence gleams in his eyes. "She's not my real sister."

"Go home," I grit out. "I'm done with this conversation."

He pokes my chest. "This conversation is over when I say it's over."

I've had enough of this fuck face. Rolling my head over my shoulders, I crack my neck in hopes to calm the building rage that's settling in my bones.

"You're going to want to hear this," he says in a smug voice. "And then you're going to do exactly as I say."

The rain continues to beat down on us. As much as I want to shove past him, I don't. His calculating stare tells me he's up to something. Considering Willa lives in his house, and it's my duty to protect her from this piece of shit, I stay rooted in place, ready to hear him out.

For Willa.

I tense when he pulls something out of his hoodie pocket, half expecting it to be a weapon. It's not a knife or a gun. It's his phone. He swipes it and then taps the screen. As soon as the sweet familiar sounds pierce the air, bile creeps up my throat.

Willa.

It's fucking Willa.

Her perfect moans that I've committed to memory are replaying back to me. They're slightly muffled but obvious that she's receiving pleasure. Levi turns his phone toward me. Rain splatters the screen, but I can see my classroom door clearly. My name is emblazoned on the placard beside the door. Sexual grunts and moans are clear as day coming through the closed door.

That motherfucker spied on us.

I knew it was reckless having sex with her at school, but I'd been so out of my mind with the need to comfort and claim her. I was careless. Now, because of my actions, this sick punk has something against me—against Willa.

I'm going to fucking puke.

The grunts and moans eventually cease. Then, you hear my voice and hers as we laugh and talk. It's disturbing to know our private moment was being watched and recorded. Our moment of happiness was being observed to later be used against us.

"What do you want from me?" I demand in a low growl.

"I already told you." He glowers at me. "Stay away from Willa."

"And let you get your sleazy hands on her?" I scoff at him. "Not going to happen. Besides, you can't prove anything. It could have been anyone behind that classroom door."

"Nice try. Keep watching. The good part is coming."

The classroom door opens, revealing both me and Willa. She stares up at me like I'm her whole fucking world. In the video, I glance into the hallway to check for anyone watching and then I steal a tender kiss.

We thought we were alone.

Otherwise, I would have never risked kissing her with the door open.

Fuck, I'm an idiot.

"It's easy, Park," Levi says with an evil grin. "Stay the fuck away from Willa. This will all go away. Your career will be saved."

"And if I refuse?"

His smile falls and his eyes darken. "Everyone will see this. The school, the press, the cops. This will blow up in your fucking face, man. Hers too."

My stomach churns at the thought of her getting swept up in such a scandal. It'll be a nightmare for everyone I love and care about. Hugo can kiss his campaign goodbye.

"Fine."

He arches a brow in surprise. "Fine? That easy?"

"You heard me," I growl. "But you have to erase it all."

"Prove to me you can stay the fuck away and I will."

This time, I do shove past him, no longer able to be an audience to his blackmail. I unlock my car and fling open the door. He grabs the top of the doorframe to keep it from closing once I drop into my seat.

"Later, Mr. Park."

I'm going to fucking destroy this kid.

My life has once again exploded in my face.

At this point, it's a joke. Nothing good ever lasts for me. Problem is, this time, it's going to drag down more than just me. Namely, Hugo and Willa. It's only a matter of time until Levi shows that recording to someone.

I continue to pace the floors in my kitchen like I've done for the past hour since I got home from school.

Willa: I miss you. When can I see you again?

Anxiety and frustration weave themselves into my brain, clouding my every thought. I need to tell her about Levi, but I can't do it over text. I need to hold her later tonight when I confess that shithead recorded something so private between us.

Me: Miss you too. Soon. I need to see my brother first and then we'll figure something out.

And we will.

I'll be damned if I actually go along with Levi's demands. Sure, I'll have to be more secretive, but I'm not going to cease seeing Willa altogether.

I crack a brief smile at the heart emojis Willa sends and then switch over to dial Jude.

"What?" Irritation drips from his single-worded greeting.

Rather than giving him shit for it, I cut right to the chase. "Did you find anything else on the Paulsons? Darren or Levi?"

"I've been preoccupied. I didn't realize it was so pressing."

"For fuck's sake, man. Our family's reputation is on the line."

He grunts. "Could have told me that before."

"And..." I pinch the bridge of my nose and stop pacing. "Someone very innocent is about to also get dragged through the mud. I have to protect her."

Jude is quiet for a moment. Then, he starts tapping away at the computer, the echo of the keys clicking the only sound that can be heard between us.

"The mother or the daughter?" he asks, irritation in his tone.

"What?"

"Which one are you fucking? The married woman or the teenager?"

I close my eyes and grit my teeth. "Not the married woman."

"She's your student?"

"Yep." Shame burns through me. Not because of her, but because I'm forced to admit this shit to my brother so he can properly help me. Of all my brothers, Jude will be bothered least of all. Still, it fucking sucks.

"I'll call you back in a few."

He hangs up, leaving me to my misery. So much rides on the hope that Jude will find me something I can use against Levi.

Willa: Darren and Mom are going to Seattle for the weekend. Can I come stay with you?

A whole weekend just me and Willa. It sounds too good to be true after two weeks of torture. But, knowing her fuck-face stepbrother, he might make an issue out of it.

Me: I'll come get you after dark. You can sneak out through the window.

Once I figure something out to do about Levi, then I'll keep her for good. Waiting until she graduates feels like an eternity, but if that's my only option, I'll take it.

Since I'm still damp from standing in the rain earlier, I toss my phone on the bar and head for the bathroom. As much as I'd love not to wash Willa's scent off my dick, I know it's only temporary. She'll be here in a few hours. I'll have plenty of chances over the weekend to sink my cock deep inside her and revel in her delectable scent.

The shower water is hot and eases some of the tension in my neck and shoulders. Memories of this afternoon when I had her bent over my desk at school flood my mind and thicken my cock. I soap up my hand and stroke myself, imagining it's her body instead. Thrusting my hips, I fuck my fist with an aggression I'd never use with Willa.

It's brutal and punishing.

Recalling the breathy moans she made earlier, I'm finally sent over the edge. I come hard with my girl's name on my lips.

God, I need her.

I won't allow some little shit to threaten me from seeing her.

Once I'm clean, I dry off and dress. I opt for a pair of gray sweatpants and a Park Mountain High School hoodie. Rather than mess with fixing my hair, I quickly run my fingers through it before throwing on some socks and shoes. By the time I make it back to the kitchen, I've effectively wasted nearly an hour.

Won't be much longer until I have Willa in my arms.

My phone buzzes on the countertop. I pick it up to see several missed calls from Jude. He also sent some texts.

Jude: Call me.

Jude: You seriously made me stop what I was doing to serve you and now you can't be bothered to answer your phone?

Jude: Whatever, man. Here. This should pique your interest.

I pull up the screenshot he's sent. It's an email from Darren Paulson to an employee at Park Mountain Lodge.

Jude: I can see you're reading my messages…

He sends another screenshot.

And another.

Holy shit.

Me: This is big. Really fucking big.

Jude: You doubted my abilities?

My brother is a finance genius, but it's his ability to find damning information out on anyone that's his most useful talent.

Me: Never. I have to take this to the authorities.

Jude: I'm assuming they have something on you?

Me: Video proof of me fucking my student. At school. Darren's kid, Levi, showed it to me this afternoon.

Jude: Dirty, kinky bastard.

Me: I love her. She's not some itch to be scratched. She's fucking everything to me. I can't lose her.

The dots move and then stop. Finally, he responds.

Jude: I've got your back, Cal. We'll bury these fuckers so deep they'll never climb out by the time we're done with them.

I let his assurance wash over me.

He's right.

We're motherfucking Parks.

Parks always prevail. It's why half this damn town is named after us.

Levi can fuck all the way off.

I'm getting the girl whether he likes it or not.

CHAPTER TWENTY-SIX

Willa

IT CAN'T GET DARK FAST ENOUGH FOR ME. I'M DYING TO sneak out and go to Callum's. Today, at school, our reconciliation was everything to me. Hearing his apology and then feeling him inside of me healed the cracks in my heart.

I quickly toss clothes into an overnight bag, though I don't anticipate I'll wear much of them. The thought is silly, but it makes me smile.

Thankfully, Levi hasn't made it home yet. I'd briefly seen my mother and Darren as they breezed out of the house earlier. Mom still hovers, though not like she did right after what Levi did to me. As much as I want to cling onto her and keep her near me at all times, it's unrealistic. Not to mention, Darren certainly won't allow it.

I'll never understand the hold he has on my mother. She's always been a strong, independent woman. When she started seeing Darren, I slowly watched her life drain away until she was a shell of herself. The pills, though admittedly less in the past couple of weeks, seemed to be her escape from his stifling control. Problem was, by escaping, she left me all alone.

I busy myself with packing the rest of my things I'll need for the weekend and then sit on the end of the bed. I'm anxious and excited. I could probably go ahead and leave, but I'd die if Levi saw me walking to Callum's. It's safest to wait in my room until Callum comes for me.

Not going insane until he shows up is going to be a problem, though.

Swiping my phone, I scroll through my messages to the last one Gemma sent. Things have been awkward since the party when I basically ghosted her after. Then, I'd gone back to school, pretending I was the same girl I was before I'd started seeing Callum.

Friendless. Quiet. Meant to blend in.

I avoided everyone.

Nibbling on my bottom lip, I debate if I should text Gemma. I really liked her and me shutting her out because of her brother wasn't fair. But now that so much time has passed, I feel stupid reaching out to her. Biting the bullet, I fire out a text before I can change my mind.

Me: Sorry for the past couple of weeks. Been kind of depressed. I didn't intend on hurting you.

She replies back immediately.

Gemma: Want to talk about it?

Me: It was a lot of things. My family, getting pulled in by the cops, and then breaking up with my boyfriend.

Gemma: I didn't even know you had a boyfriend. Do I know him? Tell me it wasn't my brother. Ick. Dempsey is a manwhore and you're better off not dating him.

I can't help but grin. I've been an idiot for not texting her sooner. She's obviously a good friend and deserves to be treated that way.

Me: Not Dempsey. Or Spencer. We got back together, though. He's older than me. People wouldn't approve. Did you get in trouble that night?

Gemma: Older? Do you call him Daddy?

Giggling, I tap out a few eye roll emojis, even if the thought does give me butterflies in my stomach. I might tease Callum about it later.

Me: Ha. No, perv. And you never answered my question.

Gemma: I stayed at Spencer's. Dad knows some kids were involved but he assumed it was Dempsey. We never told him it was me too.

Me: I miss you.

Gemma: I miss you too. Want to come over this weekend to hang out?

Me: I have plans with my boyfriend, but maybe I could escape for a little while.

Gemma: Do I know him?

Me: I shouldn't say.

Gemma: You know I won't say anything to anyone!

Guilt twists in my gut. Of all people, Gemma wouldn't want to do anything to hurt her brother. Maybe it's safe to tell her. Eventually, people will find out, especially after the school year is over. If she finds out then, she'll be hurt.

Me: You can't tell a soul….for reasons.

Gemma: I'm intrigued. Is he married?

Me: No. But...you know him.

The dots move and stop.

Gemma: It's not Spencer or Dempsey?

Gemma: Oh. My. God.

Me: What?

Gemma: Is he a teacher at our school?

Me: Yes.

Gemma: I knew it! I could tell something was off with the way he looked at you. You slut, you're fucking my brother!

I can't tell if she's angry or shocked, so I chew on my bottom lip, wondering how I'll reply. Luckily, she's already texting again.

Gemma: He could get in serious trouble for this.

Me: I know. It's why you can't tell a soul.

Gemma: I can't process this. This is craziness.

Me: I love him.

Gemma: It's about time he found someone to love him. How do you put up with his grouchy attitude? If that's some weird kind of kink...ewwww.

Me: Don't kink shame me! LOL!

She then proceeds to send me GIF after GIF of Oscar the Grouch from *Sesame Street.* It makes me laugh. Texting with Gemma certainly helps the time pass. I'm about to reply when I hear a thud at my bedroom door.

The nightstand is pushed in front of the door—a habit

I never fail to do—and blocks Levi from entering. I jump to my feet, glowering at the door.

"Willa, let me in."

His voice sends chills running down my spine.

"Leave me alone," I bite out. "Leave or I'll call the cops."

He laughs. "I live here, stupid. What are they going to do?"

Though he's right, I don't feel any better. I dial Callum's number, but he doesn't answer. I'm in the middle of typing out a text when Levi kicks the door hard. I cry out in surprise, nearly dropping my phone.

"I just want to talk to you," Levi growls. "Let me in or I'll come through the window like your boyfriend does."

My heart stutters to a stop inside my chest. He knows about Callum? Oh God. This is bad. This is really bad.

"It's locked," I lie. "And I don't have a boyfriend." Another lie.

Silence.

Panic swells up inside me. I stumble over my own feet as I race to the window. As soon as I reach it, a shadow appears. I wish it were Callum, but the terrible feeling in my gut tells me it's not. Levi presses his forehead to the glass and his lips curl into a sinister grin.

"Let me in." His fingers drum on the glass in a slow, taunting way that has every hair on my arms standing on end.

"N-No." I try to keep my eye on Levi, who's thankfully safely locked out, as I also text Callum.

Me: Please hurry. Levi's trying to get into my room and he's scaring me.

"Who are you texting?" Levi barks out. "Me and Mr. Park came to an agreement about you. He won't be saving you."

I snap my head up and gape at him. "What?"

His evil grin is back. "I know you fucked him at school today."

Bile creeps up my throat. How could he possibly know this? And of all people to find out, why him? He's the one person who can use it against me in the worst possible way. The only person who would want to.

"I don't know what you're talking about." I tear my stare from him to send Callum another text.

Me: He knows. I don't know how, but he knows. I'm so sorry, Callum. I don't know what he'll do with this information.

Bang!

I cry out in surprise. Levi's fist remains resting against the window beside his face. He hit it hard enough I'm genuinely shocked it didn't break. Darren will kill him if he breaks the window.

"You're going to let me into this room or I'm going to the cops. I'll tell them what a perv your teacher is." He sneers at me. "Your choice. Let me in and I'll keep it quiet."

At what cost?

I don't trust this monster a bit.

Still no response from Callum. I'm half-tempted to text Gemma, but I don't need her getting involved. What if Levi hurts her? I'd never be able to live with myself.

"I'm going to tell Darren and Mom what you're doing," I threaten. "They'll come back and Darren will be pissed at you."

Levi's nostrils flare. I know I've struck a nerve. Darren

isn't a good stepfather by any stretch, but he's also a shitty dad to Levi. He knows if Darren comes back, it won't be pretty.

"Text him and I'll go straight to the cops." Levi tilts his head and narrows his eyes. "How long do you think it'll take for them to arrest him?"

"I'm eighteen," I shout. "They can't do anything to him."

"Rumor has it," Levi growls, "is he's been fucking you long before that magical age."

It's a lie, obviously, but one that would be difficult to prove. Still, I have to take my chances. It's better than letting Levi try to blackmail me. I start typing out a text to Mom.

"Stop!" Levi barks out, slamming his fist again on the windowpane.

Me: Levi's scaring me—

I don't get to finish my text because glass shatters. Levi has rammed his fist through one of the panes and is now reaching through it. All I can do is stare in stunned silence as he unlocks the window. Shards of glass scrape along his bicep, tearing through his shirt and drawing blood.

Move, Willa.

Run!

I bolt toward my bedroom door and grab hold of the nightstand. Sounds of the window opening and shoes crunching glass on the carpet can be heard behind me, but I don't pause to look back. As soon as I move the nightstand out of the way, I fling the bedroom door open and dart into the hallway. I don't make it very far before I'm grabbed by two powerful arms.

"Ahh!" I shriek. "Let go!"

He's proven time and time again that he's stronger than

me. This time is no different. All too easily, he manhandles me back into my bedroom. At first, I'm pissed and my blood boils with rage.

Until he tosses me onto the bed.

I don't get a chance to scrabble away. He pounces on me, pinning my arms against the mattress and settling his body against mine. Terror claws its way up my throat and my eyes prickle with tears.

"You know, Willa," Levi croons, dipping his face close to mine so that his breath tickles over my flesh. "I can make this all go away."

I don't chase the bait, choosing instead to glower at him.

"All you have to do," he continues, "is give in to us."

"There is no us," I spit out.

He shoves my wrists above my head, capturing both of them with one of his large hands. Then, he uses his free one to tease his fingers along the side of my face. I shudder at his touch. He continues to roam his hand down until he reaches one of my breasts. A tearful sob escapes me when he roughly squeezes it.

"Do you know how long I've wanted this?" His voice is low and his eyes are glazed over. "Since I met you, Willa. I got a boner that day at the idea I'd have you in my house all the time. It felt like fate."

He's delusional.

Completely insane.

"Fate?" I hiss, spittle flying from my lips. "Not fate. Hate. I hate you, Levi. I always have. I'm not your property just because your dad moved us into your house."

He grabs hold of my shirt and starts yanking it up my body, exposing my bra. I squirm and wriggle to no avail.

Everything goes dark for a moment as he drags the shirt over my head, leaving it at my arms. His smile is vicious and cruel.

"That's where you're wrong," he murmurs. "No one's stopping me and you're right beneath me where you belong."

Seconds crawl by like endless eternities.

I stare at the open window, wondering if Callum will ever show up. Levi follows my gaze to the window and shakes his head.

"He chose his career and family name over you, Willa. I showed him the video. I'm sorry, but your boyfriend chose to protect himself. No one is coming." He grinds his hard dick against me. "It's just the two of us now. Always."

No one's coming for me.

I burst into tears and try not to puke when Levi starts kissing them away.

CHAPTER TWENTY-SEVEN

Callum

DARREN PAULSON IS DIRTY AS FUCK. I KNEW HE WAS a slimy piece of shit the day he came into the principal's office when his rotten son had pictures of Willa. He just gave off a vibe. But seeing actual proof is something entirely different.

He's a snake.

The documentation Jude dug up was plentiful and keeps coming as he unearths it. We'll never be able to use it in court, considering the means we obtained them, but it'll be enough to open up an investigation.

"What can you do about it?" I ask Sloane, drumming my fingers on the edge of her desk.

She purses her lips and studies her computer monitor. "I mean, there's enough here from this 'anonymous' tip to get a warrant. He's not some rando messing with another rando. Paulson is an esteemed attorney going out of his way to sway an election by conspiring to damage your family reputation."

The Park Mountain police station is quiet this evening aside from a couple cops barking out laughter from somewhere within the building. Sloane continues to click through the documents sent to her from Jude via an encrypted email claiming to be anonymous.

A creak resounds from the station's front door and then

footsteps squeak across the linoleum floor. Hugo rounds the corner wearing a scowl.

"Well?" he asks, gaze darting between the two of us.

"It's big," Sloane says with a tired sigh. "What did you guys do to piss him off?"

Knowing our family, the list is probably endless. We Parks are always raining on someone's parade.

When Hugo starts interrogating Sloan about her information, I pull my phone from my pocket to let Willa know I might be later than expected. Several texts sit unread.

Willa: Please hurry. Levi's trying to get into my room and he's scaring me.

Seconds later, I see she's sent another one.

Willa: He knows. I don't know how, but he knows. I'm so sorry, Callum. I don't know what he'll do with this information.

All the blood in my veins turns to sludge and then ices over. It's been several minutes since she texted. If that bastard got into her room…

"I have to go," I bark out, flying out of my seat. "Call me if anything else comes up."

Hugo scowls at me, but I don't have seconds to waste on an explanation. On the way to the car, I text both Dempsey and Spencer in a group chat.

Me: Meet me at Willa's. Now.

Before I reach my vehicle, they've both responded.

Dempsey: Is she hurt????

Spencer: Why are we meeting at Willa's?

Me: Just do it!

I fling open the car door and hop inside. My phone buzzes with more texts.

Spencer: On our way.

Dempsey: Are you fucking her???

I send a thumb emoji. They can sort it out themselves on who I was talking to. For the record, it was both. Peeling out of the police station parking lot, I haul ass toward her house. As I near our road, Spencer's midnight-black BMW 8 Series darts out in front of traffic, causing a few vehicles to honk and swerve.

Crazy little shit.

I'm thankful they're not wasting any time, though. Spencer drives like he's training for NASCAR and barrels down the road ahead of me. My heart is beating out of my chest. Worry strangles my throat to the point I can't breathe. I push the button to the window, inhaling the cold air as it whips at my face. The drive to Willa's doesn't take long and when we're in front of her house, the three of us bolt toward her open window.

As we near, I hear her whimpers.

Her motherfucking pleas.

So help me, if that psycho touched her…

I don't finish that thought as I push the curtains out of the way and step into her room. My shoes crunch on glass. I freeze for half a second, trying to process the scene.

My girl…

My fucking girl is pinned beneath Levi. Both their shirts are gone. She's struggling as he works at pulling her pants off.

He doesn't hear me or see me.

Willa's dark eyes find mine and a sob of relief escapes her. Meanwhile, I detonate like a bomb.

With a roar that is so powerful it could rattle the house, I charge for him. Crashing into him, I grab hold of him and roll away from her. We continue to roll until we land on the floor with him on top of me. Dempsey's and Spencer's voices can be heard beyond the rage ringing in my ears, but I don't stop to investigate or worry over the fact they're seeing Willa topless.

Right now, all I care about is killing this motherfucker.

I slam my fist into his face, knocking him off me. Before he can sit up, I'm on him, sitting on his stomach so I can rain my fists down on him. He's young and strong, but my fury makes me an unbeatable beast.

For every two punches I land, he gets one in on me back, most of which hit my ribs. It hurts like hell, but I won't rest until I've beat this asshole to a pulp. I bellow and scream at him as I punish him for touching her.

"Callum!"

Willa's voice, a terrified sob in her throat, cuts through my vengeful haze. I want to go to her. To hold her against me and never let go.

"I hear sirens," Spencer says. "A neighbor must have called the cops."

My throat is hoarse from yelling and calling Levi every name in the book. No wonder the cops were called. Fuck.

"Go," I growl to my nephew. "Take Dempsey and go."

"So you can take the fall for this dipshit?" Spencer bites back. "No. *You* need to go. There's a lot more on the line for you."

Levi moans in pain but keeps trying to punch me. Before

I can land another hit, Dempsey grabs me by the collar of my shirt, dragging me away.

"Let go," I snarl. "I said fucking let me go!"

He shoves me away and then Spencer takes hold of my shirt, keeping me from attacking Levi. Willa, trembling and crying, hugs the blanket to her naked chest. My heart cracks down the middle.

She'll never be safe here.

Never.

Which is why he should die.

I lunge for Levi again as he attempts to stand. Dempsey beats me to the punch. Literally. He rams his fist into Levi's gut, causing him to howl in pain. I watch with satisfaction as Dempsey lands a couple more punches, this time to Levi's battered face.

"Get him out of here," Dempsey bellows. "The sirens are getting louder. He can't be here when they get here."

I attempt to reach for Willa, but she shakes her head. "He's right. Go!"

Spencer hauls me toward the window and practically pushes me out of it. I stumble over my feet but recover shortly after going through it. He shoves me toward my car. When I make it over to it, he stops and levels me with a fierce stare.

"We'll take care of this," he vows. "Promise. Just go home."

I want to stay and continue to beat the hell out of Levi. I want to stay and hold my sweet girl. But if I stay, I'm most definitely going to jail for fucking up a minor. In his own home. And said minor is going to rat me out for being with Willa.

If I want to see Willa, I have to keep a low profile.

"Don't let him touch her," I growl.

"He won't. Now go."

As soon as Spencer is sure I'm climbing into my car, he takes off running back toward the house. I turn the ignition but don't drive away immediately. Everything aches in me to charge back inside—to finish off that piece of shit so he'll never be a threat again. I'm just considering it when I see the flashing of red and blue lights. Against my better judgment, I slowly drive away.

The entire drive home, I'm numb.

Completely fucking numb.

Not knowing anything about how Willa is doing is going to drive me insane.

I drive all the way home in a trance. I'm not even sure I remember driving at all. Just one minute I was parked outside of Willa's and now I'm in my garage. Dazed and depleted of energy after my adrenaline crash, I climb out of my car and slam the door shut.

"Callum?"

The young voice confuses me for a second. I'm almost certain it's Willa, which is impossible, but then I see my sister standing in the open garage door behind my car.

"Gemma." I scrub a palm over my face. "You should go home."

She huffs and storms over to me. "You're hurt."

"You should see the other guy."

Our eyes meet and though there's no humor in my words, she grins. "Levi?"

Grinding my teeth together, I give her a curt nod. "How'd you know?"

She rolls her eyes in that dramatic teenage way that

irritates me to no end. "I'm not an idiot. Let's go inside so I can look at your hand. Your knuckles are bleeding."

I follow her because I know my sister. Gemma won't relent. And right now, I need the company so I don't do anything regrettable like drive back over there.

"He had it coming," Gemma says when we reach the kitchen. "That guy is such a douchebag. And you're a Park. If someone messes with your girl, you're not going to sit around and let it happen."

I stiffen at her words.

"Please," Gemma mutters. "Like I said, I'm not an idiot. Plus, Willa told me you two are fucking."

"Gemma," I growl in warning.

"Chill," she sasses. "She said it…*nicer* than that, but it's what you're doing."

I don't argue or deny her words, unsure where all this is going. She smirks as she turns on the kitchen sink. I let her guide my hand under the stream of cold water.

"Now tell me everything. I need all the juicy deets."

"I love her." I bore my gaze into her. "I fucking love her."

And that's all she needs to know.

The details don't matter.

Just Willa.

CHAPTER TWENTY-EIGHT

Willa

I'M NUMB.

Completely numb.

If it weren't for Spencer's comforting grip on my hand, I'd go back to shivering. Maybe it was the terror of what Levi was doing or the shock of what Callum did to him in return or pure adrenaline, but for the past hour, I've been shaking.

"How long has this been going on?" the officer asks for the fiftieth time.

Spencer gives my hand a squeeze, urging me to answer. I blink away my daze and lift my chin, meeting her concerned stare.

"W-What?" I croak out.

Her lips purse together. "I'd feel better if you'd go to the hospital to get checked—"

"No," I hiss. "I don't need to go to the hospital."

I need to see Callum.

To know he's okay.

At first, I'd been overjoyed he'd come to rescue me from Levi's assault, but then he went mad. Lost himself to blind rage. I was certain he was going to kill Levi. Not that Levi didn't deserve it. But I was sickened at the thought of losing Callum to prison. It wasn't fair.

"Let's try this again," the officer says gently. "How long has your stepbrother been harassing you?"

A full-bodied shudder quakes through me. Levi has always taunted me in some way. It's never been this bad. Had Callum not come when he did, Levi would have raped me.

Tears well in my eyes and I swallow down the lump in my throat. "I want my mom."

The officer nods, smiling at me. "I know, honey. She'll be here soon. We've already contacted her."

"Where's…" I trail off, eyes darting everywhere.

"Your boyfriend was arrested, but I'm sure it'll sort itself out," the officer assures me. She winks at me. "He's a Park."

I tense up. Did they find out Callum was responsible for beating up Levi? What happens now?

Spencer's thumb rubs over my hand. "Dempsey just lost it and wanted to protect you. My dad is a really good attorney. Everything will be fine."

Dempsey.

They think Dempsey is my boyfriend.

Despite the relief at knowing Callum isn't sitting in a cell, I want to correct both of them. I want to tell them Callum is the Park I'm in love with, not his little brother. Admitting that, though, means undoing everything Dempsey did to protect Callum's and my relationship. He took the fall for beating up Levi.

"Levi? Did they arrest him too?" I ask, voice hoarse with emotion.

The officer nods. "They did. Once we have your statement, that ought to be enough to keep him there for a bit. I need you to tell me everything about your stepbrother and the events that happened earlier."

"Pull it together," Spencer rumbles from beside me. "Tell her everything. The sooner you do, the sooner Dempsey can be let go."

His words send steel shooting down my spine. This family has come together to save and protect me. That means I need to step up and do my part to do the same for them. I give Spencer a small nod of understanding and then spill every last horrid detail, skating over parts where Callum is my lover, not Dempsey. By the time I'm finished, I'm crying.

"I'm going to get you some water," the officer says, her features soft with concern. "Will you be okay here with your friend until then?"

I nod quickly and rest my head on Spencer's shoulder. If he weren't here to help me through all of this, I'd probably shut down completely. As soon as she leaves us alone in my living room to go to the kitchen where another officer is standing, Spencer kisses the top of my head.

"You almost had me convinced," he murmurs low enough for only me to hear.

"About?"

"Dempsey being your boyfriend."

I stiffen. My first urge is to deny knowing what he's talking about, but the jig is up. He and Dempsey both witnessed Callum's rage on my behalf. A man doesn't turn so feral to protect a woman like that unless he's madly in love with her.

"It just sort of happened," I whisper. "I love him."

We both know I'm not talking about Dempsey.

"You're eighteen, though, right?" Spencer asks. "I don't get all the secrecy."

"His position," I say with a sigh. "It could be twisted to make him seem like a predator."

"He's a Park. We're all predators."

I crack a smile, but it quickly falls. "I don't want him to lose his job, or worse yet, go to jail."

"Hmph."

"We were just trying to wait until I graduated," I explain. "Then…"

"Then what?"

"Then, I guess, we were going to see each other proudly and unafraid of what others would think."

He starts to speak again, but the front door opens. I jolt at the abrupt intrusion, ready to run if it's Levi, and then relax at seeing my mother.

"My baby," Mom cries out, rushing over to me. "Oh my God."

She drops to the sofa beside me, prying me from Spencer's grip to pull me into her loving arms. For a moment, I'm six years old and letting my mom comfort me after a nightmare. I cling to her shirt and sob against her neck. She whispers assurances, stroking my hair.

It's like old times.

"Where is my son?"

The warmth flooding through me is snuffed out as the chill of Darren's voice sweeps over me. I'm reminded Mom chose Darren over me. She married a man I knew she never really loved and let me fend for myself for years, alone and terrified.

"Mr. Paulson," one of the officers greets, voice tight and professional. "A word. In the kitchen."

"Not until I find out what the hell is going on around here," Darren bellows. "Is Willa being dramatic again? It's no secret she and my son don't get along."

Disgust ripples through me.

How dare he transform this to make me seem as though I'm a bratty child who's trying to get her stepbrother in trouble. Blood rushes in my ears, deafening me. I wait for Mom to speak up and defend me.

Nothing.

The officers, however, manage to corral Darren into the kitchen. I'm left feeling hollowed out, once again, by my relationship with my mother. If it weren't for Spencer on my other side, then I'd feel completely alone.

"Oh, baby girl," Mom says, her voice cracking. "I am so sorry."

It's too late, though.

She's chosen sides and it's not mine.

I listen to her assurances and whispered promises but don't let them infect me like they used to. It's about time I come to terms with the fact my mom picked Darren over me years ago and she always will.

"I want that sonofabitch out of my house," Darren barks, reentering from the kitchen. "You Parks are a disease in this town." He thrusts a finger at Spencer. "I will eradicate each and every one of you."

"Mr. Paulson," the male officer warns. "That's enough."

"I want him out." Darren's features are twisted into a murderous scowl. "Now."

I give Spencer's hand a squeeze. His family has done enough for me. It's time to stand up on my own.

"I've got this," I promise. "Check on Dempsey…" And him.

Spencer kisses the side of my head. "Call me and I'll be here in minutes. Got it?"

"Thank you."

He leans in and whispers, "You're practically family now."

Words have never sounded sweeter.

As soon as the officers drive away, the temperature of the living room drops several degrees. I refuse to allow Darren to intimidate me. He and his son are in the wrong here, not me.

"Our family is becoming the laughingstock of this town," Darren bites out as he paces the living room in front of the sofa where me and Mom are still sitting. "I won't have it."

"Darren," Mom starts but snaps her mouth closed when he glowers at her. "I'm sorry."

I freeze at her apology. She's sorry? Seriously? All these years, I've held in my sadness and feelings of betrayal, but today I've had enough. I'm tired of the same old routine. Something has to change.

"No," I clip out. "You don't get to apologize to him, Mom. Not now, not ever."

Silence befalls the room.

"Baby," Mom murmurs, "please don't."

"Stop!" I shake her off me and straighten my spine. "I'm tired of this hold he has over you. Why do you always choose him?" My bottom lip wobbles despite my desperation to stay strong and angry. "Why not me?"

"There's more to it than that," Mom says, voice quavering. "I've done everything for you. It's always been for you."

"Liar!" Tears well and I can't contain them. I swipe them off my cheeks with the palms of my hands. "You do everything Darren says and when he's not lording his power over you, you drown yourself in your stupid pills! I'm tired of all of this and you!"

"That's enough," Darren bellows. "Your tirade is done."

"Fuck you," I snarl, my words drenched in venom.

Mom rises to her feet, hands lifting in a placating gesture. "Darren, she's just upset. Let me handle this."

His head tilts to the side as he studies her, a cruel expression on his face. "She's not a little girl anymore. I think she's owed the truth."

Bile creeps up my throat.

What truth?

"You can't tell her," Mom whispers. "You swore to me."

I stand up despite the way my knees slightly buckle. Uneasiness has a hold of my nerves and every cell in my body feels alive. Something tells me that the big secret will have me wanting to bolt and I need to be ready.

"Tell me what?" I demand. "What have you been hiding from me?"

Whatever this is will hurt. I can feel it. Like a calm before a chaotic storm. My mother has betrayed me in some way and I need to know what it is, no matter how painful it may be.

Mom's head bows and her shoulders begin to shake as she sobs. I stare at her with new eyes, aware of how weak she is as she fumbles for her purse, locating a couple of her pills.

"I need to know," I say to Darren, unable to peel my eyes from my mother. "I need to know what has her choosing this over me." I motion at the pill bottle in her hand and then at him.

His smile is wicked as he walks over to her. She's limp but willingly goes into his arms. I want to throw up but manage to keep from getting sick.

"When your daddy died, your mother had a hard time keeping her shit together." Darren murmurs the words as he gently strokes her hair. "Damn near drank herself into the grave with him."

I remember those early days after Dad died. When I was a small child taking care of a grown woman who would never leave the bed. I learned quickly how to open cans of ravioli and other easy meals to feed us. I'd done a good job, too, until the food ran out.

"She was grieving," I whisper. "She got better."

She was forced to get better.

Child protective services were called when I went to a neighbor's house asking how to cook a frozen turkey. It was all that was left in the freezer and I dragged the rock-hard thing next door. I didn't realize that day I'd be getting my mother into trouble.

Luckily, it was the wake-up call she needed.

I spent the night with strangers, but the next day, the mom I knew and loved was back. She was fierce, loving, and protective. Since I was young, I don't remember all the details, just that she was back to taking care of both of us and going to work like normal.

And then, one day, Darren was there, filling the role of dad.

"When you have an expensive oxy habit, it's amazing how quickly you can go bankrupt," Darren states, a smugness in his tone that grates on me. "Your mom was on the verge of losing everything."

My stomach twists at his words. "What are you saying?"

"I'm saying your mother was desperate. Desperation can make you do crazy things."

I wrack my brain for memories of years back. Mom went on a vacation without me one summer, while I stayed with some people who were practically family, and when she came back, she was married to Darren.

"She married you for your money?" I rasp out. "That's what this is all about."

Darren snorts. "Hardly. You know your mother doesn't do anything in moderation. Her Michael Kors bags can attest to that."

Mom remains strangely quiet, as though she's resigned herself to the fact he's going to tell her biggest secrets—ones that are going to destroy her family.

"I don't understand," I whisper.

"Your mom embezzled from the law firm she works at. She stole money from that old man you used to call Grandpa Leo."

Mom's boss, Leo Sorrel, was the family I'd stayed with while she ran off to marry Darren.

"What?"

Darren laughs. "Right? Leo may be an attorney, but he's a great guy. Who would steal from that guy? She'd have to be a heartless, selfish bitch."

She was an addict.

A grieving addict on the verge of losing her child.

I can understand the desperation, but it doesn't make it right.

"Mom…" I trail off, hurt in my voice. "Does he know?"

"If he knew," Darren says in triumph, "your mother would be in prison for a very long time."

Mom tenses but doesn't argue his words.

"How much?"

"Enough," Mom croaks out.

"Last time I checked, it was upwards of what, one? Two?" Darren asks, his eyebrow arching.

"Thousands?"

Darren barks out a laugh. "You sweet, naïve child. Thousands? How cute."

My blood runs cold. Millions of dollars? My mother embezzled millions of dollars from someone I looked up to as a grandfather. How could she do such a thing?

"How could she take so much money and not get caught?" I demand. "He had to have discovered it."

"The old man has almost as much money as those damn Parks, so he hasn't noticed she's been stealing from under his nose," Darren states. "Plus, when your mother wants something, she's really, really good at getting it." He pats her on the top of the head. "But no matter how good she is, it would have caught up to her eventually because the oxy was beginning to make her sloppy."

Oxy made her a lot of things and sloppy was one of them. Once she got off those, she did better. The Xanax doesn't make her sloppy, just sleepy. Probably because she takes a lot more than she's supposed to. At least she somehow manages to pull herself up to go into work, even on Saturdays.

"Before I opened my own firm, I worked for Leo," Darren says. "I came in one Saturday to find her digging through Leo's office, slurring her words. She confessed what she'd done and begged for me to take her to rehab."

"That summer..." I mutter.

"That summer I did take her to rehab. But I also saw an opportunity. Your mother, despite her addictive ways, was a genius and ruthless when it served her own needs. Having her on my side could be beneficial to me. I told her I'd keep her secret if we were to marry." He chuckles. "I reminded her she had a child to think of. That I could help care for and protect that child. No one had to go to prison. She just needed to be smarter and more careful."

"You're a monster," I snap.

"No, I'm an investor. Not only do I have a beautiful, intelligent wife, but I have one who pays like interest. An annuity if you will."

"You disgust me. You'll pay for this."

"Me? No, Willa, I won't. The one who'll pay is your mother. Over the years, I've kept everything that could implicate her. As long as she skims and covers her tracks, no one will be the wiser. Meanwhile, I keep several of Leo's businesses he owns knee-deep in lawsuits with the Parks so that Leo doesn't know he's being robbed blind. Everyone wins." He smirks. "Well, not the Parks or Leo, but that's neither here nor there." Darren releases my mother and then walks toward the door. "Now, if you'll excuse me, I have to bail my son out of jail. Later, we'll sort this mess out and finally work together as the family we are. There will be no more dealings with the Parks, nor will there be any altercations between you and Levi."

He exits the house without looking back, leaving me hollowed out by his words. Mom can't even look at me. And she shouldn't. I don't think she'd like the expression on my face.

"All these years," I croak out. "You betrayed me. You broke the law. All because you wanted to get high?"

Mom's head snaps up, eyes bloodshot from tears. "My heart was broken. When your father died, I was destroyed. I did this so I could survive and keep you. I was managing the best way I knew how."

"Who are you anymore?"

"I'm your mother." Tears race down her cheeks, but her eyes are glazed over, the Xanax now numbing her to the bone. "I love you."

"I love you too..."

"But?"

"But I can't do this anymore. I'm leaving."

"Where will you go?"

"Anywhere but here."

Though I don't divulge my destination, I have no doubts where I will go.

To him.

Always to him.

"Please don't go. I can still protect you and keep you safe. That's all I've ever wanted."

I recoil from her disillusioned words. "Safe? I've been sexually assaulted under your own roof several times. You didn't keep me safe, Mom. You moved me in with a monster."

"Willa, baby..." Her face crumples. "Where will you go? You don't have anyone but me."

A burst of anger swells inside me. "I have him. Callum Park. My boyfriend." Even as the words tumble out of my mouth, I wish I could reel them back in.

Her eyes slightly widen despite the drugs creeping through her system. "That *man*? Your statistics teacher?"

"I love him," I tell her, lifting my chin. "I'm going to stay with him and I'm not coming back."

"But he's your teacher. How long has this been—"

"Don't start in on your high horse," I snap. "You don't get to take the moral high ground. Not now. Not ever."

"I should go to the police," Mom tries, though her voice is weak. "This is disgusting."

"You stealing from a man who rode horses with me that summer and promised everything was going to be okay when Mommy came back for me is disgusting. It looks like we both have our fair share of shameful secrets." I shake my head at her. "I won't tell if you won't tell."

"Willa…"

"Goodbye, Mom. I love you and I really hope you can get the help you need."

The last tether keeping me in this unhappy life of mine snaps indefinitely. I'm free. Finally free of the guilt and desire to protect my mother. Free to go to him. Free to go home.

CHAPTER TWENTY-NINE

Callum

THE DOOR FROM THE GARAGE TO THE HOUSE OPENS and in steps Spencer. His grin is wolfish and knowing. If I weren't such a mess worrying about Willa, I'd tell him to go the fuck home. But seeing someone who's recently been with her and knows her well-being, I can't help but rush over to him.

"How is she?" I demand. "Tell me."

"Aside from Gemma trying to accost her in the front yard, I think she's just fine."

The front yard?

Gemma left a few minutes ago to go home. Spencer must have given Willa a ride over here. I shove past him, storming into the garage. The overhead door is open, revealing the two girls standing in the driveway. Willa has two bags at her feet and a backpack hooked over one shoulder. They both turn their heads as I rush toward them.

Willa drops her bag and flies into my arms, knocking me against the back of my car. I squeeze her to me, afraid that if I let her go, even just the tiniest bit, she'll disappear forever. She smells sweet like honey-scented shampoo. I inhale her, hoping to keep her essence trapped in my lungs until the end of time.

Pulling back, I grip her soft jaw in my massive hand and then crash my lips to hers. She tastes sweet like vanilla and

Coke. I devour her mouth, needing to lick every part of her, claiming her as mine. Her moan is soft and breathy, speaking straight to my cock. It hardens between us, and I have the sense to feel ashamed at getting an erection in front of my sister and nephew.

Not the place.

Not the time.

"Fuck," I rumble against Willa's perfect pouty lips. "I missed you so fucking much."

"You literally saw her a few hours ago," Spencer says in an unhelpful voice. "Just pointing out the obvious."

"Shut up," Gemma sasses. "They're stupidly in love. Leave them alone."

It's humiliating to be seen like this in front of my family, but I can't find the sense to reel it back in. All I want to do is kiss and hug her. Keep her locked in my arms where I know she's safe.

"Go home," I growl, unable to keep from nipping Willa's bottom lip. "We'll talk about this later."

I don't wait for them to answer. It takes everything in me to pull away from Willa to retrieve her bags. I toss them into the house and take her hand, tugging her along after me.

"Wait," Willa says, breathless. "What about Dempsey?"

"Hugo is dealing with it," Gemma assures her. "Don't worry."

If I know anything, it's that my brother will get Dempsey out of jail before his ass even warms the bench. The main concern today was Willa and now she's here with me. Everything is going to be okay.

"Bye, children," I grunt out, smacking the button to close

the overhead door. “Don’t just walk in unless you want to see something you can’t unsee.”

“Eww,” Gemma complains over the sound of the door closing.

As soon as they’re gone, I close the garage door to the house and then press Willa against the wall, locking her in with my hips.

“Are you okay?” I murmur, studying her tearstained, puffy face.

Her smile is breathtaking. “I am now.”

“You brought bags with you.”

Pink darkens her cheeks and she chews on her bottom lip. “It was probably presumptuous—”

“You’re moving in with me.” I press my forehead to hers. “No question about it.”

She nods and closes her eyes before a sigh of relief escapes her. “Thank you.”

“I want you here,” I murmur, my hands sliding down her front to the button of her jeans. “I need you here. I don’t think you understand how much you’ve gotten inside me, sweetheart.”

A tremble ripples through her. “He touched me... I want it gone. I want you. Everywhere.”

The feral desire to claim her, marking her all over with my scent and seed is overwhelming. I’m not gentle or careful as I strip her clothes from her body. The tear of my own shirt isn’t enough to jar me as I yank it away with haste and eagerness. With one, two, three beats of my heart, she’s naked. I’m naked. We’re finally together.

“Get it wet,” I command, my voice husky. “This will be quick.”

Her nails rake down my naked chest as she kneels. A hiss rushes past my lips when her breath tickles my shaft. My dick jumps in anticipation. She curls her small hand around my massive cock and sets to licking the damn thing like it's a sweet treat.

"Such a fucking tease," I growl. "You're killing me."

Her eyes dart up to meet mine and they flash with pleasure. So goddamn gorgeous. And mine. I've claimed her and I'm not letting her go. She purses her puffy pink lips and then parts them to kiss the leaking tip of my cock. A sound of pleasure purrs from her as her tongue laps at my pre-cum.

"I like how you taste," she says, hot breath fanning over my sensitive flesh. "So good."

She takes me deep into her mouth. My eyes roll back in sheer bliss. Her mouth is hot and slick. It takes restraint for me not to buck my hips and fuck her tight little throat. I fist my hands in her hair to keep control of the situation. She sinks deeper and her throat constricts with a gag that has her slobber running down the underside of my dick.

I'm too damn big to fuck her throat. Hell, her teeth are dangerously scraping the skin around my cock as it is, but it doesn't stop me from imagining what it'd feel like.

She pulls back, sucks in a breath, and then goes back to pleasuring me with her perfect mouth. I could spend hours just like this, but I want more. I want my dick buried inside her and my tongue owning hers.

I want to consume her.

"Good girl," I praise. "Now get up here. I need your sexy mouth."

She allows me to pull her up to her feet, my grip still tight on her hair. Once she's standing, I dip my mouth to hers, kissing her slick lips. I slide my palms down to her ass and squeeze. Since she's so small, I easily lift her and guide her to my dick.

"Ease me in, sweetheart."

She fumbles for my cock and then positions the head at her wet pussy. As soon as I'm angled the right way, I push down on her hips while thrusting my hips up. I bury myself to the hilt in one hard buck of my hips.

"Ahh!" she cries out, fingernails digging into the backs of my shoulders. "Oh God!"

"Mine," I growl. "You're fucking mine."

She nods and then her head falls back against the wall as she loses herself to ecstasy. I drive into her hard, not able to take her softly or sweetly. This is a proclamation. Feral and filled with animalistic need.

Mine. Mine. Mine.

My fingers dig into her flesh as I use her small body to fuck my starved cock. So easily I pull her up and down over my shaft, drawing out unimaginable pleasure as her tight body grips mine. Her perky tits bounce and jiggle with each crazed movement. I angle her back some so I can make sure to hit her G-spot with each well-timed thrust. I know I've hit my mark when her back arches and her face tilts toward the ceiling. A howl of need pierces the air. I'm not sure if it's hers or mine or the combined sound of this furious lovemaking. All I know is her body is shuddering like she's possessed and her pussy squirts the hottest, sexiest juices all over my throbbing dick.

"Fuckfuckfuckfuck," I chant before burning my face into her neck. "Fuck, you're mine."

I bite her neck, desperate to chase that statement with something permanent. Something I can see long after this moment is gone. My teeth bruise her flesh and when I taste the tang of blood, I fear I've gone too far.

But then she's coming again, sobbing and clawing at me, coming so hard I nearly drop her.

This girl is my world.

My air and purpose and sustenance.

My everything.

A flash of white-hot pleasure seizes me. My balls tighten and then I'm unloading into her still seizing body. I continue to fuck her like I'm a goddamn feral animal, eager to fill her up with every goddamn drop.

I want her permanently mine.

Pregnant with my children. One after the other.

If I could, I'd stay buried in her forever.

She goes limp in my arms, exhausted from our bodies reuniting in such a desperate way. I hold her close to me, careful not to dislodge my cock from inside her, and carry her over to the sofa. Keeping her tight against me, I sit down and arrange her legs so she's straddling me. My dick might be half hard and spent, but it still fits nicely inside her, plugging my seed inside her.

"My sweet, perfect girl," I croon, stroking my fingers down her back and then back up again. "How are you so goddamn perfect?"

She snuggles against me and I can feel her smile against my skin. "You make me happy, Callum."

I curl my palms around the cleft of her ass and let my fingers tease at the way her pussy lips stretch to accommodate my fat dick. Cum and her own arousal are leaking out wherever it can escape. We're so fucking messy and I love it.

Her soft, rhythmic breathing lulls me to sleep where I dream of many lifetimes of us locked together just like this.

Banging on the door jars me awake. Willa jolts upright, revealing to me the damage from my teeth. Her neck is bruised, purple and blue, and the skin is scabbed over in some areas. Fuck. I tore at her neck like I was a goddamn vampire. My dick swells, still deep inside her, and her tight body resists. I'm not sure how long we slept, but it was long enough for the cum to dry into something sticky.

Knock-knock-knock-knock.

The door.

That's what I'd heard. Someone is here. Reluctantly, I gently pull Willa off my dick and set her on the couch beside me. I yank a blanket down and cover her up.

"Who is it?" she rasps, concern making her brows pinch.

"Whoever it is, I'll get rid of them." I storm over to my pants and yank them on, not bothering with a shirt. Once I'm decent, I make my way to the door.

For fuck's sake.

"We just want to ask you some questions," the man on the other side of the door barks out upon seeing my face in the window. He holds up a badge. "Won't take but a few minutes."

I glance over my shoulder at Willa. She's frozen in place, the blanket swallowing her tiny body, keeping her body hidden from anyone who might try and catch a peek. With her big, wide eyes, she seems younger than her eighteen years. It's hard to believe this was the same woman who less than an hour ago was coming all over my cock while I bit her pretty neck.

"I'm eighteen," she reminds me, clearly reading the panic on my face. "They can't do anything."

I nod, thankful for the reminder, and unlock the door. Once it's open, I gesture for the two cops to enter. They're not familiar to me. I may know a lot of people in this town, but I don't know everyone, nor do I care to. I'm not Hugo or Dad, for fuck's sake.

"Did we interrupt something?" one of the men asks, eyeing Willa.

"Actually," I grit out. "You did. We were taking a nap. If you'll be so kind as to make this quick, then we can get back to it."

"I'm Detective John Summers and this is my partner, Detective Riley Harp."

He offers his hand, but I don't take it. My girl's cum is on my fingers and I'm not about to let some man in a cheap suit touch what's mine.

"If this is about what happened earlier, that was my brother's doing, not mine." I hate lying, but Dempsey would be pissed if I undid everything he did by outing myself now.

"Actually…" Summers huffs and then crosses his arms over his chest. "We're here on an anonymous video that was sent to the station. Harp?"

Harp pulls his phone from his pocket and holds up the screen. He pushes play and I'm shown the video of my classroom door. The same video Levi took and tried to blackmail me with.

"I have to ask, Mr. Park, is this your voice in the recording?" Summers frowns at me. "Lying won't help your case here. We're just trying to clarify some important points here."

"Callum," Willa warns. "Don't say any—"

"It's me and Willa." I lift my chin. "My student."

To their credit, neither cop flinches.

"She's eighteen. We didn't pursue any romantic involvements until she was of age." I level Summers with a hard glare. "We didn't do anything illegal."

"I can see where you'd have that understanding," Summers says, frowning, "but this was recorded on the device of a minor. As you can see, this complicates things, Mr. Park."

Fuck.

Before I can utter a reply, Hugo bursts in through the door. He's slightly disheveled, but his expression is fierce. My brother is a politician second and an attorney first.

"John, Riley," Hugo greets, a million-dollar smile on his face. "So good to finally put two names to faces. Chief Glenn has nothing but great things to say about both of you."

I don't miss the way either of them puffs up at the mention of their superior's name.

"Carey and I go way back. Did you know she used to babysit me when I was a kid?" Hugo asks. "How's her new grandbaby anyway? Marla was it?"

Harp laughs. "That little girl is so cute, but she puked all over Summers's suit when Carey brought her to the station for a visit."

"I'll have to pop in and see Carey someday soon. Catch up on everything," Hugo says, never losing his megawatt smile. "Let her show me baby pics." He winks at Harp. "I'm really sorry you both had to get involved in this…situation."

Both detectives straighten their spines again, remembering they're working, not having social hour.

"We're just doing our jobs. Investigating what's brought

to us," Summers says slowly. "Just gathering statements at this point."

Hugo nods. "As fascinating as it is to some that my brother is dating a much younger woman, we all know what this is about." He sighs as though it's all his fault. "My campaign really has brought out the worst in people. They're going after my family. Though we knew they would, it still hurts. But sending an underage kid to do the dirty work? That's low, even for Mr. Paulson."

I glance over at Willa and her eyes widen. I'm not sure how Hugo is going to pull us out of this mess, but he seems confident enough.

"My father assures me that these things happen and not to let it bother me. But I can't help but want to stay two steps ahead of them. If I don't get elected as AG, that means we're headed straight for corruption. The Park family has worked too hard for this town to let money hungry bastards run the show." Hugo clasps Harp on the shoulder. "It's guys like you two who help people like me and my father keep the riffraff off our streets."

Both detectives nod, eating up Hugo's speech. I relax slightly despite the fact my girl is six feet away, naked aside from the blanket covering her body. I want to shove everyone out of my house and drag her back to my bedroom.

Not until this is cleared up, though.

"We've just uncovered some damning evidence about Mr. Paulson and his corruption in this town. It's clear to me and everyone involved that he's actively finding ways to not only set me and my family up, but participating in other illegal activities that will need to be brought into the light. Of course, this all takes time." He releases Harp's shoulder and nods at Summers. "I appreciate all you've done here."

Summers looks over at me. "It's not against the law to date your student since she's of legal age, but word is out, Mr. Park. I just want to warn you that your job might be on the line."

"I understand and am fully prepared to deal with the consequence of my relationship." I find Willa's worried stare and give her a smile. "It's worth any and all trouble."

"I'll walk you two out," Hugo says, gesturing for them to go. "I'll see you and your girlfriend at family dinner on Sunday, little brother."

When the detectives turn away, I mouth a thanks to my brother. As soon as they're gone, I flip the lock and then scoop Willa into my arms. Her blanket falls away, revealing all the silky skin on her breasts to my greedy eyes.

"What happens now?" Willa asks, her palm cupping my face.

"Whatever we want."

"You might lose your job." Her brows furl. "I don't want that to happen because of me."

When we reach my bedroom, I set her to her feet, tugging the blanket from her body and tossing it to the floor. Her fingers hook into the top of my pants and she peers up at me. I'm awestruck at how fucking perfect she is all the time.

"I don't give a damn, sweetheart. All I care about is having you."

"That's a reckless way of thinking."

"Everything about us is reckless and yet I'm still here."

Her grin is infectious. "Promise me you'll love me even when we're poor and destitute because you lost your job."

God, she's so fucking sexy when she's playful and teasing.

"We'll never be poor and destitute." I grab hold of her ass and lift her, her legs wrapping around my waist. "I'm a Park and we Parks have massive trust funds."

"I thought teaching was your calling."

"It was a job and one that led me to you. While I'll be grateful for it, I don't need it. Any more questions or can I eat your pretty pussy? I'm ready to celebrate."

She giggles when I toss her onto the bed. "Celebrate what?"

"Us, sweetheart. I want to celebrate us."

CHAPTER THIRTY

Willa

DINNER WITH MY BOYFRIEND'S FAMILY.

No big deal.

No. Big. Deal.

"You're totally freaking out," Gemma says, a wicked grin curling her lips. "You're dating my brother and yet you're worried about his family. You do realize Callum is the scary one, right?"

There's nothing scary about Callum in my eyes, so maybe I can relax.

Maybe.

Okay, so, doubtful.

"What if they don't like me?" My stomach bottoms at that thought. "What if—"

"I'll stop you right there." Gemma tugs on a strand of my hair that I spent too long flat ironing in hopes of being somewhat presentable tonight. "First of all, Dempsey and Spencer already like you. And of course, I love you."

We both grin at our reflections in the bathroom mirror.

"Hugo likes everyone, or at least pretends to," Gemma says with a smirk. "Likeability is a big part of his campaign."

He was friendly enough when he saved us from the detectives, so that's one less family member to stress out about.

Gemma turns to study me. "That leaves Jude, and well,

he's Jude. He doesn't really like anyone, especially not himself. You won't even land on his radar."

"Why doesn't he like himself?"

Her smile falls and she avoids contact. "You'll see."

"And your parents?"

"Mom will be happy that Callum's finally happy," Gemma says with a sad smile. "Their drama goes way back to high school." She waves off the rest—thankfully, all of which Callum already told me—and huffs. "But Dad? He's probably going to be annoyed and push Callum's buttons. It's kind of their thing. Every dinner, every gathering. There's always this tension. We're used to it, but it'll probably be awkward as fuck for you."

Heavy footsteps thud into the bedroom and then Callum appears in the bathroom doorway. He's dressed down in dark jeans and a tan Henley, but it somehow makes him even more hot than usual. My mouth waters and my skin flushes.

"What'll be awkward?" Callum asks, dark brow arched in question.

"Your face." Gemma snorts out a laugh and then screeches when Callum launches at her. "Do not touch me, you freak!"

He manages to grab hold of her and tickles her. All her carefully applied mascara melts away as she cackles with laughter, while tears stream down her cheeks. Finally, he lets go of her, grin wide and eyes glimmering with satisfaction. My heart warms. This is how a sibling relationship should be. It's what I always craved and never knew.

"Fix *your* face, *freak*," Callum says, smirking.

He takes my hand and tugs me out of the bathroom. My stomach is in knots with anticipation of dinner with his entire family, but with him by my side, I feel confident we can handle this together.

Gemma's house is modern and gorgeous. Where Callum's house appears to be more lived in, Gemma's is showroom ready. I feel underdressed and like if I sit on the pristine light gray sofa, I'll somehow leave a mark. Callum walks us toward the sound of voices and Gemma struts ahead of us. We eventually make our way into a cavernous dining room with far more seats at the table than guests. I breathe a sigh of relief at seeing Dempsey. Hugo bailed him out of jail the same day he got arrested, which was great, but I still haven't had an opportunity to thank him for taking the heat rather than letting Callum take the fall.

"'Sup," Dempsey says, grinning at me. "I guess this really is a thing."

This being me and Callum.

"We really are," I admit, my voice breathy and slightly high. "Are you okay after..."

"Dad handled it," Spencer assures me. "He's fine."

"Where is your dad anyway?" Callum asks.

Spencer gestures down the hall. "Study."

Gemma disappears into a door that must lead to the kitchen. Seconds later, she reappears with a woman of her same height and build. At first glance, they could be the twins, not her and Dempsey.

"You must be Callum's girlfriend. Willa is it? Gemma has such great things to say about you." She offers a dainty hand. "I'm Jamie."

Callum is stiff beside me. On principle, I want to deny

the handshake for what she did to him all those years ago. However, their family dynamic won't allow for it. She's still Dempsey and Gemma's mother. I can't be rude to her.

"Nice to meet you," I say, though I don't necessarily mean it.

"Dinner is about ready to come out of the oven," Jamie chirps, smile bright and welcoming. "I hope you like Italian food. I've made baked ziti. It's a family favorite around here."

Hugo enters the dining room and commands all eyes with his presence. Like Callum, he's tall and muscular, but there's also something authoritative about him.

"Hugo," he says, smiling at me. "Nice to officially meet you."

"Willa Reyes."

Hugo darts his gaze between me and Callum for a couple of beats as if he's trying to understand our relationship before launching into friendly chatter. I let out a gush of breath, relieved to have passed whatever test he just gave me. The atmosphere is an easy one. Everyone seems nice, though I've yet to meet Jude or Callum's father.

"We have a guest, Dad," Gemma says, drawing everyone's attention to the older man who's quietly crept into the dining room unnoticed. "This is my friend, Willa."

The man isn't quite as big as Callum or Hugo, but there's a formidable nature about him. Callum doesn't stiffen like he did with Jamie. Instead, his chest bows slightly and his arm finds its way around me.

He's taunting him. Or provoking him. I'm not sure which. It should irritate me that I'm being used in this performance, but it doesn't. Callum's father did him dirty and Callum still carries the pain from the betrayal. If I can help Callum stick it to his father in any way possible, I absolutely will.

"Dad," Callum rumbles, arrogance dripping from his words. "Meet my girl, Willa. Willa, this is my father, Nathan."

Girl. Not woman. I notice his word choice as another stab at his father, so I don't take offense.

"Kind of young, don't you think?"

Dempsey snorts, earning a sharp look from Gemma. Spencer smirks, clearly entertained by the turn of conversation.

"What can I say," Callum says, chuckling in a dark tone. "Like father, like son."

Nathan's nostrils flare. He avoids his son's stare and instead sweeps a dismissive look over me. "Tell me she's not a student."

"He's my statistics teacher," I state, batting my lashes at him. "We met in class."

Spencer smothers a laugh and Hugo shakes his head. Gemma's eyes are wide with shock.

"Callum," Nathan growls. "Do you have any idea how this will look when word gets out?"

Callum drops a kiss to the top of my head. "Hmm. I suppose it will be rather humiliating to our family. It feels kind of familiar, though. Tell me, Dad, how did you handle it when the whole town shamed you for fucking a teenager?"

Nathan's features harden and his cheeks turn crimson. "That's enough, Son."

"At least she's legal, right? That's one thing I don't have to worry about, unlike you."

"Are you doing this to punish me?" Nathan seethes. "For..." He can't even finish the sentence. *For stealing your underage girlfriend all those years ago.*

"Not everything's about you, Dad. I assure you. This thing between me and Willa is far from anything that has to do with you."

"You'll lose your precious teaching job. You've fought your entire adult life against me to keep that job that pays you pennies. Are you really ready to give up your calling for a child?"

I bristle and level Nathan with a glare. "I'm not a child." His words curdle, though, still stinking long after he's spoken them.

Callum says losing his job is fine. He doesn't care. Still, the guilt is a smack of reality, punishing me.

"I'll manage," Callum says, shrugging. "I always do."

There's a quiet standoff where neither man speaks. The rest of the family, including myself, wait out the awkwardness while biting our tongues. Finally, Nathan huffs and waves a hand in the air.

"Sit. Jamie's prepared a delicious meal. We can deal with these matters another time." Nathan walks over to the head of the massive table and takes a seat. "Hugo, did you ever meet with the city planner?"

Just like that, the awkward conversation is over.

Callum relaxes, which, in turn, makes my muscles loosen. He guides me over to a chair, pulls the seat out, and then pushes me closer to the table once I've sat down. Gemma plops down beside me and leans in.

"Told you it'd be awkward as fuck." She squeezes my thigh. "You're doing great. I'm glad you're here."

Dinner isn't as bad as I feared. Now that Nathan is essentially ignoring the big elephant in the room, the conversation becomes friendly and everyone sort of talks all at once. I may not like Nathan very much, but I hope eventually the tension between him and Callum can subside.

I'm lost in the chatter when a coldness settles over me. All the hairs on my arms stand on end. I quickly glance at everyone seated at the table, but no one else seems to notice anything amiss. Eyes bore into the back of my head. A shudder passes through me.

What the hell is going on?

I turn my head, looking over my shoulder. Standing, like a statue, in black jeans and black hoodie that covers his head and shadows his face, is a massive man. I thought Callum was big, but this guy is a giant. His shoulders are broad and muscular. With a frame like his, he could probably tackle any dude in the NFL with ease. Who is this guy and why is no one concerned?

"Jude," Callum murmurs. "He's…just don't pay any attention to him. He doesn't like it."

The man in question, Jude, stalks forward. I tense up, unable to move. It's not like he'd hurt me, but the intensity rolling from him is palpable. It's like an incoming storm—powerful and vengeful, capable of extensive damage. He makes it to the other side of the table where an empty chair sits across from me. Tattooed fingers curl over the back of the chair and he drags it back. I watch in part terror part awe as he settles his huge frame in the chair that's far too small for him. Still, I can't see his face due to the hood.

Why aren't they acknowledging him?

They just keep yapping like nothing is wrong.

Finally, Jude lifts his head and I expect to meet a face that resembles one of the others at the table. Instead, I'm faced with…well, no face.

White latex.

A mask.

What the actual fuck?

I want to ask Callum why his brother is wearing a white mask that covers his entire face aside from his glimmering blue eyes and two small nose holes for breathing. But that would require finding the words to ask the question. All I can do is stare in confusion. Was his face disfigured from the fire?

"Jude," Callum says, voice unaffected whatsoever by his brother's strange entrance and appearance. "This is Willa."

Jude makes a slight grunting sound and gives me a small nod. Okay then. I have a million questions. All of which I'm going to bombard Callum with the second we leave.

"This smells divine," Jamie chirps as she enters with a casserole dish. "Oh, hey, Jude."

Jude grunts again.

This family is strange. Really, really strange. But Callum's a part of it and now I'm a part of him. I don't exactly have a great point of reference when it comes to good families. As long as I have Callum at my side, everything else will be okay.

As though sensing my inner conversation, Callum leans over and nuzzles his nose in my hair. I smile and bask in his sweet affection.

"Have I ever told you how beautiful you are?"

This morning. Over and over while he fucked me in the shower.

My cheeks heat at the memory. I turn to meet his lips with a kiss.

"You could remind me again later." I grin and a giggle slips out when he growls under his breath.

"Eat quickly, sweetheart."

"And if I don't?" I tease, glancing down at the way his cock thickens under his denim.

"Then I'll punish you by *eating slowly*. So slowly you'll go mad."

Now it's my turn to overheat from his words.

"You're evil."

"You're evil for liking it."

Touché.

Since we're being evil and all, I take great delight in his guttural gasp when I palm his cock over his jeans. At this rate, we'll never make it through dinner.

That's okay, I'd rather have *dessert* first.

"I'm going to have to teach you a lesson on proper dinner table behavior," Callum rasps out.

I squeeze his cock. "I'll probably fail."

He grips my wrist and tightens his hold. "If you fail, I'll have to punish you."

Getting punished by my sexy, rule breaking teacher doesn't seem to be a punishment at all. I rub at his dick and flash him my most innocent, doe-eyed expression.

"Oh, it's on now, sweetheart." His jaw clenches as he eye-fucks me. "It's *so* fucking on."

And I cannot wait.

EPILOGUE

Callum
Two Months Later…

MY LIFE IS IN LIMBO AND I HATE IT.

But I deal with it for *her.*

The quiet, sexy-as-fuck girl who's dutifully taking notes in my class. I put up with her shit-face stepbrother because it keeps her life from imploding.

Jude uncovered emails, receipts, and other proof that shows Darren Paulson is into some shady shit. Unfortunately, I can't use any of it against him. Because, if I do, he's made it known to Willa that he'll throw her mother in front of the proverbial bus. Her mom embezzled a fuck ton of money that'll land her in prison for a long-ass time.

She loves her mom and though she's been neglected by her for years, she refuses to do anything to send her mom away. It's annoying, but I get it. If it were my mother, I'd do the same.

It's not just the drama with Darren and her mom that feels as if it's in limbo either.

It's Levi. He fucking assaulted her, spent one night in jail, and then was out on bail with no punishment whatsoever. Willa didn't press charges because she didn't want it to blow back on her mother.

Talk about frustrating as fuck.

Seeing him walk into my classroom every single day, a smug look on his stupid face, is infuriating. Sometimes, I send his ass to the principal's office for the hell of it.

I'm playing with fire every time I do it because he still has that recording of me and Willa. My employment status sits in the hands of a wannabe rapist twat. He could post it on social media and then I'd be fired.

He knows it too.

Holds it over me like he's some powerful god.

Sometimes I wish he'd just share that shit and get it over with. But while I can handle the bad press, Willa doesn't deserve that. Thankfully, because of Hugo's interference a couple of months ago, at least the police haven't done anything.

My inner musings are swiped away as a crumpled paper ball sails across the room. Levi's grin is evil and he cackles when it makes impact with the side of Willa's head.

And. I. Lose. My. Shit.

I storm over to him, abandoning my lecture notes, and grab hold of his T-shirt. Several stunned students gasp in shock. His eyes gleam with triumph, clearly pleased at having gotten such a response from me. I'm done playing games with this fucker.

"Apologize," I growl, spittle spraying his face.

"Fuck. You."

I twist my fingers in the fabric of his shirt and yank him closer to me. Our noses are nearly touching.

"Apologize and then get the hell out of my classroom."

"Or what?" Levi taunts. "You going to beat my ass?"

He leaves off the *again* part.

"I'll be forced to involve your father," I snarl. "I know you don't want that."

My threat hangs heavy in the air. I can feel Willa's stare on me, silently pleading for me not to provoke Levi. We're beyond that, though. He's pushed me far enough.

"Dad can handle himself," he mutters. "We both know who will really be hurting."

Willa.

"You're eighteen now, kid. I think we both do know." *Not my Willa, fuckface.* You. *I'm seconds from bashing your face against the desk.* "Get out."

I release him and take a step back. A few kids have their phones out, recording the outburst. It's not the worst thing I've done, but certainly not something that will look good plastered all over social media.

Ignoring everyone, I stalk back to the front of the room to continue my lecture. Levi takes his sweet-ass time gathering his stuff. He stops in front of me with his phone in hand.

"Oops." He makes an exaggerated show of pressing something on his phone.

My blood runs cold. "Out."

"Testy." He snorts. "See you soon, Mr. Park."

I glower after him until the door closes. Then, I drag my stare back to the girl who calms me and makes every bad thing in life manageable because she's so fucking perfect.

Her brows are pinched, eyes darting all over me in that concerned, assessing way she has down to an art. "Are you okay?" she mouths.

I exhale, letting all the fury rush out of me at once and then give her a clipped nod. Somehow, I manage to finish my lecture and am explaining the homework when the classroom door opens.

Wayne, red-faced and wearing a scowl, enters the room. "Mr. Park."

"Mr. Erickson." My voice is icy cold. "How may I help you?"

His nostrils flare. "I need to see you in my office. Now."

The class bursts out into commotion and laughter. It's not every day the teacher gets called to the office by the principal. I don't give a shit about them, but Willa's eyes are wide with horror. I want to take her hand and promise her everything will be fine. Of course, I don't.

"Miss Reyes," Wayne grumbles. "I'll need to see you as well."

This sets the classroom off even more. I clench my teeth together and give Willa a small nod to join me.

I wait until she's gathered her bag and then follow after her. Wayne watches me with narrowed eyes, lip slightly curled as though I disgust him. I don't miss the fact that he purposefully puts his body between us once we're in the hallway. Like he's protecting her from me.

This can't be good.

Our walk to the office is silent aside from the squeaking of our shoes. Wayne guides us past a couple of curious student aides and into his office. Inside, Levi sits in one chair, feigning innocence.

I seriously want to fuck this kid up.

"Take a seat, Miss Reyes," Wayne says, voice tight as he closes the door. "Mr. Park. You won't need to get too comfortable."

Willa glances over at me, eyes wide with fear.

"She can stand with me," I clip out. "Mr. Paulson continues to torment her and I won't subject her to more of it by you forcing her to sit next to him."

Wayne scrubs a palm over his face. "Fine. Suit yourself." He sighs heavily. "It has been anonymously brought to my attention that you've been in a relationship with Miss Reyes."

Anonymously my ass…

"Don't know what you're talking about," I state, features impassive.

Wayne picks up his phone and hits play. It's me and Willa. The video Levi took of us that he's been holding onto for months.

"This was sent to me this afternoon," Wayne grumbles. "It's a video of you in a highly inappropriate act with a student on school grounds."

Levi smirks at me.

Willa, on the other hand, visibly shakes and pales at his words.

"I see," I say in a calm voice. "And?"

"And it's immediate grounds for termination." Wayne throws his hand in the air. "Depending on when this video was taken, we may need to get the police involved."

I don't flinch because the police know and they're not doing shit.

"You're firing me?"

"You were…" Wayne trails off. "A student."

"The word you're looking for, Wayne, is fucking." I shrug, no longer interested in denying the truth. "Yes, I was fucking my *legal* student. Still am. In fact, she lives with me because she's my goddamn girlfriend."

Wayne gapes in shock at my brutal honesty. Quickly,

he recovers and clears his throat. "You can no longer remain employed at this school. I'll need you to gather your things immediately and leave the premises."

"I'll leave," I agree, "but not until you transfer him"—I say, jabbing a finger toward Levi—"to another class. I will not have my girlfriend putting up with his abusive shit if I'm not there to protect her."

"I'll see what I can do—" Wayne starts, but I cut him off.

"You'll do it now," I growl. "Do it now and then I'll be out of here."

"You're in no position to make demands," Wayne bites out.

"And you're in no position to deny my one, simple request." I narrow my eyes. "It's like you forget who makes the most sizable donations to this school. You wouldn't want me to tell my father you're not capable of protecting his future daughter-in-law from rapists, would you?"

I can feel the hatred radiating from Levi, but it's easy to ignore. I may not be able to smear his and his dad's name through the mud for fear of getting Willa's mother sent to prison, but it doesn't mean I have to lie down and take his shit.

"Mr. Park," Wayne mutters. "I'll handle it. Now, please leave. I'll have someone gather your belongings and you can pick them up at a later date."

"I have to switch classes because he bullies you?" Levi gripes. "Unbelievable."

"You're playing games way out of your league, kid," I state, sneering at Levi. "You've already gone too far."

"Out of my league?" Levi scoffs. "Maybe I'm just getting started."

"Stop while you're ahead," I warn.

"Or I could just send a certain video to every damn person in this town."

His threats have me fisting my hands, barely able to keep the rage at bay. He knows he has the upper hand here. Even if he shares it with everyone, I still won't be able to leak his father's illegal shit because then Darren will expose Willa's mom.

"Am I missing something?" Wayne asks, confusion wrinkling his brow.

Willa clears her throat and lifts her chin. "Levi, you won't post that video because then I'll tell Darren what you've been up to."

I stroke my hand down her back, proud as fuck that she's standing up to this twat. Wayne scowls at my touching her. He can fuck right off because she's mine. I'm fired anyway, so who gives a rat's ass?

"You know how my dad will take to you threatening us," Levi spits back. "*Who* it affects if you do."

Willa leans into me, her arm wrapping around my waist. "I don't care anymore. So be it. I'm done living in fear, though. She's a big girl and can handle herself."

"Who?" Wayne butts in.

We continue on as though he's not present.

"You're bluffing," Levi hisses, but his eyes flash in defeat.

"I can assure you, I'm not." Willa shrugs. "Your call, Levi. Do you want to ruin your dad's life because you're an asshole? Because the only person who's going to hurt is you. You won't have your daddy to rescue you anymore when you screw up. And, newsflash, Levi, that's all you do. You're a loser."

She's right. She has me and I'll take care of her for the rest of her life. Willa is mine and as soon as she'll let me, I'll marry her. Make that shit permanent. Levi, though, won't manage well without his dad. If Darren is sitting in prison, Levi, who can't seem to stay out of trouble, will inevitably fuck up bad enough to follow his dad there. He's a dumbass, but he's smart enough to know this to be true.

Levi glares at us, nostrils flaring. Then, he jumps to his feet and mutters a defeated, "fuck this shit," before storming past us. As soon as he's gone, the tension in my neck releases itself.

"I don't know what the hell just happened," Wayne says, "but it changes nothing. You're still fired. However, out of respect for your father and name in this community, I'll keep the video to myself and won't go to the media about it. Miss Reyes, go back to class. Mr. Park, you're dismissed. Indefinitely."

Now that we're no longer worried about hiding our relationship, I take hold of Willa's hand and guide her out of the office. The curious students from before stare open-mouthed in shock at my possessive hold on my girl. Ignoring them, I all but drag Willa down the hallway. When we reach the copy room, she slows us to a stop.

I glance down at her, amused by the devilish grin on her pretty lips. "Naughty girl."

"You made me this way," she sasses.

My eyes skim up and down the hallway, making sure no one is nearby, and then I open the door, tugging her behind me. Once the door is closed, I yank off her backpack and then attack her mouth with mine. She moans into my mouth, waking my cock right the fuck up.

"If I fuck you in here, you'll be late for your next class," I rumble, nipping at her bottom lip. "I can't save you with a note any longer since Wayne fired my ass."

"I don't need saving," she says, tugging at my belt. "I just need you."

The next few seconds are a frenzy of yanking at buttons and tearing away clothes. I bend her over the copy machine and bury my cock deep in her slick heat. Fuck, she feels good. Always wet and ready for me.

"Callum," Willa whines. "Oh, God."

"Shhh, sweetheart," I growl, covering her mouth with my hand. "Someone could hear. You don't want to get into trouble."

Her pussy clenches around my cock. She's a good girl, but she sure does love being bad with me.

I fuck her fast and hard, turned on by the idea of getting caught. The machine creaks and groans beneath our combined weight pushing against it. I hope we fucking break it. Sliding my hand from her mouth to her throat, I bury my nose in her hair and squeeze her slender neck. Her entire body quakes as her orgasm detonates. It sets me off seconds later. I pump into her hard and deep, shooting thick shots of cum inside of her. When she's good and filled and boneless after our quick fuck, I smile against her sweaty neck.

"Love you, sweetheart. So fucking much."

"I love you too," she murmurs breathily. "Now take me home."

"My good girl's going to skip class?"

"Mmhmm." She laughs softly. "Maybe you could punish me for skipping."

Dirty girl.

I reach over and grab a ruler off one of the shelves and smack it down onto the copy machine. "Put this in your backpack. We're going to need it later."

I'm still buried in my girl, despite my cock half hard and completely spent. I could fuck her again, but we'll be in a rush and someone could find us. What I have in store for her later requires for us to be alone and for many, many hours.

"Promise?"

I pull out of her and admire the cum that runs out of her like a leaky faucet. I snatch the ruler and give her ass cheek a quick pop that makes her yelp.

"Promise, sweetheart. Now pull your panties up before all my cum leaves your pretty pussy. We can't have that, can we?"

She shakes her head and dutifully pulls up her panties and jeans. God, she's so fucking perfect.

Perfect and mine. *Forever* mine.

No one will *ever* take her away from me.

I hope you enjoyed Callum and Willa's story!

Want to read about the sexy Spencer Park?

The Tangle of Awful is next!

He is a master of
destruction...

THE TANGLE OF AWFUL

ABOUT THE AUTHOR

K Webster is a *USA Today* Bestselling author. Her titles have claimed many bestseller tags in numerous categories, are translated in multiple languages, and have been adapted into audiobooks. She lives in "Tornado Alley" with her husband, two children, and her baby dog named Blue. When she's not writing, she's reading, drinking copious amounts of coffee, and researching aliens.

To see the full list of K Webster's books, visit
authorkwebster.com/all-books.

Happy Reading!

JOIN MY NEWSLETTER
at authorkwebster.com/newsletter

JOIN MY PRIVATE GROUP
at www.facebook.com/groups/krazyforkwebstersbooks

Follow K Webster here!

Facebook: www.facebook.com/authorkwebster

Readers Group:
www.facebook.com/groups/krazyforkwebstersbooks

Patreon: patreon.com/authorkwebster

Twitter: twitter.com/KristiWebster

Goodreads:
www.goodreads.com/author/show/7741564.K_Webster

Instagram: www.instagram.com/authorkwebster

BookBub: www.bookbub.com/authors/k-webster

Wattpad: www.wattpad.com/user/kwebster-wildromance

TikTok: www.tiktok.com/@authorkwebster

Pinterest: www.pinterest.com/kwebsterwildromance

LinkedIn: www.linkedin.com/in/k-webster-396b7021

Excerpt

The Tangle of Awful

Aubrey

There's only one person in the entire world I hate.

Spencer Park.

He's vile. A monster. Awful.

I vowed two years ago I'd never look at or speak to him again. It was a promise I'd been able to keep until recently.

And, because of my mother, I'm once again going to be subjected to the misery he creates. This time, not because I'm being forced to, but by choice.

I'm choosing this for myself.

Not because I suddenly like Spencer. Far from it. It's because something is going on with Mom and I will get to the bottom of it.

"Here?" the Uber driver asks as he slows to a stop in front of the massive structure I once called home.

"This is it," I say with a shaky sigh. "Thanks."

I climb out, pull on my backpack, and grab my overstuffed suitcase before slamming the car door shut. The home looms over me, cold and mocking. Every single detail of this house screams money. From the perfectly trimmed hedges and yard to the shiny black luxury vehicle in the driveway.

And then there's me.

The leech.

At least, that's what he always loved to call me.

According to Spencer, me and my mother were leeches, bleeding his father of his family fortune.

Old memories of Spencer's cruelty simmers to the surface of my mind, but I don't let it consume me. I'm no longer the sixteen-year-old girl I once was. I've changed. I'm stronger, smarter, and a freaking adult now. Spencer Park holds no power over me.

I'm here for answers and nothing more.

Slowly, I wheel my dented suitcase up the front walk toward the pristine charcoal gray door that will welcome me into a cold hell. My hands slightly shake as I reach the door. Since Spencer used to always steal my house key, I kept one hidden outside. Leaving my suitcase, I walk over to the gutter spout at the corner of the house. I crouch in front of it and lift the biggest of the smooth stones on the ground in front of it.

The key is there.

My stomach twists.

It's all wrong. The metal teeth no longer sharp and jagged. It's as if it's been melted smooth. Words have been carved into the metal.

Not welcome, leech.

I curl the useless key into my palm and rise to my feet. He may have intimidated me two years ago, but I'm no longer that girl. I've been living in Los Angeles with Dad ever since I left, going to school with a whole bunch of assholes rather than just one. I've learned how to survive.

With newfound fury burning up inside of me, I storm back over to the front door. Of course, when I try the knob, it's locked. I beat my fist on the solid door, anger churning at my gut.

No answer.

I glare up at the camera pointed at the stoop and flip it off. If I know Spencer, I know he always has to have the last word.

As predicted, the snap of the deadbolt unengaging echoes its way through my bones. Gritting my teeth together, I lift my chin, preparing to face off with my enemy. The door swings open and his familiar scent—expensive cologne he's worn probably since birth—swirls around me.

Spencer steps out. Taller than I remember. Stronger, too. Every single part of him perfect as usual. His dark hair is styled a little differently—less boyish and something more manly. The eyes, though, bright blue and intelligent, are icier than ever. Two windows into an arctic hellish soul. It's his mouth that sends a chill down my spine. A cruel slant of a smile, probably charming to most, but sinister to those who truly know him.

"Hello, brother," I say in a tone dripping with acid. "Seems my key stopped working."

I toss the key onto the cement and it clatters between us.

His dark eyebrow lifts, unimpressed by my attitude toward him. *Newsflash, buddy, I'm not that girl you ran off once before.* He doesn't answer, instead perusing his gaze up down my body, lingering at my chest. Since the material of my shirt is thin, I know he can see through it, judging my old black Walmart bra and nipples that are hard from the coldness rippling from the open front door where the icy asshole looms.

"You don't live here anymore, leech."

I refuse to shudder at the name, choosing to glower at him instead. "Where's Mom?"

His blue eyes narrow, hard gaze now boring into me. "How the fuck should I know?"

"I want to talk to her," I snip. "Now."

He smirks at me. "Still a bossy princess. Go back home to your daddy. You're no longer welcome here." He fists his hand and pretends to wipe tear from his cheek. "Mommy doesn't love you anymore."

The Tangle of Awful is up next!